WE ARE TOGETHER
BECAUSE

Also by Kerry Andrew

Skin
Swansong

WE ARE TOGETHER BECAUSE

BECAUSE

Kerry Andrew

Atlantic Books
London

First published in hardback in Great Britain in 2024 by Atlantic Books, an imprint of Atlantic Books Ltd.

1 2 3 4 5 6 7 8 9

A CIP catalogue record for this book is available from the British Library.

Hardback ISBN: 978 1 80546 018 3
Trade paperback ISBN: 978 1 80546 107 4
EBook ISBN: 978 1 80546 019 0

Printed and bound by CPI (UK) Ltd, Croydon CR0 4YY

Atlantic Books
An imprint of Atlantic Books Ltd
Ormond House
26–27 Boswell Street
London

WC1N 3JZ

www.atlantic-books.co.uk

MIX
Paper | Supporting
responsible forestry
FSC
www.fsc.org
FSC® C171272

*In memory of my beloved
friend and bandmate, Matt Dibble.*

We ought to be grateful to our senses for their subtlety, fullness and force, and we ought to offer them in return the very best of spirit we possess.

FRIEDRICH NIETZSCHE

Deep Listening represents a heightened state of awareness and connects to all that there is.

PAULINE OLIVEROS

By and by comes the great awakening, and then we shall find out that life itself is a great dream.

ZHUANGZI, TRANSLATED BY FUNG-YU LAN

The past is a foreign country: they do things differently there.

L. P. HARTLEY

AT ANY MOMENT DESTRUCTION MAY COME SUDDENLY AND THEN WHAT HAPPENS IS FRESHER.

JOHN CAGE

PART ONE

One

The sun never reached this part of the river.

It was cold, unswimmable. The sheer limestone cliffs narrowed to just a few feet apart, and merged into one on the water's marbled, flat surface. Elsewhere, the ancient walls were deep with moss and ferns that never lost moisture.

Caves were dug here, places of dark and quiet when there was nowhere else. Red ochre striped by fingers onto white rock. Strange shapes – lines moving outwards from one central point, webbed together. A child, buried with a polished axe and a flint blade.

Hundreds of metres above the gorge, the land was once hard in summer and hard under snow in the winter months. In the hills, past a village that prided itself on almonds and lavender, sat a farmhouse, 153 years old, and built with mountain stone. Home to three generations who spent long days amongst their sixty sheep, and short nights packed too tight into its rooms. Over a century and a half, clusters of houses appeared around it, vineyards and olive groves spreading further. The Great War came, and the family dispersed. *The farmhouse began to crumble at the edges, tiles cracking, stairs slanting, before the tourists started to arrive.*

Now, along with a third of the houses in this south-eastern corner of France, it was a summer residence. William Low had purchased it nine years ago, regularly leasing it out to friends and work colleagues when not staying there himself, which he did with less frequency than he'd ever intended.

This time, he did something new. He sent his offspring – his lopsided family, slipshod in the middle – ahead, whilst he worked on completing three simultaneous cases and tried not to worry about how they would get on.

William would not see his children again. No one would.

It was late July, and the youngest of his four progeny was currently standing one-legged on the high wall above a slanted slope of young green oak and olive trees and was, not for the first time, thinking about killing herself.

* * *

If she fell now, she would hit her head on a rock and split it open. If she tried to jump, get height on it, she might impale herself on a branch. She could at least break a leg, with enough effort.

Violet swivelled around on the heel and ball of one bare foot, to face the garden and the pool and the house. She could stand on one leg for ages. A very warm breeze lifted up the hairs at the bottom of her neck. *Do it, Violet*, it whispered. *Disgusting fucking bitch.* She could just tip back, let herself go, arms outwards.

Violet. In her etymology app, *violet* was *a small wild plant with purplish-blue flowers, c. 1300, from the Old French 'violete', from the Latin 'viol'*. The last colour in a rainbow. The name great-grannies had. You couldn't shorten it, except to 'Vile', which some girls whispered not very quietly, or 'V', which some boys demonstrated by waggling their tongues through two fingers. Up yours. The victory sign. Vee Vye Vo Vum.

Her sister's name was two of the most basic words in the English language stuck together, and yet it meant *goddess of light, mother of the sun, moon and stars*.

Big brother one: light, again. Giver of light. Big brother two: strong and wise and apparently a lover of hounds. She should have that one – dogs were her number-one favourite.

Dad had obviously worked his way down, from normal names that normal people had, to embarrassing ones. LukeConnorTheaViolet. Trust her to be last.

It was fucking annoying.

Violet had been watching trash TV with Dad back home in London – for all his lawyering and history books as heavy as bricks, he was a sucker for people marrying strangers and entrepreneurs making fools of themselves – when he proposed the holiday.

'What do you think about France with Luke and Connor this year?' he'd said, putting his hand in the bowl of popcorn.

'Cool beans!' Violet had said, before he mentioned that he'd be working in Beijing for at least the first week. She felt like she'd been trapped into it, but was still excited – they'd only ever seen each other the odd time. 'Parent-free zone. So like *Love Island* meets *Lord of the Flies*.'

'Hmm,' said Dad. 'Hopefully neither of those things. If you don't think you're old enough, kiddo, just say. You can come with me in the second week.'

'I'm old enough,' said Violet. 'I'm very mature. It's Thea you've got to worry about.'

'Be nice to your sister,' Dad said, as he often did, quite interchangeably, to both of them.

Violet tipped her face up, still wobbling precariously on one leg, and squinted through one eye.

No violet here. Blue and then some. You could absolutely one hundred per cent guarantee that the sky was going to be blue, no matter what. Even before climate was followed by crisis, not change. Big, bright, slap-you-round-the-face blue, all of the blues possible if you looked from Dad's room, which was at the front of the house and which Luke had commandeered until Dad got here. Lake. Sky. Pool.

Cyanotype blue. Her mum had put her on a photography course last summer and now she had a Canon EOS 4000D DSLR camera and a lens for it, and she liked looking at proper old-school cameras in second-hand shops and on eBay. Together, they had gone to this really cool exhibition about early photography, and it had made her look at her phone like it was a piece of Lego. Imagine seeing this stuff for the first time – things appearing on metal plates or paper, as if rising from the depths. They would have freaked out.

William Henry Fox Talbot, Cecilia Glaisher. The first photographers used salts of silver and acid, experimenting until the vase of flowers didn't turn black, until the silhouettes of ferns became crisp and alive.

Anna Atkins mixed two diluted chemicals together so that they were sensitive to ultraviolet light, brushed them onto card, and left them to dry in the dark. Then she squashed seaweed or algae between two plates of glass onto the paper and exposed it to the sun. The plants came out chalk white on a dreamy blue, like skeletons.

Ultraviolet. Ultra meaning *beyond everything, on the far side of.* She was ultraviolet, in that she was so unlike her stupid name it was untrue.

She would erase herself, one way or the other. She could forget, be someone different who it hadn't all happened to. But not different as in dead. Not yet. Fuck you, death-whispering breeze.

She lowered her hovering foot, bent her knees so that she could rest one hand on the blistered white paint of the wall, and jumped down into the back yard.

* * *

Thea was lying on her bed, thinking about sex.

This was not a new activity, to be fair – not in one sense, in that for a long time she had been thinking about what it would feel like, and whether it would hurt, and whether a boy would be disappointed in the size of her breasts or bum or hips, or be distracted by the spot on her chin – but it was a relatively new activity in that now she had finally *had* sex.

A few times, actually.

She shifted, and the sheet came with her, stuck to the backs of her thighs. The heat was a constant reminder of skin pressing down on her, of being enclosed by arms and legs, the sheer blissful terror and suffocation.

She put her hand between her legs and pushed upwards, just to relieve the pressure, to make it spread throughout her body and not feel concentrated in that one place. Bruised, in a good way.

Metaphysical pessimists in the philosophy of sexuality – St Augustine, Kant, Freud sometimes – believed that acting on the sexual impulse was unbefitting to human dignity, and a threat to one's very personhood – that either side might get lost in the sex act and become just a *thing*. Metaphysical sexual optimists – Plato, Freud again, Russell – saw sexuality as just part of human existence, and something to be relished. In your face, Kant.

It was easy. After the first time, anyway. After wondering how she would be able to accommodate anything larger than a super-sized tampon – and even those felt a bit full-on sometimes – it had really been a surprise how smoothly it fitted. She was a natural.

Thea had been behind, really, compared to others. Compared to Jade, who'd whispered in her ear one morning in tutor group, aged fifteen, that she had been – in her words – *deliciously fucked*. Compared to Mischa, who had decided to give up smoking once she'd started having sex aged fifteen and a half, because one vice was enough, and sex was cheaper. Compared to Harper, who'd started going out with the captain of the football team in their girls' school earlier this year. She was finally part of the club.

There was a loud splash that was almost definitely Violet bombing into the pool for the fifth time this morning. When her little sister was seven, she would hit the tennis ball on a string in the back garden over and over again until Thea, aged ten and fed up with the incessant *thock* every afternoon, cut the string.

She didn't know what Luke had done when he was seven. Or Connor.

She supposed that Dad wanted them to get to know each other more, as if they hadn't had enough awkward birthdays and Christmas parties. But living together, the two boys and two girls – this was different. She'd have to get used to this sort of thing in another year, sharing rooms in halls wherever she ended up. But at least she wouldn't be related to any of them.

Two days and already it felt like weeks. Jade and Mischa had gone interrailing in Eastern Europe, something they'd been planning since January. Thea's mum had said she needed to be eighteen to go and she'd sulked for a week. She would experience their holiday vicariously through her phone, and otherwise use the time here to read all five of her *Very Short Introductions* as a pre-boost to her A levels, attempt and probably fail to tan, and find a French boy to explore the complexities of Plato's thoughts on eroticism.

She peeled herself off the bed and went to the window, looking down onto the bleached paving stones and the pool.

Connor was crouched down in shorts and a black T-shirt, wearing those huge headphones, holding the recording thing in his hand. Motionless. She imagined pushing his shoulder so that he toppled over into the bushes.

Thea could hear him through the wall at three in the morning, things bumping, making his crunchy-sounding, completely impenetrable music. Not even really music, as far as she could make out. She wasn't entirely sure that *he'd* had sex.

Just one of the many ways in which she was better than him.

* * *

It was definitely there. Connor wasn't imagining it.

In the 1940s, the composer John Cage went looking for silence. He entered an anechoic chamber at Harvard University, designed to completely block out the sounds of the outside world. To swallow sound whole. Yet when he stood there, there were two sounds, one very high and one very low. When he complained to the sound engineer that the chamber was not up to scratch, the engineer explained rather patiently that the high one was his nervous system and the lower one was his blood circulating.

In his bedroom, Connor took off the headphones, breath shallow, not swallowing. He could hear the sparrows outside on the telephone wires. A dog, with a hoarse and angry bark. Luke, downstairs in the kitchen. The cockerel's toy-trumpet fanfare went off half a mile away, as it did throughout the day. Still, he couldn't detect it. Not out there.

He put his headphones back on and listened again to the recording he'd made outside. He had been trying to get something of the little sucking sound of the water in the far corner of the pool, and had got distracted by the scrape of dry leaves in the faded green bush next to it. But listening back to it on his laptop, he'd found something else he hadn't noticed before.

There, again. A high whine, just at the edge of hearing. Almost electronic. What *was* that?

Connor's left ear was very good. Highly tuned, toned as a swimmer's limbs. The other one barely worked, had never worked, due to bone forming to completely block the ear canal while he was in the womb. Atresia. An ear only hearing itself. At least with the right-hand level whacked up on studio headphones, he could get the vibrations through his skull. A semblance of stereo. He wondered what John Cage would have done with only one ear. Made some cool pieces, probably.

He stared at the laptop screen, running his fingers lightly over the keyboard. Half-deaf. Another way in which he was a half.

Little dark, sporadic peaks spiked on the track in front of him. His audio recorder had picked up footsteps, a flat tackiness of skin on concrete that got louder, stopped, started again and faded. He'd known Thea had been there, and he hadn't turned round.

She was walking in a different way. Like skinny models did, their shoulders slung back as if dislocated, arms flopping. With the same constant, dreamy smirk.

The two of them, Connor and Thea, knotted in the middle, too close in age. If anyone ever asked, he either said he had two sisters – no half – or didn't mention them at all. It wasn't like they lived together, or were even in the same city.

They overlapped. It was like a confusing exam question for primary school kids: *A brother is six months older than his sister. Explain.*

Answer: *Their father was a cheating bastard who had got his girlfriend pregnant with a second son and then got another woman pregnant before the son was even born.*

The door smashed open, bouncing back off the bookshelf, and Violet strolled in. Denim shorts and a T-shirt saying *TEENAGE APOCALYPSE*, a dirty feather tucked behind her ear. Three tight bands had been drawn around her wrist with three different-coloured pens. She did a quick circuit of the room, her fingers on the windowsill, his desk. 'What you doing, brobro?'

Connor slid a headphone behind his ear and showed her what he'd been working on – chopping up his field recordings, layering them to make textures, beats even.

'Gimme,' she said, her hand out.

He clicked on a recording he'd made yesterday and stared at the screen as the bar moved along. He wasn't sure what he'd do with them yet. Keep recording, editing and combining, playing around with modulations and filters, until something came out.

'Sick,' she said, giving him back his headphones. He was fairly sure she wasn't much interested, but it was nice that she pretended. 'I'm going to be called Hawk from now on. Here, anyway.'

'OK.'

She pointed two fingers, shot him. A book fell off the shelf as the door slammed behind her.

It was always easier to talk to Violet, because she was four years younger than him. Because she wasn't his weird half-twin.

Because she wasn't beautiful, like Thea.

Connor moved the headphone back onto his deaf ear. He sat very still and listened again to today's recording, to the long, unpulsing drone.

* * *

'Oh, God. Yes.' Luke sucked on his fingers. 'Jesus.'

The hottest part of the day. He hadn't got his body into siesta mode yet but hopefully he would soon. Instead, he was in the kitchen, with the blinds lowered.

He pressed his tongue to the roof of his mouth. Closed his eyes and swore. Blasphemed.

Degree over, it was absolutely fine to have to be lord of the manor here (*manoir*? Luke's French was sketchy, if enthusiastically delivered) for a while, and to have some distance from a certain man's suburban house where he'd ended up one too many times.

He opened his eyes and looked at the spread on the counter in front of him. The high-intensity tomatoes. The goat's cheese, thick and cummy. The tang of the wild garlic.

He was a person of different layers. He was robust, tall, a rower's thighs, and could run up and down a football pitch for ninety-plus minutes without stopping. A proper Manc lad, but also one with a penchant for wearing glitter gel eyeshadow on a Saturday night as he chugged his cheap lager. And he was obsessed with the intricacies of flavour, especially the ones that the Mediterranean sun coaxed out. Which is why he was grateful that his mum had allowed his father to be in touch after a long hiatus aged three to fifteen, and that his father was actually a good guy, if constantly awkward when looking at Connor, and that his father had a successful job and could buy a place in the South of France which had a decent kitchen.

He was given the job aged sixteen of cooking on Thursday nights, when his mum was back late from her community choir rehearsal. Ham and eggs turned into spag bol turned into salmon fillet with tarragon butter and samphire, until Connor became a vegan, and then Luke liked the challenge of making meals just as good. *You could run a restaurant,* his dad had said, the last time they were here, and Luke had flushed with pride.

He was a sucker for compliments. For anything, really. He liked that their dad made an effort. Will was an Arsenal fan, but happily took him to the City game as one of their first outings together, Luke thrumming with excitement at sitting next to his actual father. Connor, on the other side, had a stiffness that grew over the years into a stubborn refusal to share any interests with Will. Part of Luke admired his brother for it, but he always wanted to reach out, welcome in, accept, forgive. Love was love, and it was messy and complicated.

14

He put in his headphones. He and his mates shared a playlist called *dancebabydance* and a few new tunes had been put on. This one was too bland for him, with the essence of Canal Street on a Saturday night, full of cishet tourist trash. He preferred old-school Chicago house and classic disco, but hey – he was easy. He shook his hips a little as he finely diced the garlic leaf, and pictured Jamie watching him from behind, telling him what he'd do to him with the courgette in his dour Midlands accent.

No. Not good to think about Jamie. Better to concentrate fully on this garlic leaf, foraged from the shaded woodland a few miles away, its delicately rubbery texture, the full-on scent. No way of that being used aggressively.

His phone buzzed. Where are you? Why aren't you answering?

'All right,' said Connor, walking into the kitchen with four dirty cups hooked in his fingers and those massive headphones round his neck, opening the fridge door.

'Y'all right,' said Luke, putting his phone back in his pocket. 'Chuck us that mint?'

His brother didn't always say very much, but he was a good soul, underneath the furrowed brow and the permanently attached headphones. If slovenly.

'What you making?'

'Dunno yet.' He took the bunch from his brother. 'Cheers. Want some? It'll be ready at eight.'

'Yeah, maybe,' said Connor, taking a carton of juice out of the fridge and leaving the kitchen as he tipped it to his mouth, off to do his own thing once more.

Luke wouldn't have minded a bit more coherence, siblings-wise. When his dad had called about the holiday, Luke had felt cheered, responsible. In truth, he'd been vaguely committed to a Greek-island-hopping booze, beaches and boys trip with his mates, but that could wait. He'd been deemed fit to lead the party, and daydreamed of what they'd all do together, his expanded family. But then he was a team player. Mad for competitive sports, both playing them and teaching others in the future. A PGCE in PE awaited.

The other three seemed more like individual sportspeople. Violet: maybe ski jump, showy, becoming a cult figure with massive goggles. Thea: something slinky, because that was clearly her vibe at the moment. Ice-skating, so she could wear some tiny outfit. Connor: a featherweight boxer, hurling himself methodically at the punchbag, letting out all his pent-up energy.

Fuck it, though. He would make it happen. The four of them would become a family. A proper one.

Up in the corner of the kitchen by the hairline crack in the older wall, a long-bodied cellar spider rests in a tangle of thread. House spiders are diminished by its presence. For a moment, it vibrates, as it does when a predator is near. A shimmer of spider, becoming a blur to disguise itself.

Then it continues its web-making, the pattern a little more ordered, more precisely angled than it has ever been before.

Two

Leaves. Leaf-bits. A wasp. Two daddy-long-legs. Why were they dads? Mums could have long legs. Not all females of the species were short-arses, like her. Violet Little Legs.

Violet was cleaning the pool. It was her routine every morning when she was here. Up, brush teeth, eat a bowl of dry chocolate French cereal that she called *Le Coco Pops*, walk a bit on the walls and think about killing herself – although that bit was new – and then skim the surface of the water until it was clear of clutter.

She imagined the pool net pole as a spear, bent down and formed a defensive shield wall with her imaginary fellow warriors. She probably had Viking blood, after all – her *mormor* and *morfar*, her mum's parents, were Danish, though they had lived in the UK since they were young. You were supposed to say 'Norse', but Violet liked 'Viking', even if it did officially mean raiding and plundering. Her mum had been doing the family tree with a cousin for years, and would sit with a glass of wine poring over old documents on her tablet, doing that sing-song hum she did when something was interesting. Hopefully one day she'd trace back far enough to give Violet her *berserker* badge. The bear-coat wearer. *Oh, you are definitely a Viking,* her mum would say, a hand on Violet's head. *A shieldmaiden. Anyone would be terrified of you coming the other way.* Violet had grinned with satisfaction, though Thea had snorted. Thea would definitely have been a Norse-only person, sitting at home weaving on her loom and complaining that no one had noticed her new, very ninth-century hairstyle.

Violet twisted the pole back round, scooped into the water and lifted again. Sometimes, she imagined that it was a wide fishing net and that she was collecting up shoals of brown flatfish, sea cucumbers, lion's mane jellyfish, starfish, conger eels, all her thoughts, everything flapping in the fine mesh, all at her mercy. She imagined feeding them to Artoo, who would probably sniff at them and run away.

She'd video-called her mum this morning, and spent a good five minutes talking to Artoo. At home, she did everything with him. He was a cross between a Border collie and something smaller, black and tan, with the biggest, stupidest smile, tongue lolling out as if trying to escape. They'd got him from a rescue place five years ago, and he was her partner in crime. Dogs were nicer than most people. She had built up a language that was part human, part dog. She was training him to do an increasingly badass assault course constructed in the garden at home, and dreamed of winning that competition at Crufts – except that he wasn't a pure-breed and wouldn't get in. Secretly, she also tried to cajole him into doing the nerdy owner-and-dog dancing that everyone on social media laughed at, but even Artoo refused that, no matter how many treats she gave him. Thea used to roll around with him, too, but these days she absently pushed him away or told him his breath smelt, as if he could do anything about it.

Violet turned and swept the net again, catching a corner of Thea's lilo.

'Careful,' her sister said as the lilo turned her slowly, not looking up from her book, which was called *An Introduction to Consciousness*. Hi, Consciousness, nice to meet you, how's it going? She was wearing her bright-red bikini with the ties at her hips, her shoulders creamy with the suntan lotion that had been tossed in the grass, lidless and dribbling. Apart from the hair on her head, you couldn't see any hair on her anywhere.

Violet walked the net around the pool again. 'What're you reading about?'

'Transcendental idealism and the thing-in-itself.'

'Say what?'

'Immanuel Kant. We can't fully know a thing, because our senses don't have the capacity to understand it in its entirety.'

'*Right*,' said Violet. 'So I don't understand this tree because it's got some mystery ju-ju to it that I can't see?'

'Or sense in any human way. Yep.'

'So trees are magic.'

'I didn't say magic.'

'You didn't *not* say magic.'

'Double negative.'

'Which is exactly how I feel about you.'

Violet swept the net through the water, gathering up five specks that were either vegetation or insects, and let the mesh billow, a wide basking shark mouth. She aimed straight for Thea, collecting the bottom end of her lilo, beginning to eat up her feet.

Thea jerked a leg suddenly, twisted and slid off with a loud splash, the lilo tipping her before gently righting itself. All of her went under the water apart from her book, held upwards with a straight arm. Her head came up. 'Fuck's sake. *Violet.*'

'Whoops.'

Her sister trod water, one-armed. 'You're a certified bitch.'

'She who smelt it dealt it.'

They used to get on better. They would play word-based board games – sometimes with Dad, who was a total games nerd, but mostly just the two of them. Until Thea started putting down words like *quixotry* and *chutzpah* and constantly losing was no fun. By the time Violet had discovered the etymology app – and learnt the word *etymology* – Thea didn't want to play any more. Three years was a big age gap once you were a teenager.

Thea pulled herself up to the silver plastic rail at the side. 'Just leave me alone, all right?'

'OK. I'll leave you and –' she squinted at Thea's book cover – 'Immanuel Kunt to be besties.' Violet pulled the pole clear and rested it on her shoulders, arms draped over it. 'And I'm not being called that name any more.'

'Whatever.' Thea put her book down on the grass and put the flats of her hands over her hair, ironing out the water.

'Luke said we're going in half an hour.'

Thea squeezed the ends of her hair and rolled her eyes. 'Fine.'

* * *

There couldn't have been much rain so far this year, Thea thought. The fields and the vineyard and olive grove were all bleached of their colour, the ground arid. Her dad had said something about the lavender being underdeveloped, giving less of the fragrant oil that was sold everywhere around here. Some kind of insect contaminating the sap.

'*Je t'aime, mon petit cochon d'Inde,*' Luke was singing, loudly and quite badly, to the crap French pop on the radio. He was the only one old enough to drive the tiny hire car. Next to him, Violet had her filthy bare heels shoved up on the dashboard, her hand out of the open window, laughing. Connor was facing his own back window, turned resolutely away from Thea, not bothering to brush away the brown curls flopping in front of his face. The rest of his hair was short, but he obviously grew them to block the world out. Or her, at least.

'*Le grand bateau est mort,*' Luke sang, drawing out the last word. '*Parce que le bateau c'est le champignon fabuleux.*'

'Your phone keeps buzzing,' said Violet, between sniggers. 'D'you want me to check it?'

'*Non, merci,*' said Luke. 'Hey, do us a favour.' He seemed to be speaking to all of them now, and his voice had lost its sheen. 'Don't tag me on any photos while we're out here. I want to go a bit off-grid.'

'Roger that,' said Violet.

'Sure,' said Thea.

'Yup,' said Connor.

'Ta.' Luke began to sing to the radio again. *'Je suis un pomme de terre et tu es mal.'*

Violet's laugh was like an owl, hooting. 'You are so fucking funny, Luke.' She was being ridiculous on this holiday. *I would really rather you didn't swear like a sailor*, their mum would say. *It's from a Norse word*, Violet would say back. *Fukka. I'm respecting my roots.*

It was easier for them. The outer siblings. Thea and Connor were the core, two sides of a coin. She remembered standing in the doorway of her living room aged twelve, being introduced to two boys who were apparently her brothers. Connor, also aged twelve, looking like her and also not like her at all, had stared over, holding onto his elbows, mute.

Violet – or Hawk, or Tiger, or Ace, or whatever she decided to call herself next – passed back Polo mints, her own one stuck between her teeth. Connor took his without a word. There were a couple of ratty-looking friendship bands and a wooden-beaded bracelet on his wrist, and Thea felt irritated by his attempt at edginess.

He blinked a lot. Just like Dad did when he was thinking. Dad sang loudly in the car, as Luke was doing now. And in the shower, just as she'd heard Luke do this morning.

She'd always known about her brothers, in a not-quite-tangible way. She'd heard her parents talking about it once, in low voices, when she was six or so. *Them. They.* But she hadn't really understood. They weren't there in the house, after all. It came into focus only when, aged eleven, she was sat down along with Violet and informed that they had two half-brothers who lived in Manchester.

It was like being told you were adopted. Your whole life-view tilting in an instant. She was the oldest, and then she wasn't. She spent a long time, in those uncomfortable early meetings, trying to work out whether they looked more like Dad than she or Violet. Couldn't help still doing it. A competition that she had no control over.

But she could still control some things. She felt this whole holiday to be a test of her maturity, and it was one she was going to breeze through.

As they took the crest of the road, there was the usual stomach-lurch and the half-second of weightlessness, before they began to descend and the familiar turquoise corner appeared down below.

'*Le lac,*' said Violet, taking her feet off the dashboard. '*Violà le lac*, bitches.'

'Last one in there has to cook tonight,' said Luke, briefly swivelling round to the back, grinning. At the same time, a van came haring round the corner, straddling the central road markings, alarmingly close.

'*Luke,*' said Thea, a flash of panic in her chest, as they swerved.

* * *

'Jump!'

'Shut up.'

'Three, two, one, go! Go! Oh, come on, sis.'

'I can't.'

'You deffo can. I know you can. Show me your *cahones*!'

Violet was in the water, having just done a spiralling leap

23

off their jumping rock, four metres high. She didn't seem to have any fear. Connor had come downstairs yesterday afternoon, bleary-eyed, to find her falling backwards into the swimming pool, arms outstretched and almost perfectly straight. She came out quite cheerfully with red-smacked legs, and did it again.

Thea was standing at the top of the rock, having carefully negotiated her climb at a third of the speed of Violet's enthusiastic scramble. She'd obviously been trying to move as gracefully as possible, the way some girls did, as if they were being constantly observed.

They'd parked in a lay-by and come down to the spot that he and Luke knew but somehow the girls didn't, skidding down a trail half-hidden in the trees to a narrow inlet where the cliffs were ten metres high in places. You could still hear the traffic up on the lake road, but otherwise it was just the snap and slop of the water and three members of the fractured Sheridan–Low family shouting at each other, voices bouncing off the flat surfaces. Connor was sitting opposite on the long rock shelf currently scattered with towels, food and a snorkel, reading *Silence* by John Cage and pretending not to watch.

The lake was lower than last time. Easy to measure against the jumping rock, which had a couple more feet exposed, a strip of dark grey where the water had been.

Violet was whistling and shouting *chicken*. Thea shook her head, oblivious to Luke climbing up the rock behind her, his finger in front of his lips. Her arms were crossed in front of her, shoulders hunched, and she was in a different bikini, turquoise with an overhanging frill around the top.

Suddenly there, Luke grabbed her hand and jumped with her, Thea's screech ripping into the air as their bodies plummeted. A short explosion of a splash followed by silence, apart from Violet laughing, and another unleashed yell as Thea came up and swam over to push Luke in the shoulder. He just ducked under, spitting out an arc of water when he resurfaced, followed by a laugh in the same shape.

Luke could do that. Just take her hand and jump with her. He didn't care. Connor was envious of how easy everything seemed to his brother, who made friends wherever he went. Not really close ones, as far as he could tell, but plenty of them. *My son, the social butterfly*, their mum had said once, and Luke had given a bow.

Thea was swimming towards Connor now and he resolutely looked at his book, trying to ignore the fact that he hadn't turned his page in about ten minutes, and listening to her small gasps grow louder.

'Aren't you jumping?' she said, pulling herself onto the rock.

'I will,' he said, not looking up.

'Oh, my God,' she said, seemingly to herself, and lay back on a towel, closing her eyes and putting an arm over her head to shield herself from the sun. Water dripped from her elbow.

Connor stared again at his page. Turned it, even though he hadn't read the last two paragraphs. It was supposed to be fine, looking at a family member with hardly any clothes on, because you'd grown up with them, shared bedrooms and baths. It wasn't supposed to be like this.

His mum called him her Irish rose. His best mate Kaia said, with a wink, that he could audition for *Let The Right One In* or *Near Dark*. He caught a bit of colour if he was lucky in the summer, and then it promptly disappeared after two weeks back in Manchester.

Thea was pale, too, in a different way. Her long hair was a neutral shade, not quite brown or blonde, though almost as dark as his now that it was wet. But her eyebrows were paler, giving her a slightly non-human look. Pale, heavy eyelids. She had two pale scars on the side of one thigh as if a big cat had scratched her, a childhood injury he'd never asked about.

'What're you reading?' She turned her head and opened her eyes. Her irises were the same colour as the lake. Not pale.

He showed her the cover and she took it from him, reading the blurb on the back.

'Hardcore.' Pretending to have less of a brain than she did. Another sometime-girl-thing that Connor didn't understand.

He wished Kaia were here. He felt himself with her.

'Is he a poet?'

'Sort of. Musician. Composer.'

Thea flipped the book over and squinted up at it, before reading out one of Cage's nonsensical sections about breakfast and woodpeckers and Kansas. She lowered the book enough to give Connor a wry, almost schoolteacher-y look.

Connor went to take it back. 'Yeah, well, it's not all like that.' Though, in a way, it *was* all like that.

She held fast. 'Not finished.' She swatted at a fly, a gesture that could easily have been aimed at him, too.

The book blocked her face and he looked down at the shadow it made on the frilled bikini top. She made that sound she often did, a little hum as if she was responding to a very quiet question, and shifted slightly on her towel, lifting up and straightening it underneath her hips. Her stomach was moist. Water ran down her inner thigh in pearled rivulets.

A low, tugging pain in his stomach. He stood up, suddenly, and dived into the lake.

The lake had once been an inhabited valley, before it was evacuated and flooded in the 1970s to make the largest artificial reservoir in Europe. Its vast concrete dam sat at the end nearest their house, providing much of the region with its water. They had once looked at the little museum, brown and beige photos of the drowned village – streets and bars and a church. Connor liked to imagine its bell swinging, a misty underwater clang, like Debussy's 'La Cathédrale Engloutie'.

He listened for it now as he swam, keeping his head down, the lake deep enough not to be able to see the bottom. The underwater crackle, almost like static, and his breath. He liked to swim, propelling his body, the rhythm of it, losing himself.

Keep swimming. See only milky jade-blue. Not her thigh.

By the time he stopped to rest, he couldn't see them. He was surrounded by long stretches of water and modest slopes with chalk-yellow sand at their base. The far mountains soft-focus in the heat. He spun slowly, moving his limbs just enough to keep him afloat. *The water is thick with monsters ready to devour them*, wrote John Cage in one of his lectures, something to do with self-preservation and life and death. Not for Connor. The monsters were absolutely in his head.

The drowned village was much further along the lake than this, he was sure. He got a strange sense of vertigo, then took a breath and swam downwards anyway.

The water grew colder immediately, pressure stacking up behind his ears. Eyes open, he saw the light-blue surface thicken, and looked for buildings that he knew weren't there. Roofs. A church spire. Instead, he thought he heard something, amongst the intermittent crackle.

A high, constant whine. The same as on his recordings.

When he neared the shore again, he could see the three of them standing in a line, watching him. He kept his head underwater as much as he could, and finally pulled himself up, shaking out his short curls. He supposed he had been gone quite a while.

'Jesus Christ,' Thea said, holding onto her elbows.

'Swear down,' said Luke. 'That was a bit scary. Even for you.'

'Connor,' said Violet. 'That was epic.'

∗ ∗ ∗

'Why do we have to eat at the table?' Luke's younger sister was not so much at the patio table as *on* it, leaning her entire torso over to reach for the bread that he'd just taken out of the oven. The sun was setting, a peach blush spread across the horizon.

'Because we're in France,' said Thea, liberally pouring herself red wine. She seemed in her element here, touching things for longer than necessary and experimenting with various reclining positions in her array of bikinis. It wasn't that long ago that Luke remembered her with train tracks on her teeth, lurking in corners whilst glaring at everyone.

'Just because their olives are fatter and they eat more garlic doesn't make them better than us.'

'Yes, it does,' said Thea. 'We suck, remember?'

'Because we've been here three days and we haven't eaten together once,' said Luke, sitting down as Connor came in with a pint glass of orange juice. 'I thought we'd, you know, do a family thing.'

Everyone seemed to stiffen for a moment, concentrating on reaching for something, each sound a little louder. Perhaps that word would always be banned, Luke thought. They were family, and at the same time, they weren't – two sides stuck together with Sellotape.

Right now, one side continued doing what they did best.

'Are you seriously saying that –' Violet grabbed the nearest radish – 'this only exists in my head? I can smell it. Feel it. Taste it.' She bit into it with a noisy crunch.

'So you're a naïve realist,' said Thea. 'Not a radical idealist.'

'I'm not naïve. I'm telling it like it is.' Violet picked up half a fig. 'So this is just a fig-ment of my imagination?'

'*Oh*,' said Luke. 'Burn.' He held up his palm, and Violet high-fived him.

Though it was subtle, Thea's face lost a little of her superiority. 'Just trying to expand my sister's mind,' she said. She picked up a peanut and sucked the salt off before crunching it.

'My mind's got enough going on,' said Violet, and her voice had changed, too. More muted. 'Don't need any more stuffed into it.'

A moment of quiet that no one seemed to know how to fill.

Luke's phone buzzed. I miss you. Are you going to tell me where you are? He put it away.

'Why don't you drink?' Thea said to her brother.

Connor shrugged, leaning over on his forearms. 'Just not into it.'

'You are very singular.'

Connor raised his eyebrows. He wasn't exactly verbose at the best of times, but Thea seemed to make him even less so. He obviously hated her.

Luke's phone buzzed in his pocket again.

'Have you got a stalker?' said Thea, raising her eyebrows in arch amusement.

He pulled over the salad bowl. 'Something like that.' *Dirty whore*, Jamie had said. *You fucking love it, don't you?*

A sudden flat smack from behind them.

They looked at each other.

'What was that?' Violet said.

Luke rose, trod lightly over to the edge of the paving, and stood there for a moment, peering at the shape by his feet. Then, a dark scribble of movement, and he leapt back. 'Jesus.' He dashed back to the chair, his hand on his heart, before grinning.

'What?' said Thea.

'Lizard,' he said, and glanced up towards the eaves. 'Big one. Think it fell off the roof.'

They all followed his gaze.

'What was it doing up there?' Thea said.

'Wouldn't it have exploded or something?' Violet said. 'That's like, eight metres high.'

'Guess not,' said Luke.

* * *

'Y'all right, mermaid?' said Luke, the next morning on the terrace, looking delighted. 'You look dead good.'

Violet had spent the last forty minutes in the bathroom not dying but dyeing. Now her hair was green, or more specifically Sea Punk, although it had come out loads darker than she'd expected.

''Sup fam,' said Violet, letting herself be side-hugged by Luke, trying to ignore the *you're a disgusting bitch and you deserve to die* on repeat in her head. He was happy to call her whatever she told him, just like Connor, because her brothers were cool.

She couldn't call herself Ace any more because that didn't just mean awesome or the top of a deck of cards, but asexual. Put 'a' in front of anything and it made it the opposite: *ahistorical, atypical, asymptomatic.*

She wondered if she was ace. And aromantic, which meant not wanting to go out with someone or marry them or anything. Aro. Ace aro. It sounded like something Scooby Doo would say when you put them together. She did find some people sort-of-cute but she didn't want to message sort-of-cute people she'd never met like others did, and she very definitely didn't want to kiss or have sex with anyone. But wasn't that because of what had happened, or was it something from before that? You were supposed to *feel*, and she didn't feel anything. A big hollow space in her chest. Her friend Joe at school, who had a shaved head and an earring and liked making up elaborate pun-related jokes, was hilarious and kind of good-looking. It made total sense for her to feel something for him. But it seemed like acting, when she tried.

Was she just behind? She sometimes wished she didn't have to get any older, to have to deal with this stuff. Some people at school were talking about sex in Year 7, and whenever conversations went that way, or even when she saw two people hand in hand, not as friends, it was like she was looking at a complicated maths equation.

Agender was a real word, too – there was someone in Year 10 who had changed their name to Lane, though they were non-binary. Violet didn't want to be a girl, sometimes. Or a boy. Just nothing. Agender. Aperson.

Anyway. She was now Hawk. Not Violet. Hawk was talons and wings and feathers, and everyone below Hawk was a puny little dormouse, and if she'd been Hawk when she'd been caught skiving off Physics, the caretaker doing a sweep of the PE-kit sheds, she'd—

Deep breath. Gorge-deep breath, to stop the thoughts coming, the falling-backwards-drowning-looking-up-how-to-say-sleeping-tablets-in-French tumble of thoughts.

Des somnifères. For a solemn affair.

It was like a whole other part of her mind was thinking the thoughts. Trying to distract her, being evil, and at the same time she could do somersaults into the pool, or tell Luke a joke, or crack off the shells of pistachio nuts. *Weird thoughts caused by anxiety*, she'd read online, which had made her feel better. *You cannot force yourself to stop the thoughts*, she'd also read, which had made her feel worse.

They didn't seem real, except that no one else was putting them in her head. When did these things become real, things that you believed, that you actually *did*?

At least it felt different here. Her eldest brother was amazing at all sports and cooking, and he was always nice to her, and he was gay. Right now, he was looking at his phone, quite blankly, before putting it under the lounge chair, turned over so that the screen was face down.

'I wish I could have tattoos.' She eyed the two bands, one thicker than the other, around his lower calf. He also had a geometric tattoo of weighing scales on his left upper arm. His star sign.

'Plural?' said Luke.

'Definitely. When did you get yours?'

He nodded down at his leg. 'These when I was fifteen. My mate had a mate. Not very original. The scales last year.'

'I'm not allowed them yet.' *Eighteen*, her mum had said, countless times, *and I'm not open to negotiation. Twenty*, her dad had said. *She'll totally get Artoo's face on her leg*, Thea had said.

'Oh, God,' said Luke, realising his mistake. 'You're going to use me as your reasoning.'

'Hell, yes.'

'I'm trying to stay on Dad's good side, so you didn't hear it from me.'

'Why?' She never needed to. *You get away with murder, kiddo*, her dad would say, smiling.

Luke didn't answer right away. 'Oh, it's just my way.' He stretched his arms behind his head and tipped his face to the sky. Definitely a sun-worshipper. 'Go on, then, what would you have?'

Artoo's face on my leg, she thought. 'A turtle. Or a manta ray. Or a hammerhead shark.'

'Is that your thing? Sea life?'

Marine life, more accurately. She picked a thread in the lounge chair's cushion. 'It seems nicer under there. Underwater.'

Except when it was choked with can holders and condoms and microplastics. The Great Pacific Garbage Patch was three times the size of France. The eighth continent. If she were still eating fish, she'd basically have bits of plastic bag in her. She probably did anyway. They were all just walking plastic-idiot-humans.

But some humans were funny, at least. Luke seemed to sense that her mood had taken a nose dive. He nudged her leg with his toe and started singing '*Sea life...*' to the tune of that old song 'Street Life', making up the words as he went along.

'What have you done to your hair?' said Thea, coming out and glancing up from her phone. She'd been grumpy and hungover all morning. 'It's like you've swum into a load of skanky seaweed.' She was still grumpy and hungover.

Her sister, Violet decided, was alikeable. Anice. Akind. She was just an a-hole.

* * *

Everything *was* better here. More intense.

On a lounger, Thea was picking the pips out of her slices of watermelon, its flesh as red as a tongue. Her skin felt tacky with suntan lotion, chlorine and afternoon heat.

By the far end of the pool, Violet was picking all of the blue petals from a blue-and-white flower bush, having smacked her back red from tipping into the pool, trying to impress Connor, who'd gamely held out his brick-sized recorder.

Thea put her finger into one of the little pockets left by the now-absent watermelon pip. 'You feel so wet,' Michael had said, as if acting a part, and she'd prayed that he wouldn't ask her to do anal, because she wasn't quite ready for that yet. But he hadn't.

It was like a little switch had been turned on somewhere between her ribs, made each of her pores open to the sun, the smell of the lavender in the neighbouring fields, this watermelon.

Violet was now grunting like a tennis player every time she attacked another flower.

'Please can you stop destroying the flowers?' Thea said. 'Why are you doing that, anyway?'

'Because they're violet.'

'They're blue.'

'They're violet.'

'Blue.'

'My reality isn't the same as your reality or whatever.' But she stopped doing it anyway, and walked past Thea's pile of watermelon pips. 'You can eat them, you know.'

'I don't like them.'

'So you pick them out, but you'll pick your nose and eat it?'

'Shut the fuck up,' she said, with violence, glancing over at Connor, who sat cross-legged against the dry-stone wall, his chin tucked in a little, torso curved inwards. Occasionally, he'd pick up his pen and scribble in the notebook on his knee. What did he write in there? 'And can you stop with all the *fam* and *bruv* stuff? You're embarrassing yourself.'

'They're my brothers. *Our* brothers.'

'You don't have to ram it home every five minutes. We all know.'

'Just because you don't like them doesn't mean I can't.' Violet flung two fingers up and stalked back to the flowers.

Thea swore softly under her breath and looked over towards the wall again. Connor had put on his headphones now, maybe a wordless hint that they were being annoying.

A moth landed on her knee, papery and delicate, wings like dust. Or was it a butterfly? She didn't know how to tell them apart.

They were different, as well as the same. They just *were*. It was a shock when Luke, and eventually Connor, opened their mouths and these soft Northern vowels came out.

She wiped her watermelony fingers on her thigh and picked up her phone again to see what photos Jade and

Mischa had sent, styling it out in front of Gothic architecture or with hot chocolates or Hungarian boys.

Everything OK there, darling? xxxx

The third text from her mum today. She had not been completely able to conceal her worry at them flying solo for a week, or her slight resentment towards Dad's nonchalance – he did so often make a suggestion, wave his hand and expect everything to fall into place. Thea wondered what it would be like once he joined them in a week – they'd only ever been out here together with her mum as well. She childishly imagined elbowing Luke and Connor out of the way so that she could be nearer their dad. *Her* dad.

She texted back. Hey mum xxx

Yep, everyone doing what they do best ☺

She sent a pic of Violet taking photos of the scattered petals. A selfie with her shades on, a closed-lip smile and her book open. Connor under the tree, doubtless listening to something obscure. Luke had gone out shopping again – Thea should have joined him, but she was feeling more resolute than ever about doing as little as possible.

Lovely, her mum texted back. Rainy here. Going to take doggie for a walk. Take a rest from the reading! You deserve a break!

I can't help it, she thought. She liked to get ahead. And a book was always a good place to hide.

'Do you like them, Mum?' she'd asked, aged thirteen, after Dad had taken Luke and Connor to the train station. Her mum had made them all a Danish-themed Sunday lunch.

Pork, new potatoes in sugar and butter – Thea's favourite. Almond rice pudding with whipped cream.

'Of course I do, darling.'

'No, but for real.' Her mum had spent the whole time talking in a voice that was subtly higher and brighter than normal. Dad's jokes had been slightly worse than normal, and he'd told more of them. Violet kept tickling the boys and giggling – Connor flinching and looking startled, and Luke grinning and tickling back. Thea had kept her book on her lap. No one had seemed comfortable.

'For real.' Her mum took the dirty oven dish from her. 'It'll come, sweetheart. They don't have to feel like brothers right away.'

* * *

The incessant whine was on every single track. Connor had changed cables, adjusted levels on his handheld recorder, interface, laptop. It didn't make sense.

Pauline Oliveros, the other composer-who-was-more-than-a-composer that he was reading, talked about the differences between hearing and listening. Which sounds did he hear and which sounds did he listen to? Hearing: Violet muttering under her breath as she attacked imaginary people with the pool-cleaning pole. Luke exhaling through his press-ups, swearing when he'd got to the end of a particularly tough round. Listening: the sound of the bath tap running, and Thea singing along slightly tunelessly to the tinny sound of her music on her phone, a mix of blurred words and humming. Even if he didn't hear her in the bathroom, he knew when she'd been in by the unopened, steamed-up windows and the ring of tiny flecks of shaved leg-hair around the inner rim of the bath. He didn't understand how she could have baths when it was so hot.

Listening: this drone, that seemed so similar to the one he'd heard when he'd been submerged in the lake. It was pitched, but somehow he couldn't quite grasp it.

Maybe he'd need to go to the ENT department again. He kept putting off the implant – a bone-conducting hearing aid, slipped behind the skull, with a magnet to attach to the external processor. When he was a kid he'd tried out the temporary sort, and hated it. Cried all the time, at the alarming treble-heavy deluge that seemed to take over his brain. 'You shouldn't leave it too long,' the last specialist had said to Connor and his mum, when Connor had insisted he was going to wait until the quality of the technology improved. It would take six months for the brain to adjust to this new way of hearing, and he hadn't wanted to do it during his GCSEs, then his A levels. There was an obtuse side of him that liked hearing in a unique way. He'd worked hard on lowering the volume of his voice – his mum used to gently rub his cheek when he was a kid to stop him shouting. He preferred one naturally hearing ear to the sound they expected him to accept with the implant, like a shit practice amp turned all the way up.

He sat back in his desk chair and looked at the framed painting above the desk, a small rectangular abstract, four bands of colour painted on fabric. One of Josie's friends. His dad's second wife – he didn't like *stepmum* – was all over this house, worked in a gallery, maybe got given stuff for free. It was she who had stripped decades of paint from the doors, had the wooden beams encased in modern plaster, the walls painted pale terracotta. She liked ceramics, too, oddly shaped pots that sat on various mismatched pieces of furniture looking like they'd melted in the heat.

He had no feelings either way about Josie. She was excessively complimentary and made sure that they had everything they needed, but in a kind, practical way – towels, or drinks – while their dad just threw money at them. She'd tempted Will away, Connor supposed, but he only ever blamed his dad for that, not her.

Will had first come up to Manchester on his own, with a bag full of presents. He'd always overspent since, ceramic knives or City merchandise for Luke, and things that were never quite right for Connor – the wrong album, or once, a tenor ukulele, the pricey wooden kind. Connor had sold it and bought some studio headphones instead.

They'd come here twice before, just he and Luke and those two, Will clearly hoping that a nice house in France would smooth over the cracks in their relationship. Lots of ice cream and water sports. Posh red wine – maybe that's why Connor didn't drink, because his dad did. The effort was grating, embarrassing. Never to Luke, who ate it all up, but it was transparent to Connor how guilty Will felt. He never wanted to do much to alleviate it.

A tapping at the door. Violet was leaning against it, standing on one leg. Today's T-shirt said *WHATEVER BRO*. 'Can I hear it?'

'Sure.' He brought up the edited recording of Violet repeatedly falling backwards into the pool, passed her the headphones, pressed play.

While she listened, his attention drifted to the sounds outside – someone using a grass trimmer, far off, the church bell on the half-hour. He waited for Violet to say something about the high-pitched drone on the track.

She didn't.

'Sick.' She gave the headphones back and stood by the window next to the desk, tapping the wooden sill with her nails. 'That was a seriously long swim you did yesterday.'

He nodded and pretended to fiddle with some leads.

'Luke thought you'd drowned. He was freaking out. Starting to do this chain-of-command thing.'

Connor didn't ask what Thea thought.

'Were you trying to kill yourself?'

The words were delivered so brightly that he didn't immediately take them in.

'What? No.' Though it had been oblivion, of a sort, that he'd been stretching for.

'Oh.' She looked a little disappointed.

'You fed up with me already?' He meant it as a joke, but it came out a little too deadpan.

'No,' she said, turning back to him, her eyes wide. 'No way. I didn't mean that. I just…' she looked suddenly off into the distance, as if she'd heard something. 'Wanted to know what it felt like.'

It wouldn't feel like anything, he thought, but her tone

had changed enough for him to tread carefully. He looked outwards too. 'OK. Um. Why's that?'

'Just do.'

He didn't know what else to say, and remembered coming into the kitchen on the first day to find her holding the largest knife up, moving its point so that it reflected a slab of light on the furthest wall, transfixed.

She suddenly turned back to the window, puffed out her cheeks and slapped them with both hands, making a gassy sound, the glass fogging. Looked up at the sky with one eye shut. 'Do you think the sky looks a different colour today?' As if they hadn't even just been talking about anything dark.

He looked up. 'Looks pretty blue to me.'

'Yeah, but a different blue. Like there's something covering it.'

They both stared at it.

'Don't think so,' said Connor.

* * *

I want you so badly
Please don't let this be it
Seriously?

Lying on his bed – Dad's bed, until he got here – Luke watched the messages, each one adding a little brick of guilt from his stomach up to his chest. 'Please go away,' he said, quite softly. Yet he wasn't deleting them. Why couldn't he delete them?

He didn't really know how it had started. Jamie, in his straight shirt and straight tie by the instant hot-water machine in the staffroom, giving Luke a sharp, suspicious look when he'd joked about needing caffeine after his wild night out with the boys (never one for keeping his here-and-queer light under a bushel). That afternoon, he'd come to collect his class after their PE lesson with Luke and his uni supervisor and had barely looked at him. Yet a week later, Jamie was fucking his arse clean away in the men's toilet of the teachers' pub after everyone else had left.

> For fucks sake Luke, answer yr phone, this is doing my head in
>
> I know youre reading these
>
> Youre there right now

Jamie, with his extra ten years and lived-in-Loughborough-all-his-life. Jamie, with his sensible haircut and lanyard round his neck. Jamie, who couldn't get it up unless he was calling Luke *a dirty fucking fag*.

He was supposed to be forgetting all about him over here. Leave everything at Heathrow, he'd told himself as he entered the walkway to the plane, Violet bouncing ahead of him. Let it fizzle out on its own.

The sound of one of his sisters shouting in disgust downstairs snapped him out of it. By the time he got to the kitchen, the other three were standing looking at the kitchen table as if it were a crime scene. A large knife was sticking out of their second watermelon. There was a sour, sulphurous smell.

'Taste that,' Violet said, giving him a piece of watermelon.

He spat it out into his hand as soon as he'd put it in his mouth. 'Jesus.' It was rank, rotten.

'It made this hissing sound when I cut into it,' Thea said. 'Like a cat.'

'And then the major stink attack,' said Violet.

For a moment, no one spoke. There was the faint rasp of a car on the road below the house.

Luke clapped his hands together. 'Let's get pizza. I'll buy.'

'And more wine,' said Thea, following him out of the door.

A garden dormouse, spectacled black, is making a nest on the outside sill between the living-room window and the shutter. Though nocturnal, it is becoming wakeful during the day, and travels further than its memory to find materials. Beyond the house, and further still.

It lines the nest's interior with the softest things. Fur and feathers, moss and grass.

The nest grows to an ambitious size. A nest for many mice.

Three

Rock 'n' roll. Between a rock and a hard place. Solid as a rock. From the Middle English *rokke* and the Old English *rocc* and the Old French *roche*.

Their nearest big village was twelve kilometres away, down the most massive of hills, before you crossed the dam bridge and hit the lake proper. Round a few sweeping corners, and then you were there, with its *bateaux électriques* and paddleboards, places that sold ice cream and burgers, as well as posher places that Dad and Thea liked and Violet didn't. It was small and medieval, tucked into the cliff, with little cobbled steps joining the narrow lanes together, the roofs of the houses peach-coloured. Cats lolled in the shade and once Violet had watched a nest of baby swallows high up under an awning, sticking their beaks out and making tiny bleeping noises.

After parking up in the village, Violet and Thea had taken their brothers down the dusty gravel track past the boat club and the tennis courts, past the families encamped with picnics and gazebos until, a mile later, it wound through a bank of twisted trees and gorse bushes, necessitating hurdles – in Violet's case, anyway – over protruding roots and one precarious eroding section. Then left and down the slope, so steep that it had a rope to help you down the last part, until you reached the sickest piece of granite rising out of the lake, craggy and low.

'This,' Luke had said as they approached it, 'is very cool.'

'It rocks my world,' said Violet.

The rock felt like a secret. At its tallest point, it was gouged and scratched, and from the top you could see the lake stretching far away in all directions. The previous times Violet and Thea had come had been punctuated by invasions from French and German families in boats, but this afternoon it was all theirs. It was another roasting day. Violet tried to remember a time when sunshine simply equalled joy, not some joy and mostly dread. The rock used to be connected to the shore by a short, humped spit of sand, but now, due to drought, the spit was much wider. The main jump into the lake used to be five metres high but now looked like six or seven, a bit scary even for her.

They spent the next hour jumping off the rock, swimming, sunbathing, or in Violet's case, training to be a wildlife photographer. The massive dragonfly went past again, and Violet leapt up from her position at the base of the rock. First, she'd been trying to capture the golden eagle that kept coming over – once, it circled lower and lower, then suddenly dipped down to the water and rose again with a black curve of fish in its talons. But it was too far away to get anything good. The dragonfly, on the other hand, was right here. She put her camera on high-speed sports mode setting and took liberal aim.

'Any moment now,' said Thea, from her reclining position on her towel, book aloft, 'you're going to trip and fall in and that camera is going to be ruined.'

'Worth it for my masterpiece,' Violet said, treading over her.

Luke, holding his phone above his head, one elbow shielding his eyes, glanced over with a benign smile, and went back to his screen.

The dragonfly looked exactly like a tiny remote-controlled helicopter. She imagined flying it low over the water, veering round and dive-bombing Thea, her screaming and running away. Her sister didn't seem much bothered by lowering water levels and global climate meltdown, and more concerned with how flat her stomach looked when she lay down on her back. Violet was sure she was sucking it in, even though there was no one here to look at it.

The dragonfly suddenly lifted, shooting above their heads and out over the gleaming water.

'Damn,' she said. It was probably a drone. The caretaker's drone. Spying on her, checking she wasn't telling anyone.

She clambered up the rock with her camera, to where Connor was sitting with his elbows on his knees, next to one of the two tiny trees that clung on for dear life. He was recording the air again, and kept shifting the headphone on and off his good ear. Drops of the lake on his bare back from their jumps earlier – he did a backflip off the lower ledge – the ridges of his spine mirroring the ridges of the granite.

She sat down beside him and started swiping through her photos. One wasn't bad, actually, catching the fine webbing of the dragonfly's double wings, the massive turquoise eyes. She showed Connor the screen, and he nodded with a half-smile that meant he hadn't really taken it in.

'What are you thinking about?' she said. He must do a lot of thinking, seeing as he didn't say that much.

'Not really thinking,' he said, taking off his headphones. 'Listening.'

She balanced her camera beside her, crossed her legs and made herself sit still, which she usually tried to avoid. If she sat still, she would think about things. A billowy little butterfly, neon yellow and orange, went past them, then back the other way.

'Can you hear anything?' Connor said.

She glanced at him, a little surprised, shut her eyes and listened. But thoughts got in the way first. Thoughts, and images, and the feeling of wanting to curl up into a hole and be buried forever.

'I mean, not really,' she said, taking a deep breath. 'It's pretty quiet. Kind of weirdly quiet, actually. Where is everybody?'

He nodded again, as if she'd confirmed something, and gazed at the water. She snapped a quick shot of it, though she'd already taken loads earlier. Then a shot of him, though it didn't feel right to ask him to pose. Connor wasn't much up for photos. He tilted his face slightly towards her and shut one eye as she took it, and she knew he was just pretending not to mind.

'Why?' she said. 'What can you hear?'

His right ear was smaller, not smooth-lobed around the top but crinkled, like a shell. He'd described it to her once before, how sounds weren't just quieter but had less dimension, less colour. She imagined seeing the lake with the colour turned down – though it looked a bit like that anyway, at least in her photos. She was sure it used to be bluer. Now it had a greyish, lavender look.

Connor didn't speak straight away, as if he was checking. 'A high note. Really high.' He shook his head. 'Not a normal sort of sound. Can't really describe it. Like… you can feel it.'

Violet sat still one more time. Held her breath. Heard the lapping of the lake on the stones, telling her she was disgusting.

'Maybe you've got that thing,' she said. 'You know. What's it called, the ear thing that you get if you're next to an explosion. Tourette's.'

'Tinnitus.'

'Yeah, that.'

'Maybe.' He looked at his hands. His nails were very bitten, with no white at all.

'Or it's the dam.' She pointed to the shore, where the water butted the stone in slight movements. 'That means they're regulating the levels. Probably some weird electrical thing.' She tried to tell herself that this was why the shore and rock were so much more exposed than last time, and not because there was not enough rain and the planet was burning up. There'd been several wildfires already in the South of France this month.

'Maybe,' he said.

'Do you want me to paint your nails? To stop you biting them?'

A gentle laugh through his nose. 'Yeah, you probably should, to be fair.'

They looked back out at the lake. It *was* quiet.

* * *

'Incoming,' said Luke.

Thea looked over. She'd given up on her A-level books and was reading Angela Carter, imagining herself the tiger's bride – the roughness of fur, his rasping tongue on her skin.

Luke was leaning up on his elbows, gazing out onto the smooth centre of the lake, totally unselfconscious. He'd already got so tanned, and the fine brown-blond hairs ghosted up from the waistband of his trunks. The filigree gold chain he always wore settled along his clavicle. Pls send pics of the sexy gay brother, Jade had texted. In trunks, Mischa had added. Ur bad people, Thea had texted back.

Thea followed Luke's gaze, saw the shallow angle of a bent arm, then its opposite. A paddleboarder was shadowing the swimmer, moving with long, slow strokes.

'Oh,' said Violet, bounding down the jagged rock as if she was in trainers, not bare feet. 'Thought we were going to have it to ourselves all day.'

'Where did they even come from?' said Thea. 'Has he swum across the whole lake?'

'Proper stamina if so,' said Luke.

They watched them approach, the swimmer's brown arms

and head flashing, turning, the paddleboarder's lazy drift beside them.

'You need to shave your legs, by the way,' Thea said to her sister, quietly.

'What?' Violet looked down.

'Getting a bit foresty down there.' She was only trying to be helpful. No way was her sister going to be reeling in any hormonal adolescents with her current look.

Violet crossed her arms tightly over her chest and didn't say anything.

The pair curved towards them into the shallows. The paddleboarder was a white man in board shorts, with long brown dreadlocks wrapped around the top of his head, and the sides shaved to nothing. The swimmer rose from the shelving inlet like a single lean muscle, with deep-brown skin and small black Speedos. Thea was fairly sure that she heard Luke swear under his breath.

'*Bonjour*,' the swimmer muttered, in that beautifully indistinct way of francophones. Nodded up at Connor, who was still on top of the rock.

Luke returned the greeting, as did Thea. The paddleboarder jumped down, skimming his board into the cove and onto the rocks, grinning cheerfully at them.

'English?' said the swimmer, and she felt disappointed, as she always did, that it was so obvious. Wanted to apologise.

They stood around in an awkward semicircle while the swimmer drank half a large bottle of water provided by his friend, Thea trying hard not to look at the ridged stomach and teardrop-shaped thigh muscles. The sunlight, where it fell on him, gave him a coppery glimmer. He said he and the paddleboarder were water sports instructors further round the lake, and Luke told them where they were staying. Luke had a hand on the back of his neck, his bicep showing, and for once, wasn't quite his open, breezy self.

'I go finish this now,' the swimmer said, stretching languidly and looking back over the lake as if it was a modestly sized pool and not a colossal reservoir. He'd already done five kilometres, he'd said. 'Have a nice holiday.'

'Hot,' said Thea, once the swimmer and his friend had disappeared round the rock, hoping she wasn't fetishising.

'Ugh,' said Violet, opening a packet of crisps and launching herself up the face of the rock again using only one hand.

'Insanely,' said Luke.

'Could be game on there,' Thea said, hearing the slight falseness in her voice. Luke had been a bit reticent about his love life. She'd rather hoped that they would be sharing gossip and lusting after men together, but though Luke would respond, it often seemed half-hearted.

Luke looked at the frilled wake of the swimmer. 'That would be lovely.' He sounded wistful, she thought, before he glanced at her with a grin. 'Girl's got gaydar, has she?'

'Maybe,' said Thea, grandly, though she'd rather hoped that the swimmer was extremely straight, or at least bi or pan and lazily content with all types of bodies. 'He definitely looked at you more than me.'

'Bollocks,' said Luke. 'You're like bloody Venus standing in your seashell.' He upturned his palms in a self-consciously graceful movement. 'That's literally the artiest reference that uncultured little me can manage, so—' He winked.

'I'll take it,' Thea said, though she hoped to look rather less hefty than Venus. She glanced up at the rock, where Connor was taking a handful of crisps from Violet's proffered packet. He hadn't even come down to say hi to their visitors.

'Can I ask a favour?' Luke said, quite abruptly.

'Sure.'

He bent down to pick up his phone and gave it to her. 'Can you hold on to this? I could do with – a break from it.'

'Look,' Violet called. She was standing one-legged on the highest ledge and put her hands together. 'Whoa.' She wobbled, put her hands out to the side, and back into prayer position.

'If you fall off,' said Thea, 'I am not rescuing you.'

'I won't fall off,' said Violet. 'I'm a daredevil.' She raised her hands, palms still together, above her head, and chanted, like Thea and their mum did in front of their YouTube yoga. Closed her eyes. '*Ommmm.*'

'It is a bit dangerous, mate,' said Luke.

'You'll split your head open,' said Thea.

'Sick.' Her sister wobbled again.

'*Violet.* Can you stop her?' Thea said to Connor, who was nearest.

'She's fine,' Connor called down.

'Great. Encouragement is all she needs,' said Thea, and at the same moment, Violet teetered, yelped, and fell into the water.

* * *

53

Connor stared at the screen. It seemed more and more difficult to get aroused, watching porn. He used to look at what was termed female-friendly pages, but the videos still had titles like *Tight young virgin gets cream pie*, or *Nubile teen has her first DP and loves it*, and there were girls bleeding after anal sex, only they were in hotel rooms with floaty white curtains and didn't look like they'd been picked up off the street. In the end, it had been better to go with the normal stuff, where they didn't bother pretending that the girls were having a good time.

After the lake – and after Thea had yelled at Violet for frightening them all – they'd had a late lunch back in the town at a café with tables on the terrace. Thea had ordered for everyone, because she had the best French. The waiter had winked at her as she'd passed him the menus, and she'd watched him leave, straightening and twisting her still-damp hair around her fist, before catching Connor looking at her. 'What?' she'd said, her face as cool and featureless as limestone. He'd shaken his head and looked out to the lake again until their food had come. He had pissed her off, not getting Violet down before she toppled head-first into the lake. She'd been fine, though, coming up grinning, rubbing her smacked arms.

Now, headphones on, he watched a guy wearing a mask fuck an older, blindfolded woman with unnaturally large breasts in the woods. He felt completely detached.

His phone buzzed.

He wondered how much, if anything, the woman was getting paid for this. How many crew there were and if they got off on watching it.

His phone buzzed again. He sighed and closed his laptop. It wasn't doing much for him anyway.

It was Kaia.

how is Bonjour Tristesse land? xx

He pressed pause on the video, turned the screen away. Less dads, more siblings, so far, he texted back. Otherwise basically the same. A sunglasses emoji.

There'd only been her, really. Thick as thieves for the last two years, when she was one of the few girls who joined his sixth form. They'd found the same intensity in each other, sat on her bed watching videos on her laptop, shared headphones, studied in the library. She had a pierced tongue, spoke in film quotes and made stovetop espressos that tasted like tar. He loved her family, too – her Scottish dad and Thai mum, whose meals contained enough chilli to blow his head off. Everyone thought the two of them were together – she was bisexual, but commented on girls more than boys. They'd kissed a few times at gigs, held hands in the street, but it always trod the line between something proper and friends. He'd hung in there until she got a girlfriend, and then felt surprised at his level of relief.

It had got embarrassing, the absence of action. You start thinking it will never happen. The opposite of Luke, who'd started smuggling in boys from the age of fourteen before graduating to having them over for tea – an array of mostly sporty, polite lads who'd charm their mum and look longingly at Luke as he served up his latest signature dish.

Hows u, he texted Kaia.

working my arse off so fuck u, Kaia texted. She was pulling shifts in an egg-packing factory all summer, unlike him.

55

At the lakeside café, Luke had waved their dad's credit card around like he had a business account. Was Connor the only one who felt guilty about being here? It was hypocritical bullshit, their dad doing human rights law and still having this house. Did it even occur to Thea, to Luke even? The embarrassment of privilege made his skin crawl. As far as he could make out, his mum and dad's politics were roughly the same, even if he doubted very much that Will was off on protests about housing or crime bills every month like Alanna. He wondered if she would splash out on a house like this, if she had the money. He doubted it, somehow.

It wasn't just the accents – that mix of chopped London and a bit of southern posh that neither of them thought was an accent at all – it was the way they carried themselves, even Violet. More easy confidence, as if their lot were the default. A grammar-school boy, he didn't quite feel working-class, definitely not with his dad now back in the picture, but he felt a shade more so compared to them. Like he had something to prove. Thea talked about London like it was obviously the centre of everything, but he didn't get it. He didn't mind the crowds – it was busy enough in Manchester – but people were ruder, didn't call you *love* when they gave you your receipt. Less space to breathe, somehow.

He did work. His mum had instilled the importance of it in them from day one. On weekends, he did ushering in town for the Hallé Orchestra, heard a load of music for free. Luke liked having money, would take anything going – paper round, behind the till at a newsagent's, delivering takeaways on a bike. Thea had mentioned something about helping her mum out with admin for the gallery, and Connor couldn't help smarting at the nepotism.

Yeah i suck i know, he texted now, to Kaia.

love u really, Kaia texted.

but hate u just as much

living ur La Piscine dream xx

He wanted to tell her everything. He wanted to tell someone. Wish u were here x, he typed, instead.

She sent him a selfie from the factory, her middle finger up at the camera.

He smiled and put his phone face down, and opened his laptop again. Tried not to think what Kaia would say about him watching this stuff. They had only one time watched porn together – her suggestion – and she'd given a faux-serious commentary on the camera angles and the actors' motivations. On the screen, another man, shorter and fatter than the first, and wearing what looked like a homemade squirrel mask, appeared from behind the trees. The cameraman was talking in an East European language.

Porn showed you everything. You could see it all, forensically, surgically. But it still didn't tell you what it *felt* like.

'Luke says he's making food for seven thir—'

Connor half turned, turned back and flipped his laptop down, feeling the heaviness in his shorts.

'Oh, my God. Classic,' said Thea, walking out again.

* * *

Implacable, a male wall-lizard rests on the stone, absorbing heat from the baking rock. A hint of lake-colours and black etching like ancient code. His tail is unusually forked, splitting into two tails, one shorter than the other.

A fly passes, an angry little knot of sound, and is trapped, blink-quick, by the lizard's tongue. The buzz muffled in its throat, then disappearing.

Insects have been scarce in recent years, but here is another fly, and another.

The lizard cannot stop. He eats and eats, beyond what is necessary.

* * *

'*Roquette, huile d'olive*,' said Violet as she set the table.

Rocket, olive oil, lemon. Radicchio and basil with hard little green lentils. Figs and honey. The rest of this morning's baguette with *tomme de savoie*, Luke's favourite, and semi-firm. Though they'd all eaten loads at lunch, he'd spent the last hour washing basil leaves and rubbing a garlic clove around the ceramic bowl he used for dressings. Sea salt in a flat terracotta dish. Food gave Luke focus.

'*Figues* and '*onee*,' said Violet.

'*Miel*,' corrected Thea, who'd already opened the wine.

'Damn,' said Violet.

Luke thought back to the swimmer, all six foot two of him, with his blunt accent and glittering eyes. That protruding belly button. That arse.

You're a fucking slut, he heard Jamie say. *You'd give it up to anyone, wouldn't you?*

58

'Do you want your phone back?'

'Hmm?'

Thea had it in her hand. 'You, um, keep getting messages. I didn't look on purpose.'

Luke didn't make eye contact as he took it from her. 'Cheers.'

'Are you OK, Luke?' Her voice was lower, Violet having gone outside again. 'Is everything… all right back home?'

'Yeah.' He smiled what he knew was not a thoroughly convincing smile. 'It's all good. Just need my daily quota of wine.' Goosebumps had risen up on his forearms.

Thea hovered, as if hoping he'd say more, but he couldn't. Not now. Eventually, she nodded and trailed out to the table.

'Fuck,' he said, quietly, gathering the crumbs off the counter and tossing them in the sink.

He was supposed to be better than this. He was the life and soul, had mucked in with the LGBTQIA+ Soc at uni, been rainbow-dusted for Pride, supporting two other lads in coming out. With his mum always ferociously behind him – including a shouting match with his slightly obtuse Catholic grandfather – he didn't care what others thought. His football team, swim team, athletics squad – all the straight boys at uni had done the surprised, overly-nodding thing, and that had been it. Yet he'd let Jamie – he licked the tip of his finger and placed it lightly in the salt dish, bringing one crystallised square up to his tongue – he'd let him go too far.

A man in every port, he'd said once, and his mum had laughed and said, *As long as you're safe, you can have as many men as you want. Safe as houses, Mum*, he'd said.

'*Mon frère.*' Violet was whistling, loud as a sheep farmer, from outside. '*Je suis* starving.'

* * *

They'd got midway through their meal by the time Connor finally appeared. Violet was half eating, and half occupied with killing her arch-enemy, aka mosquitoes. She'd had a dream this morning about Whitney Houston singing 'I Will Always Love You' and woken up to find a mosquito right by her ear. It had been flying in a circle, round and round as if drunk, before she'd got it.

'Finished up there, have you?' Thea was smiling sweetly at Connor.

'Finished what?' said Violet.

'Researching visuals for his next soundtrack,' she said, putting one finger in her glass and sucking it as if she did that sort of thing every day. She wanted so badly to be French it was embarrassing.

She was doing that Dad-thing of talking loudly over dinner, asking questions that she knew the answer to, or playing devil's advocate by announcing something controversial. She never said so, but she obviously wanted to be a lawyer like him. That way she'd be able to argue all day long. *Debate,* Dad would say. They often went at it, Dad and Thea, while Violet rolled her eyes and her mum winked at her and mouthed something about dessert and TV.

'That's cool,' said Violet to Connor. 'I could totally film something for you, if you ever want me to.'

'Can you film squirrels?' said Thea.

Violet looked perplexed. 'I dunno. Yeah. Why?'

'Connor's into squirrels.'

'Really?'

'Not really,' said Connor, pulling a plate over.

'Do they have them round here?' said Violet.

'I've definitely seen one,' said Thea.

'What's "squirrel" in French?' said Luke, tipping the dregs of the wine bottle into his glass.

'*Le squirrel*,' said Violet.

'I actually don't know that one,' said Thea, reaching for her phone.

'*Le petit*... what's "mouse"?'

Connor was tearing apart the last of the bread, and there was an angry blotch of red on his neck.

'It's not that,' Thea said, typing, her face lit up by her screen. '*Écureuil*,' she announced, sitting back before smacking her arm loudly. 'Ugh, bastards.'

'Wait,' said Violet. 'Listen.'

Everyone stilled under the plum-blue of the sky. After half a minute, there it was again, the fleck of black, quick as a blink, from the trees at the far end of the garden and away over the roof. Then another, coming back the other way, with the faintest hiss of wings.

Another, and another.

Later, in bed, Violet looked at her photos of the sunset. From the top of the wall, she'd taken one exactly every minute for almost half an hour, until Luke had called her to help lay the table. Wide-angle, with the big single tree two fields away to the left. The cloudless sky had shimmered, *shimmied*, into twilight. It was hard to notice the changes in colour when you were watching it, but now, scrolling through the photos, it was captured, shade by shade. She would send the best to her mum.

She hoped she'd accidentally captured a bat – it was too dark by the time she'd spotted them at the dinner table. In Thea's book, someone wanted to know what it was like to be a bat – no, for a *bat* to be a bat. Sick, was the answer. You got to fly loop-de-loops in the dark, firing out teeny high-pitched sounds that bounced off surfaces to tell you where you were. You slept hanging upside down. She'd never seen so many before, though – there'd been thirty, at least. Apparently, some of the babies would be flying by now, going back to suckle their mums, whilst their dads roosted on their own.

She wondered if a bat felt its gender, or just felt really, really *bat*. She was sure it would be easier just to be bat.

Sometimes, the more she thought about her own pronouns, the less they sounded like anything. She/her became a whispering sea on pebbles, then evaporated completely. You could be they/them but that made you sound like lots of people, and she was barely one. You could mix them up, be she/they or they/he or she/they/he. But nothing felt right, really.

Making up your own pronouns would probably piss everyone off. 'Vee/vye,' Violet tried, under her breath, as she swiped through her images. Pass *vye* the salt. *Vee* is going to the shops.

Towards the end of her sunset photos, when the sky was pale lavender, a ripple of darker lavender appeared in the top right-hand corner of each photo. As if she was looking at wet paper. She zoomed in, but the ripple didn't get any more pixillated. Weird.

She peered at her little playback screen, rubbed carefully at it, and took the lens cap off to wipe the lens with her soft cloth. Maybe a mosquito had got stuck on the lens earlier and distorted the image. That was the thing with hot countries – guaranteed sunshine, guaranteed blood-sucking mozzies. On an American website, she'd found loads of different slang names for them. Swamp angels. Cousins. Drill bugs. Brassheads. Well, England would be getting their own names for them soon enough, she thought, putting the camera by her bed.

Four

Connor's notebook was lying in the grass by the roots of the oak tree. He hadn't spoken to Thea all day, barely even looked at her. Last night, she'd heard him swimming for ages, proper somersault turns at each end.

She glanced over towards the house. Violet and Luke had driven to the town to pick up a few things – Luke said the supermarket was better than a museum. Connor was probably watching more totally unsavoury porn. She'd thought herself way above it, but when she'd been with Michael, she was aware of mentally checking off all the positions. For the first couple of times, she'd felt outside herself. Still, at least she hadn't been wearing a creepy mask.

She walked over to the oak tree, tipped the notebook open with her toe, and crouched down to look.

Dates, words, drawings. The small, compact handwriting curled in on itself. *Breeze interacting with birdsong*, she read, under today's date. *Trying to hear them as one thing but keep separating them. Drone never seems to fit with any natural pitch.* There was a drawing, a loose circle with three lines stemming from it, like a crude impression of a sun.

He was always stilling, as if someone had pressed pause on him, or as if he'd spotted prey. *Listening.* Maybe that's what you did when you were half-deaf, you had to listen with much more effort. He couldn't always work out where the sound came from – Luke had called to him in the crowded airport lounge, and Connor had turned round in a circle, vulnerable and wary.

She picked up the notebook. The previous pages were more of the same, a detached analysis of noises. There were quotations, too – *'what kind of tree makes a sound?'* he'd written, with three question marks after it. And *'listen for a heart sound'.*

'What are you doing?'

She straightened in an instant and got a slight head-rush. 'Nothing.'

Connor was standing there, chewing on his lip, looking at the book in her hand.

She felt the prickle of bugs on her bare legs, reached down and scratched, still holding his book. 'God, they hate me.'

He didn't seem to hear her. 'Why did you do that yesterday?' His eyes flicked over to hers, impassive.

'Do what?' She knew exactly what he meant, and he knew she did. Because it made her feel good, to be superior to him.

'Everybody watches porn,' he said. 'You watch porn.'

A rash of heat over her upper arms, her chest. She thought about denying it, for a half a second, but she wasn't going to let him get the better of her. Angela Carter fuelled her imagination much more – you weren't going to find a woman being ravished by a tiger, at least not in the places she looked. Though it probably did exist, because every possible scenario existed somewhere online, and she was absolutely not going to look that up.

'So?' she said. 'Not in the daytime, at my desk. Like I'm *studying.*'

He took a breath, released it short and sharp, and looked beyond her. 'Can I have my book, please?' He held out his hand. His blunt nails were painted dark green.

It's not my fault Dad left your mum, she wanted to say. *I didn't do anything wrong.* 'Fine,' she said, passing it to him, and stalking back into the house.

* * *

It's hot. Tinder-dry. Drier than ever.

Behind Connor, a stag beetle clacks along the paving, mandibles curved, its segmented body swaying in a curious new dance. Returning to a central point, stalking outwards again.

A hare halts in the wheatfield. Though already in late pregnancy, she is pregnant again. Her younglings shiver and turn inside her.

* * *

'Hey, Mum.'

'Hiya, love. How is everything?'

He was lying on a lounger under the umbrella. His mum was outside the library where she worked, having a cigarette and holding up her phone.

'Oh, you know.' There was always a subtext – making sure it didn't seem like he was having fun so she didn't resent him.

67

You know we've got another dad, Luke used to say to him as kids, when they still shared a room. *He lives in London*. London seemed as far away as Japan to Connor, and the idea of a second father just as distant. All Connor had known until the age of nine had been Dave, with his plaid shirts and dirt under his nails, taking him along to rock gigs, bright-yellow ear-defenders not quite filtering out the dirty, nasty guitars and synths. Their mum hadn't been married to him but he was still his stepdad. Then Dave was gone, first out of the house and then moving back to Canada to look after his sick mum, and Connor finally understood that it had only been temporary, that he was not worthy of having a father who stayed.

He'd always been ready to hate Will, sensing his mum's stubbornness over his access to her sons. Luke had got angry at her for not letting him see them, but Connor had always stayed loyal. Hadn't much wanted to know him.

'Are you feeding the cat?' he said to his phone screen.

'Course I'm feeding the cat. Not that he needs it. Found another chaffinch on the doorstep today. Another rated-18 morning for me.'

He couldn't help feeling proud. Spike had always been his, a black cat with a modest spray of white on his chest. He still merrily scratched strangers and terrorised birdlife, but insisted on commanding Connor's lap the moment he sat down anywhere. He had the softest ears and made excellent chord clusters when he walked over the piano.

'Been out on the bike?' he asked.

'Not as much fun without you. I'm back to the walking. Seven thousand steps done today.'

'Sweet.' Connor propped up his phone on the folded towel so that he could gently clap her.

'Are you having fun, then?' his mum said. Again, the slight barb in the question.

'It's fine.' Neutral answers were best. And most accurate.

'As long as you're covered up. Factor 50 if not.'

He gave a half-hearted salute. 'Yes, Mum.' She'd always been overprotective of them both, but he didn't mind. At least he knew she wasn't going anywhere.

'Blame your Irish blood, poppet.' She gave him a finger-flick of salute back. The two dry wits of the family. 'As you were, Connor.'

As he put his phone down, he realised that Thea was standing a little way behind his lounge chair. He sat up.

'Can you do my back?' she said. She was holding the bottle of suntan lotion out, her other arm over her stomach, in the red bikini top and white denim shorts. Her face a little more open than usual. He wondered how long she'd been there, and what she'd heard.

He couldn't say no. He'd watched Luke do it, cheerfully and unselfconsciously. Or Violet, too, trying to give her a violent elbow massage at the same time. They hadn't come back yet from the shops.

'OK.'

She sat down on the end of his lounger, passing the bottle back without turning round and moving her hair over the front of one shoulder.

Connor shifted up, trying to ignore the lump in his throat. She'd seen him, watching that crap. She thought she was better than him. She *was* better than him. He squeezed some lotion into his hand and tried not to think about anything. He rubbed the lotion between her shoulder blades, working outwards, using one hand, then the other. *Natural guava and mango scent*, the bottle said, and it was a more intense version of her smell when she walked past.

She was sitting very straight. Fine blonde hairs on the base of her neck and shoulder. A mosquito bite on her thigh, dark pink. He imagined the bug planting itself upon her skin, siphoning out the blood. Wondered what it tasted like.

'So I've been reading up on him,' she said, quite brightly, still facing forward.

'On who?' he said.

'John Cage. Of Arizona fame.' She was obviously trying to make an effort, after earlier.

He watched his fingers swipe out over her shoulder blades. 'OK.'

'He wrote a piece consisting of no sound.'

'Um, not exactly.'

'Yes, he did. Four minutes thirty-three seconds of nothing. Which seems quite lazy for a composer.'

He swiped up to her neck, the hairs slicking down. 'It's more conceptual.' He sounded like an arsehole.

'OK,' she said, in that half-questioning, non-committal way.

'It's not really about silence. It's about sound.' A total arsehole.

She made that small hum that he'd begun to realise meant that she was thinking, not dismissing.

Should he keep talking? 'Like...' He took a deep breath. 'All sound is interesting. Basically.' When he wrote essays, he was articulate, fashioned long, wordy sentences. 'It could have been five minutes forty, or three minutes twenty-seven, or whatever. It's about shining a light on the things you might not normally notice. Embracing everything you hear. I think.'

She hummed again.

A final squelch of liquid into his palm. Down to the waistband of her shorts and out to the curves of her sides. He turned his hands over and wiped the rest from his knuckles onto her, above each of her hips. Too gently.

Thea didn't move. He stared at the raised bone at the top of her spine. Goosebumps had risen on her skin.

'Thanks,' Thea said to him, getting up and walking away without once looking round.

Connor looked at the milky creases in his hands. Wiped them on his shorts.

* * *

'Je crois... je crois... ce soir!' shouted one DJ into his distorted mic.

'Oh, God,' sighed Thea. 'It's so lame.'

'I love it,' said Luke.

The European predilection for open-air concerts and discos on the warm nights (i.e. all of them) in their villages suited Luke down to the ground. You'd see posters for Beckett plays and ballets in the towns, but in the big village it was pleasingly tacky: DJs rolling up from who-knows-where and setting up stages, multicoloured lights and sound systems.

It was in the marketplace by the car park, overlooking the lake and the most touristy section of beach. A promontory curved out from behind them with picnic benches and a *pétanque* area. Everyone and their aunt had come out to dance, locals and tourists, toddlers to seventy-year-olds, all unselfconsciously mad for it. Amandine, the fifty-something woman who ran the *galette* café and had become friendly with their dad and Josie, was there and greeted them all with double-cheek kisses, cigarette between her fingers. She didn't speak any English and always talked animatedly in French whilst giving them compliments along with free ice cream and touching their hair. There was the Lapsang Souchongy smell of wood-fired barbecue, the smoke mingling with cigarettes. The current trashy dance track featured a lot of accordion.

These two DJs were obliviously camp in white jeans and T-shirts behind their laptops, lovely tight Eurotrash arses, making him think of Jamie's arse, high and taut in those too-shiny teacher's trousers. (No. Don't think of him – that was why he'd dragged them all out, really. To not think of him.)

Violet was currently standing on a bench next to two old ladies in wheelchairs, taking photos of the dancers and then glaring at the screen. He'd already lost sight of Connor. It was so hard to keep them together. Connor lurked in the shade all day long, defiantly lost in the mask of book, notepad and headphones, or in his room. Thea was wrapped in a cycle of phone and sunbathing and swimming, always with an actorly sense of performance. Violet was more game, but even she'd been reluctant about tonight. *I'm no good at dancing,* she'd said, but he'd persuaded her by whacking on one of his tunes and dancing so badly that she said she'd come out if he stopped. He promised Thea they'd be each other's wingman at the hint of any hotness. He shamelessly used emotional blackmail on Connor, repeating Violet's threat of not coming if Connor didn't.

Luke scanned the masculine faction of the crowd, which mostly consisted of well-fed dads in shirts and canvas trousers wheeling their small children around, and twelve-year-olds. There were a couple of guys in their early twenties with cans of beer, all low-slung shorts and no tops, watching the dancers.

He nudged Thea and nodded towards them. 'Could be worse.' Was he allowed to pimp out his seventeen-year-old sister?

Thea followed his gaze, straightened and sounded less downbeat. Tonight she was wearing a white lacy dress that just about skimmed her thighs. 'Oh. Yeah. Maybe.'

He would dance to anything, near enough. His mum's influence. She was always grabbing him in the kitchen and dancing to the radio whilst Connor ran away. Taught him jive and swing. He'd learnt to entertain her early on, because she wasn't always happy and he'd do anything – wiggling his little kid-arse, doing pop routines with a wooden spoon – to make her laugh.

Luke used to hear his mum arguing with Dave over bills, and how Dave thought she should let Will see his sons. It was the first he knew of his dad sending them money. His mum, never one to hide her feelings, would complain about Dave's ever-changing jobs – landscape gardening, working in a record store, door-to-door carpet-cleaning – and round it would all go again. Luke had only fleeting memories of the tall man with the hairy hands and wide laugh who came before Dave. She'd always said it had been Will's choice to leave, and Luke felt that she had withheld access to him and Connor as a punishment, a feeling that he had grown more uncomfortable with over the years.

He finally looked him up on Facebook – not that Will put much on there, just a few holiday and work photos. He stalked him for a year, watched his two half-sisters' faces grow less round. Then he friended him. Will friended back. Luke wrote him a long message, then shortened it. Hello. This is Luke (your son). I just wanted to say hello. I hope you don't mind.

Luke, Will had written back. Of course I don't mind. I'm delighted to hear from you. Does your mum know you've got in touch?

Yes, he'd lied.

They continued halting correspondence, Luke's heart always in his mouth at the thought of being found out, and fairly sure that Will had known he'd lied. He told Connor about their messages, and his brother had given him a look like he'd betrayed some great clan motto.

When he was fifteen, he finally plucked up the courage to ask his mum to let him see Will. It had blown up into an argument loud with tears and shouting, two days of deeply uncomfortable silent treatment, and then hugs and apologies. The Sheridan way.

When Luke had asked Will about the long absence without communication, he'd said, *Well, your mother didn't want me to be in contact with you*. Luke did always wonder why he hadn't tried a little harder. There was always the niggling doubt that he'd have preferred never to receive that first message.

The DJs were now blasting out something with Spanish guitars and full-throated male voices yelling about some anguish or other. Violet had jumped off the bench and was bouncing around, and he felt proud of her for literally jumping out of her comfort zone.

'Right,' Luke said to Thea, and took her hand so that they could join her. 'Let's 'ave it.'

* * *

Violet found Connor down by the shoreline. 'Sick,' she said, looking at the cliff. The disco lights up above them were flaring dimly on the rock, like someone was taking flash photos of it. 'That is lit.'

She sat down next to him and Connor pointed upwards. Stars all over the place. You only had about five in South London. There were join-the-dots shapes, some sparkling faint orange, or ice green. The odd satellite zooming slowly through them like a star gone wrong. And you could see the planes, blinking red and white.

'Literally lit,' she said, before leaning over and burrowing her hand in the pebbles. She found a smooth round one and did an overarm throw. The lake gulped it up.

Connor was even quieter than normal tonight. Violet felt guilty for having a good time up at the disco, though mostly it had been with a ten-year-old Welsh boy called George and his older sister Gemma, who was twelve and had badly sunburned shoulders. They were so easy to talk to. They'd not questioned whether the music was any good, just taken her hands and wheeled around, before the three of them had dodged between all the families and stolen leftover hot dogs. Thea often said that Violet had to grow up, but she always felt better amongst people younger than her. No pressure to pretend to be interested in sticking your tongue down someone's throat. No pressure to be a girl, or a boy, just a kid.

Look where we are, she'd texted her dad, with a photo. Nooo, her dad had texted back, though he should have been asleep. I'm staying right here in Beijing. No risk of foam parties here. Last year, they'd pumped out chunky white suds over everyone, and Thea had been furious that her dress had been ruined. But u love them really, Violet texted. Yes V, her dad had replied. Yes, I do. xx

She twisted round to look back up the slope. From here, the dancers looked as if they'd been drawn around with neon-coloured pens. 'Thea is totally skanking on some guy,' she said.

Connor didn't say anything.

Yesterday, Violet had looked up another website on asexuality, and discovered a whole vocabulary of other words that made her brain hurt. There was so much choice that she felt lost. Abrosexual, akoisexual, ageosexual, apothisexual, which meant someone who is repulsed by sex. She didn't feel repulsed, not exactly, just – blank. Not like Thea, who was definitely allosexual. *Allo, sexual*, she imagined Thea saying in her very precise French accent.

It was so warm, and so still. Violet wondered when it would get so hot here that people would only socialise at night, having to stay in all day or die of a heart attack.

You should die of a heart attack, she heard, from her own mind.

Shut up, she said back.

'Sorry you don't like the music,' she said to Connor, rifling her hand through the pebbles again.

'It's OK,' said Connor, who took a big breath in and seemed to wake up a bit. He stood up. 'Coke?'

'Always. They have Coke Zero so I won't even get fat.' Fat-*ter*.

'Cool,' said Connor, as if he hadn't been listening.

She stood up, too, taking one last look at the stars to imagine joining them together like dots to make a picture. That one would be an owl's head, she thought, watching a plane move between the tips of its ears.

The plane suddenly dropped. The light literally fell, incredibly quickly, and disappeared.

'Whoa,' she said.

* * *

'*Vous aimez la musique?*'

'It is very bad. But good for me.'

Thea was participating in bilingual flirting. Her French was pretty solid, an A for her AS level, but nonetheless almost every single person here would answer in broken

English. She was mostly offended, but tonight it just seemed hilarious how resolutely they both stuck to their guns.

'*Bon pour vous?*' she said. '*Comment?*'

The guy was one of the two she'd spotted earlier. Christophe. He was now wearing a T-shirt, loose and dark green, had sallow skin and very dense blond curly hair, and a piercing in his tongue he kept toying with, curling his tongue up to his front teeth. Not really her type up close, but what the hell. He smelt of beer and weed, although he was now smoking a mint-flavoured cigar.

'Because you dance very…' He said something quietly to himself, a lazy look into the distance. Trying to work out the word. 'Sexy dancing.'

'*Merci bien,*' said Thea. Frenchmen were very direct. 'Sexily,' she said. '*C'est le mot.* I dance very sexily. *Apparemment.*'

He grinned at her. Was that a gold tooth? Either that or a black one – it was hard to tell in this light. She crossed her fingers for it to be gold.

The other guy was coming back alongside Luke with beers, breaking one open for her. They all tapped their cans together and he and Luke carried on talking animatedly in English about rugby.

There was a crutch leaning on the barriers that her flirtee didn't seem terribly dependent on. '*Qu'est-ce que vous avez fait à votre jambe?*' she said, wondering when you should convert to *tu* and not *vous*. Probably after the kissing but before the blow job. Ha ha.

'Too much sexily dancing,' Christophe said right back. Another imperfect grin. She was starting to think that it *was* a black tooth. 'No, I break it.' He drew on his strange cigar and made a small gap between finger and thumb as he turned to exhale. 'A bit. I break a little bit.'

'A fracture,' she said, and repeated it, this time with French pronunciation.

'Ah,' he said. 'The same.'

Luke kept casually looking over. Bless. He'd do some tae kwon do move he probably knew if the guy did anything out of order. Although anything out of order would have been welcome, really. Christophe didn't have to be perfect. Just functioning.

'And I break one little finger foot,' the guy was saying.

Thea started laughing. 'What?'

He lifted his sandalled foot. 'What is this? Tooth?'

His smallest toe was black. Black toe, black tooth. She was hopefully becoming too drunk to care. '*Toe*,' she said, slightly too loudly.

'Why are some words the same and some words different?' He pretended to be annoyed. 'Bad English people. Too confusing. Too sexily.'

'Which part of France are you from?' she said.

He raised his eyebrows. 'Poland.'

'Oh. Cool.' Maybe it was Kristof, then. With more 'y's and 'z's. Not Christophe. She tried not to feel disappointed. Being sad that he wasn't French basically made her a racist. He really didn't look Polish. Racist, again.

A sharp stinging pain on the side of her thigh. She'd already put on more insect repellent. She slapped it, and at the same time the music changed to something English again. Some old disco funk tune.

Luke put his can of beer down by his feet and came over, holding out his hand. 'We are obliged to dance,' he said.

Thea looked over at the guy.

'No for me,' he said, blowing out more minty smoke. 'Broken fracture toe finger.' He waved them on, and Thea let herself be taken back out onto the dance floor.

'He OK?' shouted Luke.

'Not bad.'

'Sound,' said Luke, looking suddenly more interested in something behind her.

A tall black man – definitely the swimmer they'd seen at the rock the other day – had turned up with a pizza box and what looked like a large plastic bag of blood, more likely wine. He was far fitter than Kristof. Ten times as much, she thought as she turned back to Luke to see him watching too.

* * *

Connor hated it. He hated it all. The shit speakers, far too loud. The distorted music emanating from them, the fact that the tunes changed every minute and a half. He would go home and listen to hours of Japanese noise to atone, he thought with a private gallows humour. He wanted to text Kaia and tell her how bad it was, but it would only be a reminder of him being on holiday and her very much not.

Luke was there, slinging an arm over him. Wine on his breath. Buzzing. 'Y'all right, our kid?'

'Yeah. Just not my thing.'

Luke gave a faintly sheepish laugh. 'It's not really any of ours.' It wasn't true, though. He was so adaptable, his older brother. You could drop him from a helicopter into a remote rainforest or desert or ice-plain and he'd make it work. He could do it anywhere, moving between different sorts of people, always knowing the right way to open up the conversation, never embarrassed about being gay.

'Bit loud for my ear,' Connor said.

'Yeah, course. Sorry.'

It would have been a good excuse even if it hadn't been true.

'Half an hour,' said Luke. 'Is that all right?' He'd already asked Connor if he could drive them back.

Connor had passed his test a few months ago, hunched over the wheel through Salford's junctions, though unlit mountainous roads were probably a different story. 'Yeah. Course.'

'Top one. Just a bit longer.' Luke jogged back towards the swimmer they'd met the other day.

Thea had gone off with some blond guy with a cast on his foot. Earlier, Connor had watched him and his friend as Thea and Luke had danced together, arms up above their heads, Luke twirling her around. The friend had leant over to him and said something, and the blond guy had given a leisurely, leonine nod and grinned. Now, Connor watched the dark space in the trees, as the track changed to a shit French version of grime.

He put his palm over his good ear and listened. It was still there, just, underneath everything – the pitched-yet-unpitched drone.

81

He'd looked it up. Tinnitus. *Hearing noises that do not come from an outside source.* Some people heard a rustling, a whooshing or a humming. A ringing. It could be down to anything from anxiety to new medication. It could be down to hearing loss. Ways to alleviate it included deep breathing, better sleep, and avoiding loud noises.

He couldn't bear the idea of it remaining there, as it did for some people – there were globally famous musicians plagued by it. And the thought of it being down to hearing loss gave him a tiny, bleak sense of terror. Yet there was a small part of him that was drawn to the idea of deafness, being cushioned from the world. One side of him knew what that was like already, after all.

He listened to the ringing. Even underneath the music, it was almost tangible, a miniscule presence on the deaf side of his head. The sound felt connected to something, but he couldn't work out what.

He shivered, removed his hand.

Thea and the blond guy returned, the guy's arm hooked round Thea's shoulders in a proprietorial way.

Violet was lying on a very narrow bench with her head close to the speakers and a can of Coke balanced on her stomach, her phone making her face glow.

Fuck it. He wandered over to Thea, still attached to the guy. As if he'd claimed her.

'Oh,' she said, as he came over. 'This is Connor.' Not *this is my brother.* She didn't want to associate herself with him.

'Nice to meet you,' the guy said, putting the cigar in his mouth and holding his hand out.

Connor stared at it. Shook it. 'We're going soon,' he said to Thea.

She glared at him. 'Since when?'

'I've got to drive,' he said.

'So?'

'I have to go anyway,' said the guy, still nameless. 'I begin work early tomorrow morning.' He put his hand on Thea's back, and she straightened and looked attentive again. 'I maybe see you around, yeah?'

'Yeah,' she said, lightly, ambiguously.

The guy limped off, and Connor was left standing with Thea. She turned to him, folding her arms. Her dress kept changing colour with the revolving lights. 'Are we going then, or what?'

* * *

'I think a plane crashed,' said Violet, as Connor drove them slowly up the mountain road, the headlights picking out the odd ghoulishly shaped tree trunk. Best not to think about how sheer the drop was on this side, Luke decided, his head fizzing from cheap French lager and wine and his interaction with the extremely sexy swimmer, whose name was Tunde.

'Down a gear, Con,' he said, next to his brother in the passenger seat. Connor shifted down to second with a crunch and the car settled, just about. 'When did a plane crash?'

'Tonight,' Violet said, behind him.

'A plane crashed tonight? Whereabouts?' He hadn't looked at any news for days.

'*Here.* Up there.'

'Stop being melodramatic,' said Thea, her head resting against the back window.

'I'm not. I saw it. It was there, and then it just went down, out of the sky. Can you look on your phone? Mine isn't working.'

'Probably a satellite,' Luke said, his mind divided equally between the hairpin bends of the road (he really should have been responsible and not drunk anything this evening) and the sculpted muscles in Tunde's shoulders, which had curved out of his Adidas vest.

'I know what a satellite looks like,' Violet said, sounding stroppy. 'And it wasn't that. I'm telling you.'

'What was Tunde saying?' Thea said to Luke, her voice rather downbeat.

'Oh,' he said. 'Stuff about swimming, mostly.' Delivered in an alluringly bruised French accent as he leaned on the barrier. The occasional flick of his eyes down Luke's torso. 'I invited him to our party.' He put his elbow on the side of the passenger door. 'Go real slow here,' he said to Connor, who had not uttered a word since they'd got into the car, his shoulders up around his ears as he clutched the wheel.

'What party?' said Violet, behind him.

'The party we're now having tomorrow night,' he said, and held on to the handle above the window as they lurched around another corner.

Five

Nothing.

Violet had looked at British and French news sites for reports of a plane crash, and found exactly zero. It must have been a shooting star, then, though they weren't stars at all but meteor showers. Astrophysicists probably got really annoyed by people calling them that.

She put down her phone and looked at the overcast sky again. It was never usually cloudy in the summer but today the sky was just a blur of grey, like something had been smeared across it.

Her heart felt grey, too. She imagined being in that plane, the lurch of your stomach into your throat as it suddenly dropped, the chaos and screaming, everyone's mini-cases and coats falling out of their overhead lockers, some people praying to their gods, the unbelievable roar-smash into the Alps, metal crumpling and rippling, the tumble and tear of bodies. She wondered whether she'd die straight away, even before hitting the ground, or still be conscious, trying to work out which limb was where, hearing her heartbeat fade away.

She wondered whom she'd think of last of all.

* * *

Thea would have done it.

She had gone onto the spit with Krzysztof – she'd looked up the Polish spelling – where there were benches and men playing *pétanque*. Sat on a bench whilst he smoked another cigar, which she'd tried, and he'd laughed when she pulled a face. At one point, he'd shifted and adjusted himself and she'd wondered if he wanted her to give him a blow job, had been ready to nod, go somewhere quieter, put her head down to him. But he hadn't, and she'd offered herself as an extra crutch as they'd headed back. They hadn't even kissed.

At least there was tonight.

* * *

'*Musique concrète*,' said Violet, reading the title of Connor's book as she passed him with the pool net. 'Music made by concrete? That is mad.'

He was studying again. He had a Music Tech degree to start in October as long as he got the grades, and if he was honest with himself, he was scared. It was partly stubbornness that kept him pursuing music, he was sure. Brian Wilson was deaf in one ear. Evelyn Glennie, the percussionist, was profoundly deaf and felt vibrations through the floor. Beethoven, obviously. If they could do it, then he could.

'Shame we don't have a piano here,' Violet said. 'It would be cool to hear you play. I liked the video of your concert.' She was always trying so hard to cheer him up.

'Thanks,' he said, working hard not to downplay it. He turned his page.

'What do you think about when you're playing in front of all those people? Are you like, shitting yourself or is it like –' Violet hooked the pool net in the crook of her elbow, put her thumbs and forefingers together in a yogic pose and closed her eyes – 'I *am* the piano.'

He couldn't help grinning. 'I don't know. A bit of both, if I'm lucky.'

My lad is such a romantic, his mum had said. *I don't know where it comes from, all this expression.* His fingers itched a little from not playing.

Violet turned the pool net around and bashed the end of the handle against the paving stones in a faintly rhythmic way, doing some pretty bad hip-hop moves. 'Dad always goes on about how good you are.'

He felt a prickle of surprise. 'Does he?'

'Yep.' She didn't sound jealous. She part-folded her arms and pushed imaginary glasses up her nose. '"*You* could learn an instrument, like Connor."' Her impression of him was unnervingly accurate. '"Except not drums. Drums are banned."'

He grinned again, but was aware for the first time of a discomfiting, muted sense of pride. Then guilt, for feeling it. He saw his mum, pretending not to be disappointed.

Violet carried on beating the paving stones, then stopped, twirled her pole round and took a bow. 'Boom,' she said. '*Musique concrète.*'

* * *

Gliding above them unnoticed, a short-toed snake eagle casts its hot-yellow eye on the fields. A rare bird, now. They call it 'the flight of the Holy Spirit', this fine subtlety of wing-extension and spacing of tail feathers that allows such stillness. But today, it suddenly drops twenty feet and flies up again on an erratic path. Drops, ascends. A strange, jerking flight. As if drawing something in the air.

Further down the road, underneath the young oaks that begin the forest, the fungus known as black gold constructs threads to find other rootlets, connecting, collecting. Faster than it ever has. A tiny scale insect attaches her body to the wood of a Kermes oak and makes a hard, scarlet shell so strong that moving it would destroy her. She lays her eggs and waits.

* * *

'Yow. Yowza.'

Luke had taken Violet paddleboarding. His middle siblings had not-exactly-politely declined, Connor saying he needed to fix his recording device, Thea saying she was going to read. Violet had seemed pretty chuffed for it just to be the two of them. But he needed to – Connor had mentioned something pretty dark and he felt responsible for sorting it.

Distraction had always been his coping mechanism. Forget his own bullshit and help other people with theirs. The party was the same – it was an excuse to see Tunde again, but he'd already cycled down to the village to see if Amandine fancied coming over tonight, hoping his best attempts at French had made the invitation obvious enough.

And he'd gone up the road to Philippe's house, where their neighbour, a friend of their dad's, said he'd pop in.

Violet had twice fallen into the lake at the beginning and emerged without a hint of embarrassment, hauling herself back onto the board. He was a dab hand, having done it a few times up in Manchester on the canals, where you did your very best not to fall in to avoid gashing your leg on a broken shopping trolley.

'Owza.'

Now, they'd parked up on a reddish sand cove accessible only from the water, and his little sister had finished snorkelling and was hobbling over the stones, most of which were small and spiked.

He tore another bit off his sandwich. 'Aren't you hurting your feet, mate?'

'Yep,' she said, jumping off a low log onto the stones. She was like a grungy, gothy version of the kid from *Where The Wild Things Are.*

Finally, she came and sat down and he passed her half of her requested cheese-and-crisps baguette, which he'd dutifully made.

'So,' he said. 'Been meaning to ask. If it's all right. What's with the death wish?' He said it as unobtrusively as he could.

Her face shut down. 'Don't know what you mean.' She squashed her sandwich in her hand, the crisps crunching.

'Don't blame Connor. It's not entirely hard to notice. What with the swaying on the wall and the fascination with sharp cutlery.' He gave her a smile.

Violet made her mouth into a small, gathered shape over on one side of her face.

Perhaps he'd misjudged the light-hearted approach. He wasn't a psychologist. He didn't know himself that well, after all, so why should he know anyone else? 'Look,' he said, more gently. 'I know you and me haven't hung out that much, in the whole scheme of things. But I want you to know that you can tell us anything.'

The puckered skin slowly flattened back into the centre of her face. She dug a nail very deeply into her knee. 'It's nothing.'

He nodded, and didn't fill the silence.

She stared ahead of her. The cheese of her baguette was already smelling pungent. 'I can't tell anyone.'

A spark of worry. It wasn't nothing, attention-seeking. Of course it wasn't. 'You definitely can,' he said. 'That's what I'm here for. No judging. It'll make you feel better.'

Her toes were curling round the stones, going white. She took a deep breath.

* * *

It had been the one and only time Violet had smoked. She'd stolen out on her own, having made an anguished *I'm on my period* face. The cigarette in her pocket, bought from the entrepreneurial maths boy Paulo in the year above because no way was anyone going to serve her in the newsagents. She'd used the purple lighter nicked from the kitchen cupboard at home, whilst crouched underneath the big pine trees right down the bottom of the field.

Physics was shit, anyway, and she was rubbish at it. She might as well miss the last ten minutes. Mistake. Instead, she got caught by the caretaker, a balding, blond-haired man whose reflective specs had gone dark from being outside.

'And he…?' her brother repeated, very gently, because she'd stopped talking.

Two buttons undone from his brown boiler suit. 'He made me, like – with my hand. Or he said he'd tell on me.' She felt weirdly apart from herself again, like someone else was telling Luke about something that happened to them, not her.

Use both of them, he'd said. *Your hands are small. Aren't they?*

'I didn't want to get into trouble,' she said. Other girls would have walked off. Laughed, insulted him. Gone straight to the head teacher.

He'd leant one hand against a tree. Like he was peeing. He hadn't finished, suddenly tucking himself back in and walking away.

'Jesus,' said Luke, with a sharp breath through his nose. He thought the same. The same as she knew everyone else would, if she told. *Slut.* 'When was this, Violet?'

'Two months ago.' She squashed the two halves of her baguette together and watched the cheese ooze out of the sides.

Luke seemed to be trying to control himself, as if he was really itchy but wasn't allowed to scratch. She could see the muscles in his forearms going tight. 'Have you not told anyone?' he asked. 'Not your mum? Not Thea?'

91

She shook her head. Violently. 'No way.'

'OK,' he said. 'OK. When Dad comes—'

'No,' she said. 'I don't want to. Not on holiday.' He would be tired, and he'd want to sit in his creased shirts and shorts with his embarrassing flip-up sunglasses, reading that expensive European version of his newspaper. Girls were supposed to feel empowered to speak out now, to be a proud survivor. Her dad would not want to hear about his youngest daughter being a useless slag who couldn't say no because she was too scared. 'And it's my word against his,' she said. She'd imagined the courtroom, more than once, except she couldn't picture him in anything other than that boiler suit. 'Everyone will think I wanted to do it.'

'No, they won't. And you're forgetting that Dad's a lawyer.'

'*International* law.' His main job at the moment was something to do with oil pollution in the South China Sea, which meant he was away half the time. He had four more days in Beijing before he joined them.

'He'll know what to do, is what I mean.' Luke looked over at her and gently removed the baguette from her hands. Most of the cheese had splurged out now anyway. 'There might have been others, Violet.'

She dug her fingernail into her leg again. 'Well, why haven't they said anything?' She hadn't really thought of that. Only of him, waiting for her. Every time she passed his door in the corridor beyond the canteen she felt sick. She'd mostly stayed inside at lunchtimes since then, looking at photos of the world's tallest bridges and wondering what it would be like to jump off them.

'Maybe because they're too scared. You need to be proper brave. The bravest. If you say what happened, then others might feel strong enough to say something, too.'

She wasn't brave. She was the opposite of brave.

'I'm so sorry that happened to you, Violet. Can I – can I give you a hug?'

She felt stiff and closed-up. 'Not right now.'

'No. Yeah. Sorry.' He exhaled and put his hands between his knees, clenched them. 'You've already done the right thing, telling me. He's a criminal, and he needs to be in jail. You didn't do anything wrong. I've got your back. OK?'

Violet saw him beating the caretaker up with kick-boxing moves until his face was just blood and pulp. 'OK.'

'You're nothing but awesome. I'm – I knew I had a sister, two sisters, but it didn't really feel real until I met you.' He looked across at her. 'I like you being around.'

Violet took her fingernail away from her leg. A crescent-shaped mark, the red paling again, slowly. 'OK. Please don't tell Thea.'

He looked pained.

'Please don't.'

'All right. But I can't promise not to tell Dad, and your mum. You've had the guts to tell me something really serious, and it's my responsibility to tell them.'

'Can we stop talking about it now?'

'But—'

'Fine.' She stood up. It wasn't fine. She knew he was right, really, and maybe it would be easier if it came from Luke rather than her. But she was still terrified to think of having to face that man again. 'Maybe you can tell them. I don't know.'

'OK,' he said, lightly. 'One day at a time.'

She stood at the shoreline, facing the grey-lavender lake. She nodded and looked at the sky again, to see if another plane might fall. Anything to distract her. 'You're the nicest one.' She turned back to him.

Her brother was smiling unhappily. 'What's that?'

'Out of the four of us. The other two are both moody all the time.' Thea and Connor were probably scowling at each other right now.

'They just read more books.' Luke grinned and looked at her through one eye. 'Paddle back?'

Six

'How come you're so good at cooking?' Thea was being *sous-chef*, which translated to chopping onions and courgettes for Luke's ratatouille.

'It's not so hard,' Luke said.

'I can't even – OK, I can boil an egg, but I don't really like eggs, so I don't really boil eggs.'

'Mum—' He glanced over. 'I mean, my mum is pretty good.'

He and Connor had been round a few times, over the years. Picnics and barbecues and after Christmas. It wasn't reciprocated. Their mum, Alanna, had never properly forgiven their Dad. Understandable, she supposed.

Violet stuck her head round the door. She'd been quiet since getting back with Luke, shrugging and not saying much. Turning into Connor. 'Does anyone want to play something? Computer or IRL?'

'Busy,' said Thea, and Violet began to withdraw.

'In a bit,' said Luke, after her. 'Definitely. If there's time.'

'Like father, like daughter,' Thea said, a little archly.

Luke glanced over.

'Dad really likes board games,' she said. 'And computer games, but especially board games. I mean, sorry, you probably knew that.' It still felt awkward to talk about the parent they shared.

There was the slightest pause as Luke added her onions to the sizzling butter. 'I didn't, actually,' he said. 'Maybe it's only for special occasions.'

'No,' she said, with emphasis. 'It's a total pain. He's so competitive.' *You know I'm too old for this*, she'd said, aged fifteen. *Never too old for Bananagrams*, said her dad. *You're only saying that because I'm winning.* That would be enough for Thea to sit down again. 'He probably only does it when he's bored. Count yourself lucky.'

'Yeah, no doubt,' said Luke, with another slightly forced smile. He seemed distracted.

'What did you do with your mum?' She tried to sound natural. 'When you were younger?'

'Went on marches,' Luke said.

Thea looked at him, surprised.

'Protests, you know. Proper banner-waver, my mum. Fair play to her. And gigs – like, alternative, sort of indie stuff. It was the only time I rebelled.' He raised his eyebrows. 'Fled screaming towards dance music, while Connor went in the other direction.'

At his name, Thea gave a neutral hum.

'I'm sorry you two don't get on,' Luke said.

'Oh.' She was taken aback. She'd hoped she appeared civil, most of the time. 'No. I mean, there's no reason why we should.'

'You just seem really similar, that's all.'

'Really?' She gazed out of the window, and tried very hard not to seem insulted. Was that how he saw her? Them? 'I don't think so.' She pushed over the pile of courgette pieces with the heel of her hand. 'I guess me and Violet aren't exactly a picture of harmony.'

Luke gave a vague, indistinct response. He really seemed off today.

'How was it, anyway?' she said. 'This afternoon?'

Luke stopped finely chopping garlic, sniffed, and nodded. 'Yeah. It was… it was nice.'

'Yeah?' He didn't sound very convincing. 'It's OK, you can say. I know she's an annoying little brat.'

'She's not,' he said, quite abruptly. 'Sorry. I mean, I don't think she is.'

She felt chastened, suddenly. His tone had changed.

'Can you do me a favour? Can you – just keep an eye on her? I will too, but –' he seemed to work very hard to muster a smile – 'all hands on deck.'

'Yeah, sure. OK,' said Thea, feeling bewildered.

'Sorted, ta.' He let out a long breath.

'Is everything all right?'

'Um,' he said, and gave a half-laughing, half-anguished sigh. 'Not exactly. I'm a colossal fucking disappointment to myself.'

She was startled. He was always so rangy and cheerful. 'What d'you mean?'

He put his chin to his chest and looked at the shine of garlic on his fingertips. 'You won't tell anyone, will you?'

* * *

'Made you a coffee.' Violet was standing above Connor, holding a mug.

'Oh. Thanks.' He took it and put it in the grass by his ear. She'd already given Luke one, too.

'Where's mine?' said Thea, from under the sun umbrella, but not as unkindly as usual.

She and Connor had steered clear of each other all afternoon in the others' absence. She'd lain outside reading, or texting on her phone with that smirk on her face. She'd been talking to friends at some point, laughing and then her voice dropping, becoming a blur, apart from a loud *no way*. He'd taken his whole portable recorder apart, put it back together and recorded a fly butting itself against the glass. He'd listened and heard the high whine. Removed his headphones, and could still hear it in his head. Just like before. Then he'd watched a film that Kaia had been telling him to watch – an art-house one set on a Yorkshire farm – and texted her a running commentary.

Later, he'd decided not to hide away like an idiot, but when he'd got to the sliding door, he'd seen that Thea had taken off her bikini top and was lying front-down on the lounger, hands under her cheek, shoulder blades pushing against the skin like the beginnings of wings. He'd gone back inside.

'You don't drink coffee,' Violet said to Thea.

'I might start.' Thea was speaking with a false, bright levity. 'Get it yourself.'

The pretence lifted. 'Oh, my God.'

It was a performance, the two of them. They always talked as if they had to perpetuate this sense of spiky rivalry. He and Luke had never been like that – his brother had always been so encouraging, never diminishing the excitement of a debut activity by saying he'd done it already. There were rambunctious days as kids, but when Connor didn't fight back, Luke stopped his amiable roughing-up. He just loved having a brother, and Connor had followed Luke around like a puppy until a few years ago. He only had him to thank, really, for not becoming a complete recluse.

'Is it OK?' Violet asked Luke.

His brother had been texting Tunde about tonight's party, getting him to bring friends. He took a sip. 'It's mint,' he said.

'Huh?'

'Fantastic. Just like you are.'

'Safe, bruv,' she said, looking a little embarrassed, and hopped away on one foot.

Luke seemed shaky this afternoon. He'd looked ashen on his return from paddleboarding, and then he and Thea had been having some heart-to-heart in the darkened living room, their heads close together, and had stopped murmuring to each other when he'd walked past the doorway. Connor wondered, with slight dread, what they'd been talking about. He'd watched from behind his sunglasses since they'd been back outside, Thea giving Luke a warm, sympathetic look.

Connor rolled over and tried his coffee. It was horrendously strong.

Luke quietly tipped his own coffee into the bush beside his chair.

Along the road in the olive groves, a Cleopatra butterfly is in its single summer flight, a radiant yellow and orange amongst the forest's faded colours. It is drawn to the crimson flowers of knapweed and thistle in these higher places. At rest, its closed wings resemble leaves, but they are changing, becoming non-reflective to avoid the birds attracted to ultraviolet light. This would normally take place over centuries. It is happening in weeks.

In the squat oak, the scale insect's eggs hatch. The young feed on her, and as she dies, she releases a lasting scarlet liquid onto the bark and her offspring, staining them forever.

The liquid does something new. It darkens to lavender.

* * *

It wasn't exactly the best party Luke had ever hosted, but it would do. A modest gathering of eleven, mostly in the living room or out on the terrace. The neighbours had arrived first – Amandine, cigarette in hand, heavy crucifix necklace above her cleavage, rattling on to Connor and somehow getting away with squeezing his upper arm and not embarrassing him. Philippe, who worked in engineering and whose wife and teenage daughter were away. Violet had got those two red-headed kids from the car park disco to come over, and was showing off her lilo-surfing moves.

Thea came into the kitchen for another bottle of wine. Tonight she was in a light-blue wrap dress, sexy 1940s tea-dance vibes. 'You OK?'

'Yep. Just coming.'

She gave him a sweet, rather maternal smile as she left.

He did feel better for telling someone. Finally. Hearing about Violet had set him off. She was just a kid. It was almost as if she'd been reading from a script, she was that detached. She'd been completely powerless with a grown man – it made him realise how much stronger he should have been with Jamie.

He didn't really know how it had started, the acceptance that Jamie could only fuck him whilst verbally abusing him. Luke was aware that he had a bit of a praise kink, but dirty talk was also fine, was great, and somehow being called *a filthy cunt who wants to be fucked in every hole* flowed seamlessly from the tamer end of things, and somehow having his hands held down became having his neck clamped so tight that he wondered if he might be about to die.

After the first time, he'd suggested having a safe word, and Jamie had just laughed. *Where would the fun be in that?* Luke had vowed to not do it again, except that there was an affectionate, vulnerable side to Jamie, too. The softening of his jawline and his Cambridge-blue eyes, the odd surreptitious glance at school, a hand once briefly touching the lobe of his ear on the stairs just before the Year 4s rampaged past.

Luke hadn't known straight away that Jamie was married – he didn't wear a wedding ring at school. It seemed to get Jamie off further, being in his suburban three-bed with its chaos of toys, a child's safety gate at the top of the stairs. Luke couldn't deny the thrill of two fairly straight-acting men fucking each other's brains out in a very straight setting. He kept going back.

The last time, his head had been pushed between two pillows, a belt round his neck. Things had started to blot and flash – the musty smell of Jamie and his wife in the down of the cotton, glimpses of the mirrored wardrobe – until he'd found the courage to kick, hard, and rolled over, gasping and crying.

Jamie had followed him out of the house, contrite, baffled. *Fuck. Luke, I'm sorry. I got carried away.*

Seriously, Luke had said at the gate. *Let me go now. I've had enough. Just fucking do one.*

When he'd dared turn at the end of the road, eyes blurry, chest still thick with panic, Jamie had been standing there, watching him, and by the time Luke had turned the corner, his phone had started vibrating.

'That's awful,' Thea had said, her hand on his knee. 'I'm so sorry.' Though he hadn't spilled every lurid detail, she'd revealed a kinder side compared to her usual highly polished sheen.

He couldn't tell her that his guilt at being a grown man and not standing up to Jamie, when Violet had no choice, made him feel so much fucking worse. He would ring Jamie tomorrow. Not just message him. Wrestle his self-worth back. Tell him to fuck off.

'Maybe you need to get back on the horse,' Thea had said. 'Horse being sexy swimmer man.' She pulled a self-deprecatingly amused face. 'Bad analogy.'

'I could do with a pony,' he said, feeling shattered. 'A really sweet pony.'

Now he was here, Tunde, wearing a tight-fitting black vest, leaning against the kitchen counter and definitely watching Luke through those sage-green eyes. He'd brought the paddleboarder, who was called Zaf, and another fellow instructor, Gael, a short, light-skinned black guy, both of them currently chatting next door to a delighted Amandine.

When they'd arrived, Thea had come to the door, asking whether Krzysztof was with them. Her face had fallen when Tunde had said that he couldn't come because his girlfriend had just got in from Poznań.

Zaf had brought some incredibly pungent-smelling weed, or maybe skunk – Luke had never been much interested in anything beyond alcohol and the very odd happy pill. Every time Tunde drew on the joint, his stomach arched inwards. He said he was at nursing school, and doing the master's programme next year.

Despite Thea's setback – she had worn a very determined expression before hearing about Krzysztof's no-show – she was being an unnervingly excellent host, giggling at something Philippe was saying, topping up his drink, answering him in what sounded, at least to Luke, like flawless French. Even her pauses sounded French.

Violet was still happily lording it over her new friends, Ron Weasley Junior and his shy sister.

Connor – oh, he was around somewhere.

* * *

Violet found Connor standing by the edge of the pool, staring at it. Everyone else was now inside.

'This party is weird,' she said.

The air felt weighted tonight. Her head hurt. George and Gemma had been picked up after two hours by their mum, and more than anything Violet had wanted to go with them. They could have eaten liquorice strings and watched an animated movie and gone to bed.

'Yep,' said Connor. He was dangling a bottle of beer by its neck from his first finger.

She couldn't help feeling disappointed. 'You're drinking.' He wasn't supposed to be like them.

'Yep.'

Luke kept trying to hide from her the fact that the tall black guy and the dreadlocked white guy with the little circle tattoo on his forehead were smoking in the house, but not very well as the whole kitchen stank, and she knew it was weed.

She did feel better for telling Luke. She was scared that he might look at her like she'd really wanted it to happen, but he kept checking on her, asking how she was, and very carefully not touching her. She didn't want him to tell her mum, or their dad. But she knew he would, and that was OK.

She brought up her camera and took a shot of the artificial light reflected on the surface of the pool. Adjusted the settings and tried another one. It reminded her of the ripple on her screen in the sunset photos. She was like Connor, she thought. Noticing small things.

There was a loud ring of laughter from their sister, and they both looked over towards the sound. Thea had been trying to flirt with the one called Gael, but he was obviously not interested. Now she was talking to Philippe again, and for some reason finding him totally hysterical.

Connor half turned at Thea's laughter, then turned back and drank from his beer again.

'I know,' Violet said.

* * *

It wasn't so bad.

He was clearly into her, because he kept looking at her breasts. Quite subtly, but not subtly enough. Thea couldn't work out if he wanted her to notice that or not. It was hilarious really, flirting with someone even older than Dad, but it was totally working. She had actual flirting skills, with someone who had probably been around the block a few times, not some stupid Polish guy with a limp and a sudden girlfriend. She was a clever, pretty young Englishwoman and he would go home thinking about her and not about his absent wife.

OK, so he wasn't exactly the perfect fifty-something silver fox, but it was worth it to see Connor keep giving her filthy looks.

* * *

Please don't sleep with him, Connor thought, from the doorway to the living room.

Thea was sitting on the side of the armchair next to Philippe, attentive as he droned on about Cistercian monasteries. Occasionally she would say, '*Qu'est-ce que c'est le mot pour...*' and put her hand on her chest, looking questioningly into the distance. He'd help her out, give her three or four possibilities, and she'd nod, earnestly, and end up laughing again, as if she was watching a fucking sitcom and not talking to an old man who'd put on too much aftershave.

She walked past Connor in the corridor to get more corn chips, a cursory glance becoming an abrasive one. 'What?'

'Nowt.' Just like his mum, getting more Mancunian when he'd had a few.

'Stop staring at me, then.' She gazed at him, more shrewdly. His skin itched. 'Someone can't take their drink.'

'At least my standards don't sink to the bottom of the lake.' Of the lake? What was he saying?

The side of her upper lip curled, slowly. Opal eyes and an almost gleefully incredulous expression. 'What is *with* you?' The middle of her bra was visible at the base of her sternum. Pale pink.

'You're embarrassing yourself.'

'I'm not embarrassed.' She seemed taller. 'No one's embarrassed. Except maybe you. For some reason.' She raised her eyebrows. She'd missed a bit of sun protection on the left side of her collarbone. Also pale pink.

In the other room, there was the sound of a wine cork popping and someone laughing. Connor wanted to walk away, and he wanted to stay right here, antagonised and antagonising.

'I know what your problem is.' Thea stepped closer, close enough for him to feel her heat. A hand on his shoulder. Her mouth, close to his ear. His deaf ear. The press of her breath on it as she whispered something. Her hand remained there a little longer before she removed it.

'Can't hear you on that side,' he said.

'I know,' she said, and walked off.

Connor sat on the armchair in the corner, shovelling crisps into his mouth to try and soak up the alcohol. Tunde was looking over Luke's shoulder at his phone, saying something about Luke's music collection being shit and where was the black metal. His brother laughed, not caring one bit about being insulted, and cued up another one of his rare disco tracks.

He hated being drunk. Being drunk meant losing control. Losing dignity, frankly, not that most people seemed to care. He'd read up on straight-edge once to see if that was him, but it seemed too tribal and anyway, he didn't have tattoos and the abstinence wasn't ideological. To have to give a name to something, to have to still *belong*.

He roused himself as Amandine came over, standing to kiss her goodnight. She put her hands on his cheeks and said something including the words *adorable* and *charmant*. He blushed, smiled and glanced over to Thea, who wasn't looking.

He couldn't bear it. Thea, arching her neck and wrapping her hair around her finger. Talking earnestly about the southern French accent with Philippe, and then laughing at Gael's joke, purely for the benefit of how it made her look. Doubling over. She put her hand on Philippe's knee and Connor looked away.

Violet came and stood beside him, her arms folded. 'Can I borrow your headphones?' She looked tired. 'I'm going to bed, but I don't want to listen to what they're listening to. Yours are better.'

'Yeah. They're in my room,' he said. 'What're you going to listen to?'

'Anything but this,' she said. 'Really loudly.' He watched her go upstairs, taking two steps at a time.

* * *

A hummingbird hawk-moth flits against the kitchen lightbulb, over and over. It emits a tiny, almost imperceptible hum, high and ringing.

Warm air. In the verge outside, the dormouse eats a snail far too big for itself, holding the shell to its mouth and turning. Then, for the first time, it devours the shell, too.

A barn owl, watchful, lifts from its post. The silence of the bird into the silence of the night.

* * *

There was a sudden deep sound, like an explosion far off. Everyone stilled, in perfect unison. It had sounded incredibly low. Unearthly, somehow.

'Wow,' said Luke. 'What was that?'

Philippe, Tunde and Zaf talked rapidly in French, all shrugs and understated head-shaking. 'Military, probably,' said the neighbour. He explained in English about the military zone south-west of here, and Luke remembered the small tank they'd seen last summer, soldiers sitting in light camouflage colours on the top, guns visible. How incongruous they'd looked, driving on a path between perfectly aligned cypress trees.

'Spooky,' said Thea. '*Un – un frisson.*'

'We are all safe,' said Philippe. 'It is only practice exercises. They do not operate their artillery near any houses. *Effrayant*,' he said to Thea. 'This might have been the word.'

'I should hope not,' she said. 'And thank you. Any more wine?'

'Of course,' he said. 'Let me help you.'

Tunde and Zaf were still talking about the military, and the destruction of hundreds of hectares of forest in a wildfire not far from here, after using artillery fire in training during yet another heatwave. When he was sixteen, Luke had considered the army for a week or two, before realising that however modern modern life was, it possibly wasn't fully ready for queer folks.

Gael, who'd gone to smoke outside, came in to say his farewells.

'Is it OK that I use your toilet?' said Tunde to Luke, once he'd gone.

'Course,' said Luke. 'Upstairs, first right.'

'OK,' said Tunde. 'Next to your room?'

'Mine's straight ahead,' he said.

'OK,' said Tunde and seemed to look at Zaf for a moment before getting up, rolling one shoulder back.

'OK,' said Luke, and looked at Zaf.

* * *

Boom. A sound that she felt in her stomach.

On her bed, Violet lifted off a headphone. Another plane, she thought. Falling. But she could only hear the thud of old dance music, *duh-duh-duh-duh*, and Thea's voice in the hallway.

Footsteps on the stairs, and shushing.

* * *

'Once you have tried it, nothing else suffices,' Philippe was saying in the kitchen, because Thea was having a grown-up conversation about rosé, because she was a grown-up. 'It's the fine balance of grapes that makes it so appealing – the *mourvèdre* gives it something special, I think.'

'I'll have to have some, then,' she said, grandly, putting her hands underneath her hair and letting it fan back out. A quite drunk grown-up. It wasn't just the wine – that sonic boom had made her feel queasy.

'Well, you must come over another time,' he said. 'And I will give you a bottle.'

'I *will*.'

He was looking at her, amused. 'A girl who has sophisticated tastes,' he said. 'Forgive me. A *woman* who has sophisticated tastes.'

Everything sounded more amusing in a French accent. 'Forgiven,' she said. 'Just this once.'

He glanced behind him – at what she was not quite sure. '*Venez ici*,' he said, and she realised that he was checking that the door was shut.

* * *

The voices had all stopped.

Luke's music was still pumping away in the living room, but Connor couldn't hear anyone. That strange, deep boom had reverberated under the soles of his feet. Made the drone appear in his ear again, louder, brighter.

Maybe they'd all left. Finally. He rose, collecting the two Dr Pepper cans that were in the grass by the pool on his way in. The wind was picking up.

The kitchen door was resting ajar, and gave a gentle creak. He went to shoulder it open, before catching a glimpse of light blue.

A moment in which nothing seemed to move. In which the drone in his ear was penetratingly focused. Thea, pressed against the kitchen counter, not smiling, and the back of Philippe, his wideness concealing much of her, leaning down strangely, one shoulder much lower than the other, because his hand was up her dress. Thea was making that humming sound, except it was higher in pitch than normal. Her hand was on his other shoulder, and Connor realised that she was not holding him, but pushing him.

Or trying to.

Connor threw open the door hard enough that it banged against the big jars on the floor, and Philippe was straightening, Thea walking right past Connor out of the kitchen, not making eye contact.

'Another drink, yes?' said Philippe.

'Everyone's gone,' said Connor, putting his foot on the pedal of the bin to dump the cans, wanting to pick the whole thing up and smash it in his face.

Philippe turned the tap on and put his fingers under it, before wiping them on the front of his thigh. 'Then I will leave also,' he said. '*Bonne nuit*, Connor.'

Connor followed him out. Philippe stood outside for a moment in the glow of the sensor light, turning round and glancing upwards. Connor stepped forward, putting his hand on the side of the door. Philippe saw him, and casually looked about him in other directions, as if noticing the wind. Gave him a nod, and walked away down the path.

Connor shut the door. Locked it and leaned against it.

* * *

Turning over, being turned over.

Choices. Unspoken agreements, and dark-blurred questions in two languages. Ceiling, bed, headboard. A manic giggle.

Different tastes. Synthetic coconut. Intense salt and oniony sweat. And once, accidentally, with his mouth on his own arm, the numbness of mosquito repellent.

He was lightly stoned, and less lightly pissed, and yet he still knew that neither of them were going to do anything to him that he didn't desire.

The audacity of three, Luke thought, delirious.

Seven

Violet was lying under one of the cypress trees by the front, her T-shirt ridden up above her stomach. Partied out. Part teed-out. The branches above her swayed in the strong wind.

Philippe had told them once that there was a saying, *dormir sous un cyprès* – to sleep under a cypress – that meant *to be dead*. He also said that farmhouses in this area often had three trees planted in a triangle, which meant that the people living there welcomed travellers. One tree meant, *No way are you coming on my land.* They had two here, which meant somewhere in between. Hi, come in, have a cup of tea, now fuck off.

Cypress. From the Old French *cipres*, from the Latin *cupressus*, from Greek *kyparissos*, from an unknown pre-Greek Mediterranean language. From a time when people didn't have words for things. When people weren't people but distant relations and not even the world's main predator. Who had just discovered that they could sharpen stones, and drew on cave walls with minerals, experimenting with mixing like the first photographers did.

She lay looking up at the dark green. It didn't much feel like being dead, unless being dead meant you had a small rock digging into your back.

There was an odd feeling in the air today. Maybe the cypresses knew something that they didn't. Pointing up to the sky like creepy fingers.

Over her head, the neon butterfly she'd seen by the lake, dressed as if going to a festival, fluttered past, doodling in the air. There were fewer butterflies than there used to be, she was sure. The buddleia bush used to be full of them, like extra flowers.

There it was again. She'd never seen it up here before, but she couldn't be bothered to get the camera. She watched it doodle in the air, coming back to a central point each time and going out again in a different direction. Imagined drawing its path with a black pen.

A squeak from the house and, rolling her head, she watched Tunde step out of the patio doors, pulling his tracksuit trousers a little higher over his hips. Violet stayed very still. He cricked his neck from side to side as he took the path round the side of the house, not noticing her.

Violet tried to imagine being a boy. Tracksuits and trainers and caps for the rest of her life with no questions asked. But that didn't really make you a boy. Boys could wear dresses. Boys who wanted to be girls tended to act like very girly girls, and girls who wanted to be boys tended to act more like lads. But there were plenty of boys who wanted to be boys but definitely not lads, like Joe at school. Like Connor. And girls who were happy being girls but didn't act much like girls. Violet didn't want to change her body, but she didn't like it. She didn't want it to be anything. Abody.

Tunde had stayed over. They'd probably had sex. Luke was a boy who wanted to be a boy but was also gay. Violet had heard them come up the stairs, then turned up her music. Later, she'd carefully taken off the headphones because it was hard to sleep in them, but then she'd heard a man – she couldn't tell who – giggle, and put them on again very quickly.

Anal sex: how did that not hurt a million times over. But it wasn't just boys who did it – she knew that well enough from talk at school and the few times she'd snuck onto porn sites, feeling sick. It was like having eight thumbnails of horror movies on her screen at once. People did all sorts to each other, and sometimes they used toys and metal things and scary stuff and they put them everywhere and said the worst things possible and it didn't seem any different to what had happened to her.

On the way here from the airport, they'd passed two Love Shops on the motorway, which were called adult stores back home. But none of that stuff seemed to be much about love.

All sex hurt, she thought, one way or the other. It didn't make sense to her why anyone would want to do it.

* * *

Thea lay in bed until noon, every inch of her leaden. The proportion of ratatouille to wine had definitely tipped out of balance last night. Her skin felt filmy. She really needed water, but the thought of being upright was not good.

115

Much worse was the memory of the kitchen, and lifting her eyes as Connor had barged in. Her stomach shrank and she curled up under the sheet. It had been unexpected, Philippe suddenly changing his tone, she finding the base of her spine against the sink. He'd said some things in French, too quickly for her, a hand on her side, sliding round. Sliding *under*, a finger at the seam of her pants. She hadn't been ready, and it was suddenly too real, and he was too old, and—

The look on Connor's face. A mixture of hurt, and anger, and something else. It confirmed what she'd said into his deaf ear last night.

* * *

Connor had been up before everyone else, loading the dishwasher, using the dustpan and brush. Getting the upper hand on the others, and atoning for drinking four beers.

Trying to clean away the presence of Philippe. Any trace of his fingerprints.

Male voices in the hallway. The sound of a kiss. No, two kisses – the quick, French, on-the-cheek kind – and the door shut.

'Morning.' Luke's voice was a croak. 'Afternoon.'

'Hiya.' Connor glanced out of the window to see Zaf leaving along the path, the longest dreadlock trailing down the middle of his back.

Luke was drinking orange juice with the fridge door still open. He sighed and rubbed at his mouth with a thumb knuckle, before blinking and seeing the tea towel in Connor's hand. 'Oh, God, thanks, man. You should have waited. I'd have helped.'

'It's OK.'

'Morning,' Luke said again, as Thea came in.

She was wearing a hoodie over her vest-top. A pale, chalky shine to her face. She walked past Connor without looking at him. 'Yeah,' she said. 'Where did you get to?'

'Suddenly crashed out,' Luke said.

'Liar,' said Thea. 'I've got ears.'

'Please don't say anything to Violet,' he said.

'I'm going to make posters and put them on every fence,' said Thea, her eyes sweeping over the cleaned kitchen counters and resolutely not over Connor. 'Joke.'

'Very funny.' Luke moved a hand over his face. 'Think I need a run. After another quick sleep.' He disappeared back upstairs.

Connor started putting the glasses in the cupboard. There was the sound of Violet launching into the pool.

Thea opened the breadbox and took out the empty croissant bags, the paper patched with oil. She leant down to the fridge, staring into it. 'How are we out of fucking food again?' she said, her words utterly featureless.

'Are you OK?' he said. She couldn't have wanted to. The man was grotesque.

She shut the breadbox and turned, blank-faced. 'How d'you mean?'

He'd spent half the night awake, imagining Philippe doing what he'd begun to do to her in the kitchen and much more, and the other half thinking of ways to kill him. 'I just – wanted to check that you were all right.'

Her eyes narrowed. 'I'm fine.' Words tight. She snatched the glass that he was holding and filled it with water. 'Thanks.' She stalked out of the room.

* * *

'You were snoring loudly last night.'

Luke had made it back down to the kitchen, just in time for the bad cop to start her interview. 'Was I? Sorry, mate.'

Connor was at the table, eating probably his third bowl of cereal, and reading.

'No worries,' said Violet. 'Probably weed makes you snore more.'

'Sorry about that,' he said, defenceless.

Violet folded her arms. 'So did you have a nice time with Tunde, then?'

'Mm-hm. Yep.' Luke looked at his brother, the merest glance, and Connor didn't alter his body language at all, staring down at his book.

'Cool,' said Violet, but she sounded detached. 'Xbox?'

'Yep.' Luke followed Violet into the living room, where she'd already set it up.

He couldn't quite believe they'd both stayed the night. The three of them, in his dad's bed (definitely some sheet-washing to be done), with him blissfully sandwiched in the middle. A triple-spoon, at least for a bit, with Tunde stroking his hip. They'd got too warm and moved apart a couple of inches, and Luke kept craning round to look at him.

'What?' Tunde had said.

'Just checking you're real.'

'I'm real.' Tunde's words had been gentle, amusedly pleased. 'Sleep, English boy,' he'd said in his ear, as Luke had drifted off.

At 8 a.m., Tunde had whispered that he'd got work, and that he'd jog down the hill.

Zaf slept for ages, and Luke had watched him on and off between dozes, the guttural rasp in his throat on each inhale, his thickly haired calf sticking out from the sheet. He'd woken up again to find Zaf pulling the sheet back and sucking on Luke's balls. He'd had to put the pillow in his mouth.

* * *

A bloody-nosed beetle marches through crisp grass, raisin-black and blue-sheened. Heading for the foaming leaves of bedstraw. The shadow of something winged and much larger than itself passes overhead and immediately it halts, spews a defensive, noxious liquid, orange-red, from its eyes and legs. It waits. The threat passes. The beetle goes on its way.

Behind it, the liquid hardens, crackles, ripples. Turns lavender.

* * *

'Mistral wind, also known as Miserable Wind,' Violet said, standing by the window.

A grey sky again. The wind was making the shutters rattle and the leaves play tag with each other over the patio stones, and the mood seemed the same inside. Violet had beaten Luke in about two seconds, and he hadn't wanted to play any more. It was hardly worth Violet even trying to win. Now, he was sprawled on the sofa, looking pale.

Mistral was the one from this part of France, and it swept up northwards. There was the scirocco, which takes loads of desert with it from North Africa and gets wet as it comes across the sea. One which had the same name as a helicopter, chinook, which made sense, and one with a stupid name – haboob. The sort of thing that a Year 8 boy would yell after running up and squeezing your chest, something that actually happened and always hurt. Maybe she would spread that around, so they'd all shout it whilst not realising that it was a circular dust storm in Sudan.

Often the wind, the miserable mistral, did suddenly pick up in the afternoons here, making a calm day go grubby. But this had been going since last night.

'Proper Stormzy,' she said, turning round.

Luke was rubbing one of his temples.

'You're really hungover, aren't you?'

'I guess.' He smiled, though his heart definitely wasn't in it. 'I'm a terrible example to you.'

'Shall I make you a cup of coffee?'

'No,' said Luke, very quickly. 'Ta. But tea would be magic.' He winked.

* * *

It was as if stones were being pressed into Thea's cranium. The weather, maybe. Luke didn't seem much better. Ever since that boom last night, she'd felt dizzy, like her body had been subtly destabilised. Ever since what happened in the kitchen.

120

She could feel Connor, in his room. She could feel his silence, even if John fucking Cage said it didn't exist.

Her calves were itching. She scratched and scratched.

∗ ∗ ∗

Later, Thea was sitting with her elbows on the kitchen table, fingers on her temples.

Connor went over to the cupboard under the sink and took out the open plastic box, its collection of first-aid paraphernalia and sewing stuff, a couple of spare buttons and a pen-torch.

He took out the paracetamol. One left.

The drone barely stopped now. It was all he could think of, and he couldn't tell if he was imagining it or not. He felt like he was hearing – listening to –something beyond all known perception. In Oliveros' book, the story about John Cage had a lesser-known flipside. Cage only heard his blood and the ringing in his nervous system because his body was developing a condition that would lead to the massive stroke that he died from decades later. Was this what was happening to Connor? The first sign of some disease eating its way through him?

'Does your head hurt, too?' Thea was running her nail along one of the grooves in the wood, her knuckle taut.

'Yeah. A bit.'

There was the sound of the TV from the living room, and Luke coughing upstairs.

'Shouldn't drink more than your body can cope with, then,' she said, to the table. Her voice became more drifting, ambiguous. 'Or you might do something you regret.'

Was she talking about him or her?

She gave the tiniest outbreath, either bored or tired, and briefly glanced up at him. 'Why do you always have to stand there like a silent fucking movie?' Her hoodie was slipping off her shoulder. 'Aren't you going to say something?'

Floored again. He never knew quite what she would say next, or how to answer.

'It doesn't matter. I know what you want to say.' She dragged her eyes up again. Pool-blue. 'I know your secret. I said it last night.'

His heart plunged. Did she mean the porn thing? Because, while it made his skin crawl off his bones to remember her walking into his room, her knowledge of it had already been established.

She was staring at him, still leaning on one elbow. A blink. 'Don't you want to know? What I said?'

A faint coil of panic, far down in his stomach. 'Not really.'

Thea rose from her chair, its scrape against the tiles abrasive and brassy. She took two steps towards him, her finger dragged behind her and trailing off the table. He wanted to run. Her lip curled up in a way that made the skin underneath her eyelid deepen. She said each word deliberately, as if whispering an important message to a spy. '*You want me.*'

His dick bruised. He felt sick. 'You're an egotist,' he said.

She just stood there, almost triumphant.

A creak. Violet was in the doorway, and a thin line of nausea spread through his gut at the idea that she'd heard. But she looked between them oddly, and her voice sounded fragile and distracted. 'Something is happening,' she said.

PART TWO

Eight

First, it was sea. A bed of limestone and ammonites.

Then the rock rose, the water warmed, and corals appeared. The gorges found their first form.

Then the mountains and the sea drew back, leaving remnants in pockets of the land.

The earth's lithosphere shifted, fractured the limestone, made valleys. The ice came and went. The sea dried, rock eroding, and the river, jewelled blue-green by clay, micro-algae, and fluorine, dug itself more deeply into the gorges.

Wild juniper, mulberry. Trout, roach, carp. Vipers, roe deer, wild boar. Humans.

Then, a great cull, as there is from time to time, and the earth renews.

* * *

The four of them stood in front of the TV, not talking. On the screen, there were shots of famous main streets and city squares from around the world – buildings with huge adverts, marble lions, monoliths – empty, the odd person standing there carrying a shopping bag or on a bike.

'That's very weird,' said Luke.

'Where did everyone go?' said Violet.

There was Nelson's Column, fountains, open newspapers flapping across the pavement like pigeons.

'What are they saying?' Violet said. 'Is it a lockdown?'

'We'd have known if there was going to be a lockdown,' said Connor.

'Maybe it's like really bad air pollution and everyone's staying indoors?'

'Yeah, maybe,' said Luke. He glanced at Connor.

'*Disparitions massive*,' said Thea, and said the first word again, thoughtfully, emphasising the sibilance.

No one asked her to translate.

They all pulled out their phones.

'Look at the clouds,' Violet said. They were all on the sofa individually scrolling, Connor's laptop streaming British news.

They all looked up. On the TV, the clouds formed a thick ripple, like a ruched sheet, and had a strange sheen. They sat very low, with a band of normally coloured sky just underneath.

'*Are* they clouds?' said Violet. She looked to the window. The sky was normal, if very grey.

'Of course they're clouds,' said Thea, but in a quiet, drifting voice.

Connor didn't say anything, still reading local Manchester news.

'What else would they be?' said Luke. He could feel his

heart, beating more roundly and reverberantly than it ever had. An alarm call. He knew something was very wrong and he couldn't say what it was.

Shots of empty city streets, ambulances. A police chief, and a message rolling along the bottom of the screen. *Stay calm. Stay indoors.*

'So everyone *is* indoors. And that's why there's no one there?' said Violet.

Luke got up, suddenly. 'I'm going to call my mum.'

'My mum's not answering,' Thea said. 'Is yours?'

'Not at the moment.' Luke gave her an uneasy smile.

'I can't get hold of anyone,' she said.

Connor came back in, holding his phone and chewing on a nail, and they looked at him. He gave the slightest shake of his head.

'Look,' said Violet. Nodded at the TV. Connor muted his laptop. Thea stopped thumbing her phone.

The oppressive clouds were shimmering. Part grey, part lavender. Long shapes.

'What is that?' said Violet.

'What?' said Luke.

'*That,*' said Violet. 'Them.' She got up and put her finger on the screen, but then wasn't sure herself if there was something there or not. Clouds or not clouds.

The reporter's voice with a strain of urgency and bafflement under the detached professionalism. Repeating the same words.

Do not travel. Stay at home.

No one breathed.

The same vast, shimmering ripple over different cities. Day or night. Dark lavender.

Disparitions massive.

Drone shots of the empty square where the Pope usually addressed thousands. Of the empty square where the student had once stood in front of the tank. Where their dad was right now.

'Shit,' said Luke, quite lightly, still holding his phone to his ear.

'He's not answering either,' said Thea.

Luke by the pool. Thea in her bedroom. Violet, still staring at the muted TV. Connor in the kitchen, laptop out. All of them on their phones, listening to endlessly ringing tones. Leaving answerphone messages. Texting. Trying again.

'Could it be a volcano?' Luke said to Connor, quietly. 'You know, didn't that happen a while back? In Finland or somewhere. Downed planes and that.'

'Iceland,' Connor said. 'I think.'

'So yeah, everyone's indoors and…' He glanced outside again. No ripples. No low clouds.

'Why would it just be in the cities?' Connor said. 'And all at once, not more gradual?'

'Is it…?' Luke lowered his voice further, as if he couldn't quite believe he was saying it. 'Nuclear?'

'I think we'd have known about it.'

Luke was biting his lip. 'Then what the fuck is it, Con? Where is everyone?'

Thea came and sat back down, next to Violet.

'They keep showing the same things,' Violet said.

'OK,' Thea said.

'Are they all just hiding? Because of... whatever that is? Whatever... they are?'

'What do you mean, *they* are?'

'I don't know.'

'Things are never as bad as they seem in your head.' Her voice sounded very far away.

'What if this time they are?'

They heard Luke outside, saying, *Dad*.

By the time they'd all got to the patio, Luke was looking at his phone again. He glanced up. 'It was hard to hear him. He said the phone networks weren't coping.'

'But he's OK,' said Violet.

'I think so. Yeah.' His phone buzzed. He stared at it for quite a while, before passing the phone to Connor.

'What?' Violet said. 'What does it say?'

Connor looked at Luke, who shook his head, before swallowing and nodding.

Connor gave it to Violet, and Thea looked over her shoulder.

Not sure what's going on but it's dangerous here.
Don't try and go home. Best to stay put. I love all four of you so much. Tell the others.

xxxx

Connor watched all the missed-call messages to his mum stack up, felt strangely detached, someone else's finger pressing the phone icon. Thea was repeatedly trying her mum's mobile, and Violet her mum's landline. Luke was walking around with his phone aloft in the air.

The shots of the sky again, and the dark-lavender ripple. Violet thought of William Henry Fox Talbot's first photographs, the flowers in the teacup seeming to hover in the air. *La police est mystifiée,* Thea heard, wondering where the police were in all these shots. Luke tried to think of other weather phenomena, fish falling like rain or weird pressure fronts. Connor thought of the hot-air balloon festival, Dave getting them up early to watch them from the park, dozens of teardrop shapes silently floating across the dawn sky.

Connor turned on the old FM radio in the kitchen and immediately flinched. The drone. His drone. More pure and piercing than he'd ever heard it, penetrating right through the breastbone. The radio should be tuned to the French jazz station, the one with the silken-voiced jingles they always laughed at. He moved the dial. White noise, then the drone again, on a lower frequency.

Thea was at his shoulder. 'What is it?'

'It's the same as—' In his head, he wanted to say. But she was looking at him blankly. 'Can you not hear that?' he said.

She stood still, holding onto her elbows, looked sideways to the wall. A tiny flicker in her throat as she swallowed. 'Hear what?'

He pointed to the radio. If he could hear it outside his body, it wasn't tinnitus.

She looked at it as if tranquillised. 'Is it not working? Can you get a signal?'

He shook his head, felt numb. Turned it off.

'Mum?' Luke had got hold of her. Video call. 'Where are you?'

'Hello, love.' She was doing that thing of pretending everything was fine, though she seemed harried and breathless, holding her phone quite close to her face as she walked. 'I'm on the way to Granna and Grandad's.' Thea and Violet had appeared either side of him. 'Oh, hello, you two. Are you all OK?' Almost as if it was an ordinary call and she was just a little late for something.

His sisters mumbled vague, awkward acknowledgements.

He felt irritated that they were there, glued to either side of him. They weren't hers. 'Yeah. Everything's – yeah. Mum?'

The screen was juddering. A lot of dark, rippled sky and houses. Perhaps she was running. Why wasn't she on the bus? 'Yes, love.'

His innards felt paralysed. 'Mum, what's happening?'

'Just stay indoors, love. Just be sensible. All of you.' There was the sound of one or two sirens, loud and distorted, and someone shouting. 'I'm sure you're in the best place.'

His sisters murmured an *OK*.

'It'll all—' His mum gave a strange laugh. 'Where's Connor? Is he there?'

'I'm here, Mum,' Connor said.

Thea and Violet moved to let him in, next to Luke. Arms touching arms. The four of them waiting to be told what to do. Children, nothing more.

'Give over,' his mum said suddenly, in a harsher voice. 'Are you seriously doing that right now?' She was talking – remonstrating – with someone beyond her screen. The same voice she had when someone had pulled out in front of her, or in her residents' meetings.

'Mum?'

'Someone is nicking a car,' she said. 'Broad bloody daylight. Unbelievable.'

They all looked at each other.

'I'll give you a call when I'm inside,' his mum said. 'Fifteen minutes or so, all right? Hold tight, love. I'll be back in a jiffy.'

She signed off, and they all stared at Luke's screenshot of him and his mates gurning at the camera.

There was the beginning of a low, indefinable roar outside, getting louder.

'No,' said Thea, the word tiny.

They went to the window. Felt the rumble in their bones. The house rocked. A massive sound, right over their heads, like a rip in the atmosphere, as a recognisable black shape streaked over the roof. Then another. Smooth, winged.

'*Militaire*,' said Violet, and they all watched as the planes disappeared over the hill.

'It's not…' said Luke to his brother, voice low again. The two of them in the kitchen. He couldn't finish the sentence. Couldn't make it real. Violet kept saying that the clouds on the various screens looked like shapes, and he couldn't see them. 'What the fuck is happening?' It was as if the earth, that had always sat under his feet and simply turned, had been given a shake, like a snowglobe.

Connor opened his mouth to speak. Closed it again.

Luke looked at his phone. It had been over an hour since the call with his mum. Now she wasn't answering.

There was a knock at the door.

* * *

Philippe looked grey, Connor thought. Ill. His wife and daughter were in Paris, and he couldn't get hold of them. *London, Paris, Berlin*, they had heard from Thea's phone. *All major cities and many towns. North and South America. Asia.*

Manchester, Connor thought. Beijing.

'I might drive up there,' Philippe said. 'It is not recommended, but—'

They had all crowded around him and he had stepped backwards, looked anywhere but at them.

Thea was wrapping her hair around her fist again, but in a childlike way. Nothing of her tall, flirtatious self from the party.

'What do you think we should do?' Luke said. 'Stay here, or...?'

'I cannot tell you,' Philippe said.

'Should we come with you?' Violet said. 'To Paris?' She looked at her siblings. 'Then we'd be closer, anyway.'

Thea shifted onto her other foot. 'I'm not sure,' she said, in a small voice.

'There's not enough room in the car,' said Connor.

'Yes,' said Philippe. 'Perhaps you should stay here.' He didn't want them to come, not really. 'I wanted to make sure you were all right. Your father would –' he took a breath – 'want me to. Er...' He shook his head. 'I think perhaps you should make sure you have lots of food.'

Luke looked at Connor.

* * *

No one was on the roads.

They drove down the hill, past the undulating rows of lavender and the olive groves. Past the churchyard, where an old man in dungarees stood by a gravestone, watching them. He slowly put up a hand, and Violet turned to watch through the back windscreen. He remained standing there, hand raised.

No one spoke. Thea, in the front passenger seat, had her phone to her ear. Connor's, to his. Violet had BBC News playing on her phone, but reception wasn't great and it kept stopping and starting. *Very difficult to understand*, she heard. *Recommended to remain – churches and mosques—*

'Come on,' said Thea, frustrated, to the road, to her phone.

They'd still not got hold of their mum. The shots of London had been the first they'd seen, and the gallery she worked at was in Zone 1. Violet had searched for *Farringdon* and *disappearance*, but it just kept saying 'various parts of the capital', and not naming anywhere specific.

It was like lockdown and not like lockdown, because in lockdown everyone was online, doing gym classes and baking and school. There were empty streets but everyone was still *there.*

As they turned a corner, there was a silver car in their lane, coming at speed right towards them. Violet's heart vaulted into her throat and her shoulder bashed into the door as they veered across the road and up onto the verge. She rocketed into her seat belt, hand slamming into the front headrest, and everything was quiet again.

'Fuck,' said Luke, putting his hand on his forehead. '*Fuck.* Is everyone OK?'

The car was angled so that Violet stared right up into the sky. There was a lavender tinge to it.

'Yeah, I'm OK,' said Connor.

'Yeah,' said Violet.

Thea burst into tears. 'I don't understand what is happening.'

Further along, they joined a line of cars. Still several kilometres from the town with the supermarket.

Luke asked Connor to go and see what was happening. The three of them watched him jog down the middle of the road and disappear round the corner.

A little way further up, a camper van had a large hand-painted banner on the back window saying *AMOUR-PAIX.* Someone was blaring 'What a Wonderful World'.

Five minutes. Thea shifted, made a small whimpering noise and rested her head on the window. They'd had French radio on, but they were talking too fast and she turned it off. There'd been no adverts. They always had loads of adverts.

Luke stared at the corner, the dry trees and the starched fields. Ten minutes. Twelve. No one was beeping.

Here he was, his brother, with his gentle loping run back towards them, his mass of black curls. Violet exhaled.

Connor got back in. Shut the door. 'It's a queue for petrol.'

'Fucking hell,' Luke said.

* * *

Back at home, they sat on the sofa again, the blinds pulled shut. Luke, Violet, Thea, Connor. Phones on laps or at ears.

They'd waited in the queue on the road for two hours, crawling along for a while until eventually not moving at all. Some cars had turned around, and in the end Luke had done the same.

'I feel sick,' said Violet.

'You need to eat summat,' said Luke, who had his arm around her. 'None of us have eaten.'

'I can't eat,' said Violet.

The same footage repeated on the TV and on BBC News on Connor's laptop and on their phones. The shapes in the sky, their cloudlike sheen, not moving. The flight and train booking websites were all down.

'My wrist hurts,' said Violet.

'Let me see,' said Luke.

She held up her forearm, and hissed as Luke touched it. 'When we went off the road,' she said. She hissed again. 'Ow.'

'Sorry,' said Luke. 'Just need to check for breaks.' He felt carefully round the wrist.

'Ow.'

All of them watched as Luke gently moved her hand, got her to wiggle her fingers. If they all just concentrated on Violet's swollen wrist, they wouldn't have to think about anything else.

'Might be sprained,' said Luke. 'Need to wrap it up.'

'Why didn't you say anything?' Thea said to her sister.

'I don't know,' Violet said.

Shots of someone throwing a brick through a shop window. Elsewhere, a woman hurrying along with a pushchair in one hand and a child in the other. Elsewhere, army tanks. Elsewhere, someone talking to camera, a hand in their hair, looking slightly high.

Shots of the empty streets, and the glossy ripple in the sky.

Violet sent all of her friends the same message. kssjhfkd kdfhsjkdsjjdjdkd H.O.L.Y.S.H.I.T. She wondered about posting a photo of herself with her mouth open, and decided not to. Instead, she scrolled through other people's photos, which were a mix of words and pictures of the sky at an angle and lots of #pray and #wtf and #endtimes, which was already an official hashtag with an emoji. She looked at famous people's accounts and watched half a video of an actor best known for playing a superhero who seemed to be crouched in his wardrobe, talking to camera about togetherness and hope. There was quite a lot of religious stuff.

Tell me ur ok, Thea sent to her friend group. Jade and Mischa were in Prague now – had Prague been on the news? She didn't remember seeing it. She sent the same message to everyone in her address book. She had a reply from someone who wasn't really her friend, but who at that moment she felt a new, desperate connection to. She started to reply that she was in France on holiday, but it seemed too ridiculous and she deleted it. Sent hearts instead. Got hearts back.

Connor received a message from Kaia, mostly swearing, and gifs of various apocalyptic scenes from films. He recorded a voice note to her that was mostly stumbling and silence. U fucking French-residing fucking dickface, she texted back. I love u.

Luke wrote long, heartfelt messages to each of his friends and watched the two grey ticks appear. Only a few of them turned blue. He waited for his mum to phone back. Kept trying her.

* * *

The smell of lavender was stronger in the dark, sweet and heady. Thea stepped onto the stones, an echo of the sun's heat still in them. Rolled dry pine needles under the soles of her feet and took another swig from the wine bottle.

Luke said they would try to get food and petrol tomorrow. Hopefully the road wouldn't be jammed this time. They ate hummus and bread without talking. Turned off the TV. Had taken it in turns trying Dad's phone, trying their mums.

The first thing her mum would have done was call them. Or text them, or email them, or leave a message on their social media accounts. The networks were all down, or hardly working, but even so. There was a landline at the gallery. A landline at home. She would have been able to walk home by now, or use a city bike, if she'd had to. It would be the very first thing.

Her skin itched. The light flicker of insects.

She took off her shorts and slid into the water in her pants and top. Full of wine and a fear that felt like a dream. The water was cool, buttery. Indigo-black. She went under, swimming against the walls. It was like a cave. She could just stay down here, her ears dulled with water, until it was all better again.

Jade had texted her. Babe ru ok? Wtaf??!!!! So scared rn. She'd replied and waited for the second tick to appear. Waited, and waited.

She let the bubbles come out, one by one, feeling her stomach constrict. Her ribs tightened, closed. At the last possible moment, she slowly floated up, and Connor was there.

She inhaled, a gasp that reached her gut.

'What're you doing?' His voice was very quiet.

It was always so hard to tell what he was thinking. Except about one thing, she thought, arcing an arm past her ear as she backstroked. 'Swimming. Like you do. At night.' She turned onto her side. The wall of the pool gently tilted.

He picked up the empty wine bottle. 'You should probably come out now.'

'Don't want to.' Here it was safe. Night-time and dark water and quiet. She went under again for a long time. There was a Buddhist word she couldn't remember, that meant emptiness. Void.

Hands on her, Connor's hands, and she flailed against them. Slipped. He was saying her name and pulling her up to the surface, and she tried to wrench free of the fingers as she was lifted out of the water. She put a foot against the wall and pushed, still being held, and Connor toppled into the pool, glancing off her shoulder.

He swore, splashed around in a blur before becoming smoother and swimming to the shallow end away from her.

She followed more slowly, full of bubbly giggles, the tears just underneath. She knew she should be apologising. But she hadn't spoken to her mum. He'd spoken to his.

He turned and faced her, standing waist-deep, his T-shirt stuck to him. 'What's wrong with you?'

She straightened right in front of him. He took a step backwards, the pool water bumping up around him.

'Nothing is wrong with me,' she said. 'Everything else has gone wrong. Everything else is beyond *fucked*.' She made the last word a poem, each microsyllable drawn out. 'Tell me it's not.'

The water flattened.

'Tell me what's happening,' she said. 'Who it is. What it is.'

He was a dark, wet shadow.

'You don't know anything. *Do* you?' Thea moved closer, and this time he didn't go backwards, because he couldn't any more, because the wall of the pool was right behind him. Captured. She could smell him, heat and chlorine. She could see the T-shirt against the skin of his chest.

She leaned forward. Kissed him.

He let her. He was letting her and she felt a ridiculous sense of validation and then he pushed at her shoulder, hard, so that she swayed backwards into the water, going under, coming up again in slow motion. 'Fuck off, Thea.'

'Yeah. You're probably right,' she said, lightly, distant.

She floated away from him until she reached the rail and pulled herself out, walked into the house and up to her room, where she lay down in her soaking clothes on top of the duvet.

* * *

Connor sat on the side of the pool, calf-deep in the water. The drone faint, but continuous, making his head hurt.

Her tongue had unfurled into his mouth. For a split second – it had been more than a second, more than five seconds – he was glued to her.

He stood, and bent over the bushes, thinking he might retch. Nothing came up. 'Please,' he said, to his stomach. He wanted it to come out. 'Come on. Please.'

His phone buzzed on the paving stones. He stumbled to the small, glowing screen.

It was Dad. *Will Low*, it said on his phone. Connor let it ring seven times before he could answer.

'Connor.' It was half statement, half question.

'Dad?' He'd never spoken to him by video before. It had been easier not to look at him. It was early evening in Beijing, he thought. He was supposed to be flying out to Paris tomorrow, then a train south. The screen froze. *Trying to reconnect.* 'Dad?' When had he ever called him this?

Back again. 'Are you OK? Is everything all right there?'

'It's OK,' Connor said. It wasn't OK. 'There's nothing happening here.' Nothing had happened here, in the pool, just now, he told himself. He felt sick again. 'There's nothing—' *out there*, he wanted to say. 'We're all here.'

It wasn't clear if Will had heard. His face kept pixillating, expressions impossible to make out. He was in a shirt and tie, as if taking a conference call.

'Is it – are you...' Connor swallowed, '... all right there?'

'I don't know. I'm glad you're OK. I'm really glad, Connor. You've got to—'

The screen froze, his dad's mouth hanging open.

'Got to what?' Connor said.

Trying to reconnect.

In his ear, the drone dug gently into the space on his deaf side. A sheer, crystal tone.

'Dad.' He felt his stomach knot. Needed to know the answer more than anything in his life. 'Got to what?'

Trying to reconnect.

'– you, Connor. I love—'

'I know, Dad,' he said.

He watched the screen freeze again. Sat there for two hours, waiting for his father to reappear, to come back to life in the palm of his hand.

Nine

The shelves were empty of most dry goods. The lights bright. Tinny jazz was playing, a lone saxophone.

Luke had barely slept. Every sound in the house had made his heart heave and he'd spent every half-hour checking his phone. His mum still hadn't called back, and his thoughts had spiralled – how to get home, drive except what if there wasn't any petrol, hitch to an airport, hitch all the way north to who knows what, except that their dad had said to stay put. His mum had, too, the only thing she and Will had ever agreed on.

They'd been running low on food, everything demolished at the party. He decided to get to the supermarket early, on his own. He didn't want them to get more frightened, though he felt like he was barely functioning. He had to be the adult and he didn't know how to be any more.

The roads were clearer, the queue only round the first corner from the town. The two petrol stations were shut, notices over the pumps.

He took what was there – tinned green beans, kids' cereal, bacon crisps. A pile of fruit had spilled and no one had bothered to pick up anything. The few other shoppers moved listlessly, not making eye contact. The person at the till had an unreadable expression.

There was a faint, foul taste in his mouth. Dry, too.

He checked his phone again.

He drove to the medieval village, where a few people were drifting along the street that fronted the lake, eyes up to the sky. A line had formed outside the little shop there, a young man shouting at an elderly woman coming out with five or six boxes of fudge, people crowding around to defend one or the other. Someone knocked a box to the floor, and when he looked in his rear-view mirror, people were scrabbling on the pavement.

He checked his phone. He wanted his mum. His dad. Dave. He wanted Jamie to message him, harass him, be violent. The battery was almost dead.

* * *

Violet looked at Luke's two half-empty shopping bags, and knew what it meant. Hardly any food left on the shelves.

'The Internet's stopped,' she said.

He stood there, holding the bags. 'You mean it's slow?'

'I mean it's like, stopped. Two hours ago. Not working for any of us, anyway.'

She watched Luke's chest rise once, fall once.

'Luke, what do we do?'

He sat down at the kitchen table and gazed at his hands. Back up at her. 'I'm really sorry, but I don't know.'

They'd taken it in turns to try and book flights or trains or ferries, watching the same holding messages on the sites. Connor's laptop screen just showed the same things as yesterday, over and over again. Then the five curves of Wi-Fi had gone to light grey, and the bars of their phones had flickered, uselessly.

'Where was everyone going yesterday?' she said. 'On the road?'

'Everyone's panicking,' Luke said, his voice dull. 'That's all. It'll settle down.'

'Why isn't anyone answering?' She'd listened to Thea leaving longer and longer messages for their mum. Wondered what Artoo was doing now, and whether he was on his own. She wanted to put her face in his neck and hide there. 'Are they dead?'

The word didn't feel like it had any meaning. She'd been trying to think of other explanations. A single evil magician had cast a spell because they were bitter and twisted and hated everyone, and they'd bring them all back eventually. Or it was a huge, coordinated stunt by people, like a global flash-mob, except instead of dancing in a crowd of shoppers, they'd all hidden away as a joke or a protest. But when she said these things to her sister, Thea had just stared at her with empty eyes.

'What were the things?' she said. 'In the sky?'

'I didn't see anything,' Luke said, shortly.

'But are they dead?'

Luke made a noise that was partly a laugh, and partly disbelief. He looked smaller, somehow.

'I made a list,' she said, and showed him what she'd written.

* * *

Connor heard it first. A crying that was almost animal, and Violet calling out.

He jogged downstairs to the kitchen to find Luke already there, crouched in front of Thea. She was bent over almost double, shuddering, filling up with heaving gasps of air that seemed to give her no respite. As if there wasn't enough air in the world. Her face patched red, eyes and nose streaming.

Violet was hovering by the door. Connor looked out of the window to the grey sky, but he couldn't see anything up there.

'It's OK,' Luke was saying. 'It's OK. Thea.' He craned his head to try and catch her eye. 'Thea. Look at me.'

Her gaze was flying around the room, past Connor and Violet without seeing them, seeking something that wasn't there. A glass had smashed on the floor, tiny shards catching the light. There was a modest line of blood coming from her toe.

'Breathe through your nose. Look at me,' Luke said, kneeling in front of her, and finally Thea's eyes settled on him. 'Do it with me, OK? Breathe through your nose.' He inhaled, loudly, and she tried to do the same, but the breath caught, and she sputtered, almost laughed, began crying again. Those loud, inhuman breaths.

Violet had her thumb and forefinger in her mouth, was chewing determinedly, eyes wide and fixed on her sister.

Luke reached over to a tea towel. 'Here.'

146

Thea took it, blew, and for a moment everything was normal. The simple, practical sound of someone blowing their nose. Then she began sobbing into it. The judders rising in her breath and body again, a wave of something beyond herself.

'Breathe in with me,' Luke said, and Connor realised he must have done this with others, fellow students maybe. 'In through your nose. Out through your mouth. I'm going to count, OK?'

Connor watched as Thea copied Luke, her body levelling. She let out a tiny whimper. All her angles had disappeared, left her soft, deflated. Her shoulders curled inwards.

'Con.' His brother was looking at him. 'Get a plaster?'

'Yeah. Sorry.'

Connor fetched the plastic box from under the sink and a cloth that probably wasn't clean enough, and knelt down next to Luke. He roughly swept the broken glass away with the side of his hand, and looked up at Thea's damp, wild eyes. He picked up her foot, which was warm and tacky, and rested her heel on his thigh. There was a mosquito bite on her anklebone, the size of a cough sweet. Carefully, he cleaned the blood away with the cloth, listening to her breathe. A splinter of glass dug into his knee, and he let it.

He tried not to think about the two of them, in the pool. That had been a different Thea to this one.

Luke was still counting her breaths.

'I'm sorry,' Thea said. A ghost-voice. Unclear who she was addressing.

'You had a panic attack,' said Luke. 'That's all.'

'That's all,' she repeated, in a whisper.

The blood welled up again, and Connor dabbed at it until it slowed. He put on the plaster and carefully placed her foot back on the floor.

She wiped the pale mucus away from her mouth with the outside of her hand. 'I want to speak to my mum,' she said, and the words were small and hard, seemed to come from a different place. 'You've talked to your mum and we've not talked to ours and it's not fair.'

A long, silent moment in which they all looked at the floor, waiting for Luke to answer in a way that would make them feel safe.

He didn't.

* * *

Noumenon, thought Thea. That which is unknowable.

* * *

It was like living in a dream, Violet thought. A movie. A game. It was unreal and it was real and reality had exploded and become something different entirely, like there had always been something on the other side of the mirror, lurking, waiting, and now *bam*.

Luke had driven down to the village. Said that they should stay here, look after Thea. She didn't know how to look after her sister.

She'd never seen Thea do that, something suddenly erupting in her. A monster she needed to get out. It was almost as scary as everything else. She wanted the old Thea back, bitchy and cutting and reading her difficult books so that everyone knew how clever she was. Now she was holding a cushion to her stomach on the sofa, pressing the same button on her phone, over and over, and staring at the muted TV. Shots of walls or the sides of buildings with the odd missing person photo and handwritten message pinned on. Nothing new.

'Are you OK?' Violet said. She thumbed the material of her wrist support, her tendons gently throbbing.

A dry sound in the back of her throat as her sister swallowed.

'Thee.'

'No.' Thea's voice was lower. 'Of course I'm not OK. Are *you* OK?' A shade of her old, challenging tone.

'I don't know.' Violet heard a sound, stiffened. Two hours ago, a helicopter had flown over, the world's biggest dragonfly. In the past, they would do manoeuvres, and you'd see them circling several times, but today it had gone right overhead.

Another sound. It wasn't from the sky, but from the garage.

Thea rolled her head around to listen, almost uninterested.

There was something moving out there. Metal against metal. Where was Connor?

A crash. Things were being shifted, thrown. Something wasn't bothered about being heard. Connor usually moved quietly, hardly made a sound.

'Stay here,' Violet said.

Thea took in a loud breath and released it in bits.

Violet picked up the rolling pin from the kitchen on her way out.

It was a movie. A game.

Her bare feet stuck to the paving slabs as she crossed between the house and the garage. Another crash from in there. Her heart was twice its size.

The side door to the garage was ajar.

Connor's head, amongst crates. The two bikes had been dragged out, and the tyre pump. A toolbox.

He looked up, his face flushed from exertion. 'Thought we might need a few things,' he said.

* * *

'*Bonjour?* Amandine?'

Amandine's house was halfway up the medieval village's slope, on the corner by some uneven steps. Here the terraced stone houses were separated by narrow, bumpy lanes. Luke hadn't been to her house in a couple of years. The great fifteenth-century door was open by a crack.

'*Bonjour?*' he said again, as he stepped inside. It sounded ludicrous. The first word you learned in any language. A useless thing.

He wasn't sure why he was here. Philippe had gone and this was the only other person they properly knew. A maternal presence, maybe. He'd tried every number he could think of – his granna and grandad, his aunt in Leeds, his aunt in Galway, the family friends, the library where his mum worked. The initial reports had reeled off cities, including his own. Now, they didn't name individual cities any more. 'Worldwide,' Thea had said, from her curled position on the sofa, clutching her phone to her chest. '*Mondial.*' She'd repeated the word over and over, until it became a whisper, until it disappeared inside her.

Amandine's kitchen smelt of detergent. There were some sandy flakes of baguette on the table. An umbrella hanging by the door, next to a turquoise scarf with tiny mirrors sewn on it. A photo on the wall of her two sons as teenagers, beaming at the camera.

You, his mum had once said, her hands on his cheeks, *are going to break so many boys' hearts.*

Luke stood at the top of the stairs down to the lower floor – these old houses were built from caves, the bedrooms in the damp dark. He opened his mouth to say her name again, but knew she wasn't here. She'd have come bounding up by now, talking nonstop, neither of them caring that he couldn't understand her.

He turned back to the kitchen and read through Violet's list. *Tinned food, food in jars, cereal, crisps, nuts, protein powders like you get in health food shops idk, seeds, vegetables in pots (like tomatos??), batteries, candles, matches, lighters, jungle juice, torches, sun cream, first aid kits, painkillers, cellatape, string, DIY kinda stuff, tools + shit.* He stepped forward and opened a cupboard. Jars of artichokes, tinned carrots. Biscuits, illustrated on the front cover alongside a smiling cartoon figure.

His blood had slowed. His mouth dry. He picked up a tin.

A sound behind him, and his heart lurched. When he turned round, a man in his thirties was standing in the doorway. There was a stricken moment in which nothing moved, breathed, beat. The man's shirt was half-open.

Eyebrows furrowed, dark. His mouth ajar, chest rising and falling. He said something, very fast, a stabbed enquiry.

'Sorry,' Luke said, putting the tin down. 'Sorry.' He held up his hands and got out of there, pushing past the man, into the shaded alleyway, running down the steps.

* * *

Thea thought about the Poe poem she'd read last summer. *What if all that we see or seem, is but a dream within a dream.* Everything felt real – she could smell the sweat under her arms, and feel the dried tears and snot tightening her face, and the insidious itch of the mosquito bite on her ankle, spreading up her calf – because that's what happened in dreams. You didn't know you were in a dream until you were out of it.

She'd been staring at the rust-red floor tiles, mind numb. Before, the thoughts had raced and whirled until they'd blown out of her body in a gust. But she could feel them beginning to form again, words clotting together. *What if – it's going to – I'm – they're—*

What was that thing she had read? Philosophical presentism. The future was not real. The past was not real. The mind was not real. Only what was happening physically, right now in the present.

She scratched the mosquito bite until it bled.

* * *

High above the house, a griffon vulture spirals on a thermal. From underneath, it looks like two creatures – one cream bird shaded by a larger black form, the flight feathers splayed like outstretched fingers. Its nestlings, in an eyrie lodged in the crag of a cliff, demand more. Though a scavenger, it is beginning to feed on live prey.

A carpenter bee, equal parts sleek and furred, burrows among the lavender. And another. Usually solitary, they are joining each other. Hoverflies are in the mint flowers and the pompom heads of the purple scabious. The flowers' colours are deepening, the petals glossy. An increase of nectar.

On the other side of the house's walls, a collection of bramble buds, fuzzy and pumpkin-shaped, suddenly burst open as one.

* * *

They waited for something to happen. Sat in a line on the loungers and watched the horizon. On the second night, it seemed like the sky in the east, the direction of a large, historic city, glowed more than usual. Then darkened, more than usual.

Nothing came.

* * *

Violet's etymology app didn't need the Internet to work. *Al*, from the Proto-Indo-European root meaning 'beyond'.

The Sanskrit *anya*, for 'other'. The Greek *allos*, for 'different, strange'. The Old English *elles*, for 'otherwise, else'.

She hadn't said the word aloud, because to say it might make them real.

There had been shapes in the sky. Clouds-that-weren't-clouds. Violet didn't understand why the others hadn't seen them. When she asked, they all went quiet and didn't have any other ideas.

There was a second meaning, too. *Al*, from the Proto-Indo-European root 'to grow, nourish'. The German *alt*, meaning 'old'. The Old Norse *ala*, meaning 'to nourish'. The Gothic *alan*, meaning 'to grow up'.

They really had gone, hadn't they? The people, the population, the world. They weren't just hiding from the things in the sky. They'd have come out by now, and would be talking to cameras, even just the single camera now on the French news channel on TV, because there was nothing people liked more than telling other people what they thought.

Violet wondered whether the prime minister actually was in hiding, because usually they got a warning about the really bad stuff, but what if there hadn't been any warning? Were the heads of governments in bunkers coordinating their armies like they did in movies? Forgetting their differences and coming together to Save Planet Earth? Somehow, she didn't think so. People weren't clever enough to compromise.

The Internet was down but there was still phone signal, and their mums and their dad hadn't rung. If he could, their dad would be on a plane to London or Paris or Marseilles. Alanna, who Violet had always found a bit scary, would be shouting at people to give her a lift. Maybe she'd get down to south London, and she and Violet's mum would come together and become best friends, and that sounded like a movie as well.

Hello, my little shieldmaiden. I'm right here with you. You're going to be just fine.

You've got this, kiddo.

Violet could imagine them, hear their voices. She didn't usually because they were always there, in the morning or after school, but they sounded so clear. Was she channelling their spirits? She hadn't really ever believed in ghosts. But if there were ghosts, now there were hundreds and thousands and millions of them, all suddenly in the atmosphere, bumping into each other, apologising politely, trying to get to their loved ones. Could ghosts travel? Were they all freaking out? Was Artoo in there, too?

'Don't be a ghost,' she said, to the air. 'You're banned from being a ghost.'

* * *

'Do you think we should still try and get back?' said Luke. He was lightly trembling. A faint waver in his voice.

He was sitting on Connor's bed, shoulders hunched over.

'No,' Connor said. There's nothing there, he wanted to say. He knew it, deep in his gut. That a massive bit of fake news on all media wasn't possible. 'We need to stock up.'

Luke had been staring into space, dragging his fingernails along his forehead.

'They know where we are,' Connor said. 'If – if anyone can, they'll get here. However long it takes.'

'But they're not going to, are they?'

Connor couldn't answer.

'I can't do it,' Luke said, abruptly. He'd told Connor of the man at Amandine's, how it might have been one of her sons, or a neighbour, or a stranger. The horror of being seen as an intruder. 'They might come back, and need all that stuff. I just can't.'

'I can,' said Connor.

* * *

'Do you know how to grow things?' said Violet.

'I don't know owt, mate,' Luke said, with an almost-laugh. 'Not a fucking thing.' He coughed.

'Are you ill?' Her brother wasn't allowed to be ill. Not now.

'No. My mouth's just dry all the time. The air is…' He gave a small, delicate sigh. 'Isn't yours?'

She shook her head. 'Shall I get you some water?'

There was a silence, and she knew they were both thinking the same thing. How long would the water last, and what on earth would they do then?

Ten

He had never walked on this road. They always drove. The newer parts of the tarmac glistened, looked oiled. The white noise of cicadas came from the fields.

Connor had spent an hour watching the featureless sky from the living-room window. Another half an hour watching from the gate. There hadn't been a single car.

The drone in his ear rang like a finger round the rim of a wine glass.

Philippe's house was a hundred metres further up. Shocking-pink flowers lined the gated driveway. His sports car wasn't there.

Connor checked up and down the road. The next house along was not quite visible. He gripped the gate, the metal warm, and tested the brick pillar with his foot. He threw his rucksack over, and hefted himself upwards. The rough, scudding sound of his trainers, gripping onto the brick. He arched in his stomach to avoid the railing spikes as he scrambled over.

He knocked on the front door a couple of times, just to be sure. Tried the handle, and the sliding doors at the side.

Locked. The tarp was pulled over the kidney-shaped pool. Two sun loungers with the backs upright. He circuited the house, scanning the first-floor windows, and lifted plant pots until he found one heavy enough. He stood in front of the kitchen window, the only one with single glazing.

Strange, how focused he felt. How disaster of an unimaginable, not-graspable kind had made everything fall away. He didn't know why his body wasn't reacting as Thea's was, or at least Luke's – his brother was constantly, subtly shivering. Violet seemed somewhere else entirely, but not in a bad way.

He held the rim of the pot in both hands and smashed the base as hard as he could against the pane. It didn't even fracture. He tried again, and again, a force appearing in his arms like rage, like fear, until the glass began to weaken, until a diamond-shaped hole appeared, enough for him to angle his arm through.

Everything was modern, clean. Far more ordered than their house, even before all their holiday stuff had been chucked everywhere. The remotes in a neat line, facing the TV. The books on the shelves arranged by size. All the wall switches had been turned off.

An odd, suspended feeling in the air. The recent human presence seemed to linger, as if at any moment there'd be the sound of a washing machine being turned on, or someone calling to another, or music emanating from the radio.

There was an envelope placed flat on the dining-room table, next to a photo frame and a bowl of dried flowers.

Handwriting in blue ink. *Cécile, Charlotte.* The photo was of Philippe, his wife and daughter in a desert climate. His daughter was about the same age as Thea.

The drone in his ear became briefly intermittent, then smoothed. He'd tried the FM radio again, and the sound had soared out at him. He'd brought the volume right down, turned it up very slowly, but it was too much almost as soon as he heard it. A ringing as intense as a torch in your eyes. It wasn't just in his head.

In Philippe's kitchen, the fridge was humming. About a diminished fifth and several octaves lower than his ear-note. The devil's interval, it used to be called, a sound that went against traditional harmony. There were vegetables, still good enough, some cheese, open jars of sauces. Half a banana in its skin. Plenty in the cupboards, too. He ate the banana as he took out every tin, jar, packet of pasta and cereal, and carried them down to the cellar, shoving them behind some boxes in a corner and covering them with a green tablecloth for now. There were at least thirty bottles of wine down here. Well, maybe they'd need them just as much, he thought. Even him.

He went back upstairs and filled his rucksack with the fresh things. Wondered what Kaia was doing at this exact moment, if she was doing anything at all. She hadn't replied any more. His mum hadn't replied.

The staircase to the upper floor was wide and curving, a high-gloss wood, the cream carpet pristine. Connor took off his trainers and went up in his socked feet. The beds in each of the three rooms were neatly made. In the largest room, he slid open the drawer of the bedside table. A couple of chunky gold rings, anchor-shaped cufflinks, folded tissues, and at the back, under an old diary, a packet of two condoms.

He stared at them. Wondered if Philippe and his wife used them, or if the neighbour had them for another reason. He briefly closed his eyes, swallowed.

Then he pocketed them, and stood up.

The side door to the garage was unlocked. A humming of something in here, too, about three and a half octaves lower than his own drone. It smelt musty, comforting. Oil and dust. He rifled through the toolboxes, finding a few things he could come back for. There were folded inflatables, a bucket and spade, a wooden baseball bat.

He slotted the bat into his rucksack.

* * *

Luke plugged in his phone charger again. Watched the battery symbol pulse. Tried his mum. Wrote a message to Jamie, nothing like the one he'd imagined sending, for when the Internet came on again. Swiped through photos. Him and his mates out on the lash, the Diwali festival lights in Leicester, he and his granna in matching reindeer headbands, the half-marathon. His mum, holding up a posh champagne glass, pointing at the camera.

His phone buzzed in his hand and his gut lurched.

Dad. A text. Look after them. I love you so much.

He stared at it, felt blank. The time that the message had been sent was thirty-six hours earlier than it had arrived.

Another buzz and his heart jammed upwards. But there wasn't another message, just the battery symbol, losing its lightning bolt, becoming a single bar. He wiggled his charger, turned the switch at the wall off and on again. Stood and turned the light on.

The bulb remained dark.

* * *

Near the house, a lesser horseshoe bat swims through the night air, gathering a moth as delicate as cigarette paper into its mouth. More moths, more bats, thronging the air. A frog, with an oil-and-mustard sheen, lowers the floor of its mouth, expands its throat, breathes a deep, endless chant.

Below the village, in the ditches by the roads, the tiny coils at the tops of ferns unfurl and fan out overnight.

The blurred hum of bees thickens.

* * *

Truth and illusion, it said in the John Cage book.

Thea woke up in darkness. Curled up on the sofa with a blanket over the lower half of her body, her stomach wrung out.

If she didn't breathe, it might wake her body up. Even coming to France had been a dream. She'd jerk awake and find herself at home, in her own bed, spooning the blue fluffy monster she'd had since she was nine. The sound of the P4 bus hefting itself up the hill outside. Her phone, just by her head on the bedside table, fully charged.

The sound of Luke coughing upstairs, and Thea was instantly here again. A sound that sealed her to this place.

Violet called out that none of the switches were working.

She rolled off the sofa, lay curled on the cool tiles for a while, her face against them. She pressed her left cheekbone down against the stone as hard as she could, allowing the pain to expand.

She thought of her dad, reading her stories in bed in ridiculous accents that made her roll her eyes. She thought of her mum, helping her cut little hearts and triangles in paper to send to her grandparents at Easter.

Eventually she rose and opened the sliding door.

The night air was cool, tacky. Something lightly dashed against her neck and she slapped it. Her cheekbone throbbed.

She stood on the door ledge, put her chin up to the sky. Wished she knew what she was looking for. It was deep grey-blue. No strange clouds.

She wanted to have been at home. Even if the very worst things had happened, whatever they might be, she wanted to have experienced it with other people, been amongst them, awash with terror. Not here. Away. She felt a deep, jagged rage at her siblings, in their rooms with the lights off, quiet.

A clicking sound. She turned around, looked out at the night. The profound stillness. Her skin still itched.

A dog barked. Then, a motion in front of her, as if the sky was breaking into tiny shards of black glass. Coming towards her.

A sudden rushing, beating sound and then there was something flung in her face, her hair.

* * *

Luke took the stairs two at a time, twisted his ankle in the dark, swore.

By the time he got down to the living room, Thea was slapping at Connor, pushing him, shrieking. Violet was in the room now, jumping up towards the curtain at something.

'What's—?' Luke said.

Thea turned to him. 'How can you sleep? How can you fucking sleep? What's wrong with you? There's something *here.*'

She was dashing her hands through her hair. Connor tried to take them and she shoved him away.

'Please,' she said. Eyes a diluted version of their old selves. 'There's something here, Luke.'

'It's a bat, sis,' said Violet, from behind them. She had one hand cupped over the other, something fluttering between them.

'It wasn't,' said Thea. 'It was—'

'Just a bat. Look.' Violet lifted her upper hand a little. A flash of grey-black, rubber and fur.

Thea shrank. 'Get it away from me.'

The three of them watched as Violet went to the door, released her hands. The shadow flicking away, one moment there, the next gone.

'I wasn't sleeping,' said Luke to Thea. 'Not really.' He felt his own shivers return, the faintly rotten taste in his mouth.

'Me neither,' said Connor.

'Nor me,' said Violet.

'I want to go home,' said Thea. 'I want to go home right now.'

There was a silence. Luke tried to think again how to do it – to drive until the petrol ran out, steal another car or beg someone for theirs, to get to an airport when they didn't know what was there. To be stuck. 'I know. But we can't,' he said. 'Dad wanted us to stay here. We just have to wait. Everything will settle down. Like the pandemic. Might just – take a while.'

He wondered if they could hear the lie.

* * *

Batshit crazy.

Violet lay in the dark, the sheet up to her waist. Her headphones on. Giving herself tinni-whatever. She'd had two albums downloaded on her phone, was saving the last bit of battery for a particular moment, and decided that moment was now.

The bat had been almost nothing but air. Delicate rubber and matchstick bones. It had vanished from her hands as if she'd imagined it all along.

The ripple in the sky had seemed like nothing but air. Almost, but not quite.

Do cats eat bats? she remembered, from *Alice in Wonderland*. Do bats eat cats?

She wanted to be a bat right now. Night and bat and nothing else at all. They didn't give a literally flying fuck what was happening.

The song changed, a track with the nastiest guitars, the fastest drum patterns. She turned it up, filled her head. It wasn't loud enough. Nasty enough.

She didn't hear the door, jumped when the sheet moved and she felt a weight next to her. She kicked out at it, hard.

'Ow,' said Thea.

'Jesus,' said Violet, plucking out her headphones. 'Shit, Thea. What is wrong with you?'

Thea let out a tiny, detached laugh that became a sob. 'Please can I sleep here?'

'It's a single bed,' Violet said, but moved over anyway, right against the wall, facing her.

Thea got in, pulling the sheet up to her chin. She lay there on her back like a dead person. They hadn't been in the same bed since Violet was four.

'Tell me it's not real,' Thea said, hardly more than a whisper.

'I can't, can I?'

'How do we know it's real?'

'Seriously? You're going to do this, now?'

'It can't be, can it?'

'You saw the TV. Heard the news. You saw the people doing the same as us out there. All the cars. It's not in your head.' She knew, though, that she hadn't cried yet because she hadn't seen it happen. She hadn't seen her dad or her mum or her friends die, or disappear. She couldn't cry until she knew for sure. Wouldn't.

'It's still in my hair,' Thea said.

'What is?'

'The bat. I know it's not. But it is.'

They lay in the dark. The sounds of Connor or Luke going to the bathroom. A short stream of pee.

'Can we listen to your music?' Thea said.

So Violet disconnected the Bluetooth, put her phone on top of Thea's stomach, and they played the album until her battery ran out.

Eleven

She wasn't in the living room, or the kitchen.

Connor always needed to be aware of where she was, to check that she was still breathing. Not to crowd her, but just crane his head round a door, see her, move on. Before, she made her presence known, was utterly aware of the shape and weight of her body in the world. Now she was so wraithlike that it was becoming harder to sense her.

He took the stairs, the tiles clinging to his bare feet with the slightest resistance.

Thea came out of his room in his T-shirt. The one that faded from dark to light grey down its length. He stopped on the penultimate step.

She looked down at herself. The frayed ends of her denim shorts visible. 'Do you mind?' Her voice flat.

His almost-twin. 'No.'

'I don't like any of my clothes any more.' She put her hand on the banister and tapped it with her nail. A hollow, insistent little thud. 'I'm sorry. About yesterday.'

'It's OK.'

'I'm not coping very well.'

Bizarre, to hear her speaking with such detached articulacy, after her mania last night. Her skin had been clammy. Mosquito bites and scratches up her thighs.

'That's... understandable.' He wanted to say so much to her, and nothing ever came out. 'Have you eaten today?'

She didn't seem to hear him. 'What's going to happen?'

'I don't know.'

Thea breathed in, soft and textured. Sighed it out again. 'Can't you just say everything is going to be all right? Like Luke. That they're all OK. That everything will go back to –' her eyes met his, wryness in the despair – 'normal.' It didn't even end as a question. She shook her head, a minute gesture. 'How are you OK?'

'I'm not.' He swallowed. 'I promise.'

'Fucking nihilist,' she said, and there was a little of her old self, spiky and mannered, though it was gentler too, and he didn't mind it.

* * *

Violet and her camera stood on the wall, both feet flat, looking over the valley. On watch. At least one of them was always by a window, looking up at the sky. Looking for clouds that weren't clouds but smooth shapes, with a sheen like clingfilm.

The sky was a very faded mauve, purple, indigo. Violet. She took a photo of it. Her battery had been on charge until the electricity had run out. She wondered how long it would last. But maybe if whatever was happening everywhere happened here, her photos would be evidence for people in the future. If there were any people in the future.

At least *he's* probably gone, she thought, imagining him there by the edge of the trees at school one moment, the next vanished. Except that she could still feel him on her hand sometimes.

Today, the hot water had stopped while she was in the shower. Luke had already said that they had to be quick, but it had only been half a minute before the water cooled.

'It's like the temperature of the lake,' she'd said to Thea, who'd begun crying again when she'd told her. 'It's not that cold.'

'Not that cold *yet*,' said Thea.

At least she was thinking ahead, thought Violet. That was an improvement.

It was so quiet. You wouldn't know that anything was any different. If you didn't have a phone or radio or ever watch TV, if you were a hermit and never went into the village or to the shops, you'd have no clue. *None the wiser*, as her dad would say. Apart from there being no cars around, or people. It hadn't even been cloudy, just this one-dimensional murkiness, as if a blanket had been thrown over the globe.

She angled her camera and took another photo.

The kitchen appliances were all electric, so Violet told Luke that they would need wood for the fire, for cooking and boiling water, and he'd just nodded, looking at the floor. He usually lived on tea, which he called *a brew*, even here where it was hot and he said the teabags were weak and tasted weird.

There was a flutey, fluttering sound, like someone playing broken panpipes. She wanted to laugh. A wise owl, none the wiser, making its normal noise like it was a normal evening.

No tea without wood, she thought. No homemade mochas heavy on the chocolate. No pasta, no soup. She didn't really mind about showers because she didn't much like washing. But Thea loved her baths, would stay in there for two hours on her phone or reading, unless you banged on the door.

Another photo, and this time she glanced at the screen.

There was the tiniest sense of a ripple in the top left-hand corner. Like the sky being stretched too tight. She zoomed in. Not cirrocumulus clouds, which she'd looked up on the second day. She looked again with her naked eye. There just weren't any clouds up there.

She drew a deep breath, and took another photo. This time, there was no ripple on the screen.

But a flicker of light caught her eye, lower in her vision.

She looked over the long sweep of hill, the terraced olive trees. There were lights down there in the deepening dusk. She squeezed her eyes tightly shut, making every part of her face twist, opened again. Still there.

This must be it, then. Annihilation. *Dispiration.*

But as she concentrated, she realised that there were shadows down there, too, on the curving road. Human ones.

A line of them.

* * *

No one spoke.

Every person carried a candle – a tea-light in a bowl or jar, or a long, tapered one, the flame cupped with a palm.

Dark figures, thirty or so, walking slowly down the hill, their hands glowing.

Luke had no idea where they'd all come from. None of the gently lit faces were recognisable to him.

The four of them had joined the end of the procession – Thea, holding her hoodie round her with tight arms. Violet, picking at her nail polish. Connor, carrying the baseball bat. Luke, limping from his twisted ankle, his thoughts blunted.

A bewitching silence. What was there to say, after all?

He hadn't told the others about that final text from their dad. Couldn't.

There were around twenty people already outside the church in their hilltop village, seated or standing in the faded amber glow of the walls. More jarred candles on the ground, underneath a lopsided yew tree. The priest was standing there, holding a lantern and nodding at everyone, as if it were a Sunday morning.

Thea sat down, her legs folded sideways beneath her. Violet hovered at the edge of the group. Connor quietly laid the baseball bat in a flowerbed.

After a while, the group grew no bigger. About fifty people were gathered under and around the yew tree, the polite shuffle of gravel as they settled. The dance of light on chins, chests, spectacles.

The priest began to speak. His voice was low, the consonants blurred.

Amen, murmured the people around him.

Again. The priest's incantation, and the shadows responding. Again.

A bat flickered overhead.

Dad, Luke thought. Mum. Granna and Grandad. His friends, the ones he'd known forever, the ones he'd made recently, the ones he slept with, the ones he ran with, partied with. Jamie.

Amen.

He felt a twist of shame in his gut. *I'm going to split you open.* He swallowed, the acid suddenly sharp in his throat. Wanted Jamie, wanted to be held by him, hurt by him, have the life squeezed out of him if it got Jamie off, because why the fuck not.

Amen.

'Let's go,' he said, under his breath. He wanted to cry.

'I want to stay,' Thea said. She remained resolutely on the ground.

He felt the need to run, back to the house, *past* the house, to keep running north until his legs gave out, until every part of him was broken. He took in a huge breath, panic rearing up in him, and put out a hand. The night tilted. Someone in the dark was holding his arm, speaking in an undertone.

'Get off me,' he said, flinging their hand away. 'Fuck. Sorry. *Désolé.*' The ground was undulating. He stumbled away from the group, round the side of the church into complete darkness, stood against cool limestone. He lightly bashed the back of his head against it.

Amen, he heard.

He hit the back of his head again. Harder.

'Hey,' said Connor, suddenly at his side. 'Stop.' His hand was on Luke's shoulder, pulling him away from the wall, so that there was space between his skull and the stone. 'Stop it.'

'I can't do it,' he said. *Look after them.* 'I haven't got the fucking balls.' He laughed. 'I can't do it, Connor.' First, electricity. Now gas. Next would be water.

'You don't have to,' said Connor, and put his arms around him. 'It's not your job.'

Luke clutched onto the skinny angles of his brother's body. Couldn't cry. The people round the corner were singing now, a quiet hymn.

'We're going to die,' he said, his ribs aching, Connor's T-shirt warm underneath his cheek.

'At some point, yeah.' Connor's voice was understated, wry.

'Our kid, the Zen monk.'

Connor responded with a small, near-amused hum.

Luke listened to his brother's heart, slowing. When had he last hugged him like this?

'One day at a time, all right?' Connor said.

* * *

'Is he going to be OK?' said Thea.

Outside the church, Connor had squatted down to her, said quietly that they needed to go, and something in his voice made her obey without question. The four of them had walked in the silence and the dark back to the house.

'Yeah,' said Connor.

'Liar.'

She tucked up her legs on the sofa, rested her chin on her knees and shut her eyes, trying to put herself back on the gravel, amongst those other people. The priest's words she'd recognised – *Dieu, pitié, pardonner, donne nous, espoir* – like flitters of flame.

Flames. She'd watched Luke fiddle with the boiler, pressing the ignition button again and again. Hearing herself pray for the small blue plume to appear, she who had argued with her religious aunt against saying grace one Christmas, whilst her dad admonished her and looked proud all at once.

'Maybe it's God,' she said, eyes still shut. 'Gods. Goddesses.'

'Maybe,' Connor said.

Liar, she thought again. *Chaque jour, à chaque heure,* the people had sung. *Oh! j'ai besoin de toi. Viens, Jésus, et demeure / Auprès de moi.* She opened her eyes. 'Don't you wish there was a God?'

There was a long pause, in which neither of them moved.

'I don't think they would really help at this point,' Connor said.

* * *

'It's kind of funny.'

Her sister was in Violet's bed again. This time, it had only taken fifteen minutes before the door opened and she climbed in wordlessly. Violet didn't mind, even though last night Thea's knees kept digging into her hip.

'What is?' said Violet.

They were both lying on their backs. A soft, deep-grey light in the room.

'You know.' Thea waved a hand above the sheet.

'What?'

'This. Everything. It's funny.' She let out a breathy giggle through her nose.

A pause. '*Right*,' said Violet, drawing out the vowel. Maybe she'd been drinking more wine. Connor had brought back some bottles from Philippe's house, along with the remaining tins and jars. 'Thea.'

'*Thee*,' said Thea. '*Uhhh…*'

She used to do this. When Violet was seven or so, her big sister would get her to think of words that would transform her name into a job. How the first syllable became *thee* if the next word began with a vowel. Thee-architect. Thee-undertaker.

'The… arse-licker,' Violet said.

'Oh, nice.'

'The army recruitment officer.'

'Hmm.' Thea slapped her arm, and scratched it several times. She was scratching herself a lot.

'The arsonist.'

'Preferable.'

'It is kind of funny,' Violet said.

'Yeah,' said Thea.

* * *

The click in the wall. The house, shifting. A car, very distant, revving suddenly and then nothing. The dog started up again, from somewhere on the other side of the valley, a sharp, high bark. Barking was not the right word. More like a cry.

Connor lay in the dark, every cell of his body open to sound.

At the church, the hymn had blossomed from the shadows. The words indistinct, no one quite on the same pitch as anyone else. Heterophony – together, but not quite. It had woven itself into the drone in his head, which sat embedded like a tiny bead behind the bone of his ear. Pure, singing.

He tried to feel something, for his mum, his friends. Couldn't even begin to gather an emotion that could encompass it. The blankness of not knowing, and knowing all the same. Instead, he just listened. The church bell, on the quarter-hour. Was someone going up there to do it, or was it automated? Another dog started up, lower, more intermittent. A sporadic hocket with the first dog, calling to each other. No answers, just calls. The cockerel had stopped two days ago.

Maybe he *was* a nihilist. He couldn't remember exactly what that meant, except that there was more to it than the popular meaning. Now he couldn't look it up. There was a grim satisfaction, somehow, in that.

Another sound, completely new. Tiny, bubbling, growing.

Thea and Violet, laughing.

Twelve

The next days were humid, the pressure immense. No wind, not even a breeze. The gaps between Thea's panic attacks stretched a little longer.

They watched the windows, but nothing came. Not even military planes, or helicopters.

The sky remained flatly grey, without rippled clouds. Violet took an occasional photo and magnified the camera screen, narrowing her eyes to try and find something, before turning the camera off again.

They didn't see anyone.

The drone in Connor's ear, however, wavered, then grew as tense as a tautly bowed string. Didn't let up.

* * *

Violet found Connor slinging his leg over the bigger bike. The baseball bat sticking out of his rucksack. He'd gone further every day, returned with fresh-ish food, tins. The garage was filling up, everything kept under blankets and out of sight.

'Can I come?' she said.

They cycled away from the village, along the level road where rows of lavender stretched to the horizon. Purple porcupines. Violet pedalled hard on the smaller bike, watching for cars, but they hadn't seen any in ages. It somehow felt better not to see any.

They rode for a couple of kilometres, the houses spaced far apart, before Connor stopped outside a large bungalow framed by short, scrubby trees. No cars in the drive.

'Haven't tried this one yet,' he said.

Shopping, new style. Looking up at gates and windows, knocking on the front door, listening with your heart in your mouth. Finding the weakest window. Tapping it with a little hammer. Then one hard, precise hit.

Being in someone's house without asking made Violet's skin sing with thrill and dread. Everyone's normal stuff sitting there – TVs, plants, toiletries, candles, free-standing lamps, birthday cards. It felt more churchy than the night with the priest and everyone singing.

Upstairs, Violet looked in the wardrobe at the row of men's shirts. She picked up the sleeve of a black one printed with large turquoise flowers, slipped it off the hanger and put it over her T-shirt. It smelt of mud and human. A person had worn this, not long ago. She took it off again, before Connor saw her.

He had a method. Kitchen cupboards, fridge, bathroom, garage, shed. Essentials: bottled water, other liquids, food, matches and candles, first-aid stuff. At least the list she'd given Luke wasn't going to waste.

She volunteered to take the shed. It was big and unused, the windows smashed or missing completely. Old pipes stacked against one wall.

There was a crunch in the layer of dust underneath her feet. At first, she thought she was treading on snail shells. She leant down and picked up something small and round, found a hole either side, realised they were eye sockets and it was a skull. She looked at the floor again, and it all came into focus, a blanket of tiny bones. Mice, maybe.

She walked very quickly away.

Connor was in the garage, hiding the tins and jars to collect another time.

'I tried the radio again,' she said, behind him, speaking too loudly to try and make herself feel better. She would cruise along the FM dial, batteries in the radio, the white noise occasionally flaring into speech. 'Thea won't translate for me any more.' *It's the same as before*, she said the fifth time, before going back to the sofa, clutching Connor's book about silence.

Connor didn't show that he'd heard.

'She's not very well, is she?' Violet pulled out a box of nails. Would they need nails? The nails were serrated like those skulls' teeth. 'Or Luke.'

'It's hard for them,' he said.

'But not for you.'

'Just different.' She watched the points of Connor's shoulder blades rise and fall underneath his T-shirt as he took a big breath and pushed his hair out of his eyes. He spoke more kindly. 'How about you?'

Today was the first day that she hadn't automatically picked up her phone. There was a strange freedom in the not-knowing. 'Yeah. Just different.' She wondered if she should tell him about the ripple in the sky. She didn't stare at the photo of it for long, to save the battery, and couldn't tell if she was imagining it or not.

'Here.' Connor straightened and passed over his baseball bat, handle first. She saw the iron bar in his other hand, curved over at one end, forked. 'Upgrading,' he said.

She took the bat. The weight of it in her hand. 'Cool,' she said.

* * *

Thea ran her hand along the bookshelves, looking at the things that had gathered amongst the bulbous coloured jars, the Jerome K. Jerome book in French and the empty bottle of Kraken rum.

The panic attacks came in swells – what was it her dad had said once, about the waves being in sets? They'd gone surfing while on holiday in Cornwall a few years ago, and she'd loathed the restriction of the wetsuit, the cold, battering sea. She refused to do any more after the first day, lying on the beach reading instead, holding in her stomach when any boy passed. Violet and their parents had come back from the sea glowing each day with their hair in strings, and she'd felt envious of their willingness to get back up every time they fell off. She'd always needed to do things perfectly or not at all.

So much for that. Now, Connor was going about his day like he relished what was happening, and Violet seemed strangely energised. Thea felt dismantled, her skin tender to the touch, ribs aching. The feeling of the bat in her hair, the insects biting. Every time she had another panic attack and fit of uncontrollable crying, she thought that must be it. Her body couldn't have any more water to release.

She could hear Luke next door. He'd brought in all the wood from the shed and lit a fire in the living room, balancing filled pans over it on oven grilles shoved into the brick, and talking methodically to himself. She knew she should be helping him, but she couldn't face seeing it fail.

Instead, she sat at the dining table, having gathered objects from the shelves. Five tiny, felt-soft pine cones. A rusting pendant with a jewelled eye in a triangle that she had found in the road when she was younger and might have worn round her neck once. Shells and feathers. The flat, three-pointed pale bone with the brown dots, which Violet had always insisted was a shark's tooth. She laid them out in different formations, the pendant in the centre and everything pointing to it. Totems to some old gods. God is telling you to go fuck yourself, as Nietzsche never said.

A gentle scuff of dry skin on stone. She had no idea how long Connor had been standing there. He wasn't looking at her but at the objects on the table.

'I found that one.' He nodded at the long, sealed mussel shell, which would have had no right to be in an inland reservoir. Odd now, to think of Luke and Connor being here at a different time. Thea remembered finding new things on the shelves amongst Violet's shark tooth and her mum's feathers, unsettling remnants of their presence.

She picked up the shell. The brown and cream were swirled together like a hazelnut truffle. It rattled, a high, woody sound. Of course it did. He liked things that made a sound.

She added it to her collection of objects. Brought over the framed photo of her mum and dad – his face pink from the sun, a glass of red wine in his hand, she leaning into him.

'Do you think he'll come?' She knew, somehow, that her mother wasn't here any more. Calling them would have been the very first thing, the only thing she'd have done, if she'd been able.

'I don't know,' Connor said.

'You never liked him anyway, did you?'

His chin dropped to his chest, dark curls dropping down. 'That's...' he sighed. 'That's just not true.'

'You never forgave him.' She didn't say it to hurt Connor.

'It doesn't matter now.'

'You never forgave me.'

He was looking at the table, shaking his head.

'It wasn't my fault,' she said.

'I know that.' He took in a long breath, and she expected him to stalk out of the room. Instead, he sat down, and she listened to his measured exhale, as if he was waiting for his organs to settle into place. He put his palm flat on the table. 'I'm not going to let anything happen to you,' he said.

She looked at him. The thick calligraphy-swipe of eyebrow. The mole to the right side of his mouth.

'To any of you,' he said. 'If I can help it.'

The veins in his forearms were high, riverine.

'OK,' she said.

'OK.' He looked at the objects on the table again, before quietly rising.

'Connor.'

He turned to her.

'Can you still hear it? The thing from the radio?'

'Yeah.'

'I think I feel it. Out there. But I'm not sure.'

Connor nodded, waited, and when she didn't say anything else, left the room.

She stared at her mum and dad. They were gone. Everyone was gone.

And here it was – the groundswell, beginning from a deep, unfathomable place.

The sea rose, consumed her again.

* * *

A line of ants ribbons from one crack in the paving to another. They have spent the day separating small leaf-shapes from their larger selves. They hold up the pieces like idols as they file, top to tail, back into a gulf in the paving. They carry two at a time. Three. The concrete begins to shift as their colony grows.

A Western whip snake is wrapped around itself underneath the shed, a long dream in the dark. At two and a half metres, it is longer than its kind has ever been. It stirs.

The ivy on the house's walls begins to grow at a faster pace, upwards, outwards.

* * *

It wasn't sensible to use the car. They needed to conserve petrol.

Luke took one of the mountain bikes – Connor had pumped up the tyres – and headed towards the village. He crested the hill, began the four kilometres of increasingly vertiginous descent without braking, not thinking how hard it would be to get back up again. No cars passed. He sailed down, allowing the possibility of veering off and juddering through the juniper trees and over the cliff, into the jade-blue trunk of water far below. Willing it to happen.

It feels weird out there, Connor had said to him the other day. *Like the air's different.* Luke had wanted to ask what he meant, but he knew, really. A heaviness, as if each molecule had significance.

Before he reached the village, he saw two figures walking towards him along the main road.

People, he thought. They hadn't seen anyone since the church. He wondered why he didn't feel relieved.

As he neared them, he realised that one of them was familiar. Tunde.

'Hi,' said Tunde, as Luke stopped at the verge and got off his bike. He was carrying a large rucksack.

'Hi,' said Luke. Almost as if nothing had happened. Almost.

Tunde was smoking, the scent of the weed pungent, a laughable throwback to the party that felt like years ago. He offered the roll-up.

Luke took it, drew on it.

'Why not, huh?' said Tunde.

Luke nodded, feeling the tears rise. The sting of pain, the sting of the weed.

'Hey,' said Tunde, and put his arm out.

Luke hesitated, glancing over at the other man. A short, wiry white guy with piercings all the way up one ear. Ridiculous how, even now, he needed to gauge whether hugging another man would be socially safe.

Tunde turned to his companion and said something in French, nodding up the road. Luke suddenly registered the long gardening fork in the man's hands. The knife handle sticking out of Tunde's front pocket.

The man murmured something back, took a last assessing glance at Luke, and began ambling away from the village.

They looked at each other for a moment, Tunde's expression thoughtful, a hint of some bleak amusement. The tang of the weed on Luke's tongue mingled with the lingering odd taste in his mouth.

Tunde beckoned Luke in with such a graceful, generous gesture that Luke felt himself crumble before he'd even made contact. Every fibre slipping. He couldn't do this with his siblings – not even with Connor, not properly. He'd seen how disturbed Violet had been by Thea's first panic attack. But now he let himself crack open, head spinning, a mess of tears onto Tunde's shoulder, the hard muscle of Tunde's chest against his own. If he could just stay here, Tunde's palm cradling the back of Luke's skull, in a fog of weed-smoke like an enchantment. If he could just stay right here.

'Crazy shit, huh?' said Tunde, his voice low.

'Yeah.' His mouth was so dry. 'Pretty crazy.' It would just

be temporary, he told himself again. Humans just always got back up. The gas would come back on before they'd used up the wood. The electricity. The phone networks. His dad's voice on the end of the line. His mum's.

'Your family OK?'

'I don't know. I don't think so.'

'I mean, your brother and your sisters.' Spoken as if it was nonsense to suggest that anyone further away would be all right.

'Oh. Yeah.'

'Just be ready, OK?' He glanced upwards.

'Um,' said Luke, trying to bring himself back into reality, not wanting to know what he meant. 'OK.'

'I talked to a friend of mine. From just outside Marseilles. On the… *téléphone fixe*. Fixed telephone.'

'Um. Landline.'

'Right.' Tunde took another tug on the joint over Luke's head. 'Yeah. That's gone. The city.' He made a gentle expulsion of breath between tight lips. 'It's everywhere.'

'Right.'

Tunde gave a ragged, garrulous sigh. 'Whatever the fuck this is, huh?'

'Yeah.'

They began to pull away from each other at the same time.

Tunde held on to Luke's forearms for a moment longer. A firm grip. 'Be safe, OK? People are…' He shrugged. 'You know what people are like.'

Luke didn't know, but nodded, wiped the underside of his

eyes with his thumb knuckle. He wanted to stay with Tunde, to not have to be the older brother.

'I'll come and see you,' Tunde said, lightly placing his hand on Luke's upper arm. A benediction, far more than the priest could ever have done.

Then he was gone, a gentle jog back in the direction of his friend.

* * *

All the music Connor loved. Vanished. It only existed in people's bodies, in whoever was left. On paper, except there were no scores here. He tried to hear all his favourite pieces, but nothing gathered together.

Kaia liked the music he'd play her. Steve Reich's *Music for 18 Musicians*. Brass-tinged electronica, the drums kicking in unexpectedly. Dark soundtracks with detuned strings. He thought of them, lying on one of their beds, heads glued together. *It's wank*, Kaia would say. *But good wank.*

He tried to pare things down, think just of melodies – the keening bassoon that kicked off *The Rite of Spring*, Miles Davis's solo in 'All Blues'. It was better, but underneath it, always, was the drone.

It was changing. There was texture to it now, no longer a clear tone but something ridged, jagged. It had expanded from one note, but it was hard to focus on any pitch. As if they were jostling each other, overlapping cells. When he dared try the radio again, he heard the same broadening sound.

He thought about the questions Cage asked of a sound – high, low, in the middle? An aggregate, a constellation?

What is it communicating? He found himself unable to answer.

He could hear Luke sobbing again. Wondered why he hadn't cried yet, felt the brief rash of shame at not doing so. Somehow, he knew he would – but just not yet. There was a space growing inside him where grief was being stored.

Will it never stop? Cage asked. *Why won't it?*

* * *

'It shouldn't be this cold.'

Violet was wrapped in a blanket on the terrace, her breath coming out in clouds. Watching the sky, clutching her camera like a teddy bear. It was still August, wasn't it? She'd lost track of the days.

'I know,' said Luke.

He had come back exhausted from hauling his bike up the hill, lain on the sofa for hours, staring at the black screen of his phone. He hadn't brought anything back, and Violet wondered what he'd been doing.

'It makes sense, though,' she said. They were sitting in the dark, and it was cool how your eyes adjusted, could see loads more than you'd think, though they'd all stumbled into each other a few times in the house.

Luke looked over. 'What does?'

'That everything's gone wrong.' She glanced at him, as if it were obvious. 'We're a shit species. We suck.' Goodbye, humans.

He laughed, as if it would be too much effort not to.

'We suck so hard,' she said, clearly wanting him to continue.

He obliged, but the moment had passed. They both knew it. He coughed instead, shook his head at himself.

She put a finger to her mouth, methodically chewed it, then took the loose nail off and placed it on her lip like a ring piercing.

Energy. Water. Violet had brought a few yanked-off branches from the stunted oak trees on the verge up the road and stored them in the garage. Kept imagining standing at the cliff-edge of the gorge, lowering a bucket down to the river, though that was probably dumb. They lit a new candle just before the old one went out, to save matches. They were going to run out of candles, though not for a while.

She looked over. 'Can I have a hug, please?'

'Yeah,' Luke said, the word breaking, and he seemed to need it just as much.

Thirteen

'Where's Violet?'

Thea had been staring at the John Cage book again at the kitchen table. *This is a situation which is no more and no less serious than any other life-and-death situation.* Now, she glanced up to see Luke at the kitchen door.

Her brother's skin was slightly waxen. He coughed a lot, drank pints of water. Was eating copiously, though in the past he'd always thought about what he ate, as much as she had. 'A lifetime on the hips,' he'd say, looking wistfully at the *tomme* cheese. 'Or in my case—' and he'd patted his flat, ridged belly. Today, she'd watched him shoving crackers into his mouth, the remaining corner of hard cheese, the yielding tomatoes, as if needing to cram in the last fresh food before it went off. He'd said they needed to eat as much cold food as possible, to save on the wood for now.

She wanted to suggest rationing, but couldn't bring herself to utter the words. To make it more real. Anyway, she was the opposite, her stomach small and hard, unwilling to digest much apart from a few crisps. Connor had come back the other day with a rucksack full of foraged figs, and she'd watched the other three eat them, Violet's fingers growing gummy.

'Thea.'

'Hmm?' she said, now.

'Where's Violet?' Urgency in Luke's words.

She tried to wrench herself from the mind-fog, the weight in her chest. After every panic attack, part of her was somewhere else – still fluttering in the storm, and preferring it there. 'I don't know.'

'When did you last see her?'

'I don't know,' she said, trying to remember, shrinking a little from the bluntness in Luke's voice and expression.

He made a sharp, breathy sound in his throat and disappeared from the doorway. She heard him calling for Connor, the two of them speaking, Luke's voice raised in a manner she'd never heard before. He was always kind to his brother. Connor's voice remained quiet. There was the sound of the side door as they stepped out.

From the patio, Luke called Violet's name, the word travelling around the exterior of the house, to the far wall where her sister would balance, trying to get a rise out of them. Thea ran her hand along the bobbled cotton ridges of the cushion she was holding. Luke had told her it was good to concentrate on touching things when the panic began to intensify.

Eventually, Luke came back in. 'Connor's gone out to look,' he said, sitting at the table.

They remained there for some time. Thea couldn't ask why he was so worried right at this moment. He didn't seem to be able to keep still, tapping his fingernails on the table, on his leg.

Outside, the grey sky began to deepen, grow dull.

Connor returned, shaking his head. 'She won't have gone far. It'll be fi—' He stopped, unsure, as Thea was, how to deal with this newly brittle version of their brother.

Another half an hour or so, and there was the skid of a tyre, the crash of metal on concrete. Violet was in the house and talking before Luke had even risen to his feet.

'Check it out, motherfuckers,' she said, out of breath. She threw a handful of paper packets onto the table, where they fanned out like dealt cards. *Courge. Laitue romaine. Carotte rouge. Tomate Jaune Flammée.*

'And…' said Violet, pulling out a hardback book from her rucksack, with photos of fruits and vegetables on the cover. She grinned.

'Jesus fucking Christ,' said Luke. 'Don't do that.'

The inner points of Violet's eyebrows raised as the rest of her body stiffened.

'We didn't know where the fuck you were.'

'I just felt like going out. I kind of wanted to surpri—'

'Without telling us.'

'Connor goes all the time.'

'He tells me he's going.'

'I'm sorry.' Violet looked young, something of the five-year-old in her face. 'I forget we don't have our phones.'

'You just fucking—' Luke shook his head as he sat down again. 'You can't do that any more, OK? Just – you can't.' He ran his fingers over the top of one eyebrow. His hand was shaking.

'Luke,' said Thea. 'She was just trying to hel—'

'I know,' he said. 'I know you were. But...' He looked towards the dark pane of the window. 'I don't think we should go out any more.' The words were low, impassive. 'If we can help it.'

Thea felt her cells delicately contract.

'Why?' said Violet, carefully.

'It's dangerous,' said Luke.

'How do you know that? I mean, I know it is for – how do you know it's dangerous right here? We haven't seen anything.' Her voice grew smaller. 'They've – maybe they've gone.' *They* again. No one bothered correcting Violet.

'I just do, OK?' Luke couldn't meet any of their eyes. 'I just do.'

* * *

A Southern swallowtail floats between the flowering semi-evergreens in its last sweet days. But down the road, rows of pupae have attached by silken girdles to a concrete barrier. In silent, astonishing unison, they hatch, billowing out from each chrysalis, and wait for their wings to dry.

Moss felts the paving stones by a neighbouring swimming pool. Quietly, far too quickly, their silvery leaves rise.

* * *

'I feel really guilty,' said Thea. 'About being here.'

'Yeah,' said Connor. He'd brought her crackers and peanut butter, which sat untouched in front of her. He'd not seen her eat anything for days.

She was draped on the chair, bone-pale and exhausted-looking – no one was sleeping enough. Dried mucus on the side of her cheek. Holding the photo frame of their dad and her mum to her chest again. 'In our dad's villa with a pool,' she said. 'Way to see it out.' She sighed. 'Maybe we did this to ourselves.' Thea didn't seem to expect him to answer any more. 'In the whole scheme of things.'

He noticed two new scratch marks on her legs. Raised, reddish, and deep. 'Shit, Thea.'

'What?' She followed his gaze. 'Are they not biting you? Just me, then.'

But there weren't any fresh bites anywhere, only the scratches over the dried raised skin of the old ones.

'You need to stop doing that.'

'I tried a salt bath. Cold water, obviously. That felt good.' Her voice was so different these days, all the hard edges shorn away. 'But they started itching again as soon as I got out.' She resumed her scratching.

'Stop.' He sat down on the arm of her chair and tugged her fingers away. She resisted, with surprising force. 'Please.'

Thea allowed her hand to fall. Chewed on her bottom lip, one cheek taut, the other gathered almost comically towards her mouth – Violet did that, too. The skin of her lips looked jagged and papery.

'I'm sorry I've been mean to you.'

'It doesn't matter.' His voice emerged with more fragility than intended.

'I'm sorry I kissed you.'

He swallowed. Knew somewhere, deep in the recesses of

his gut, that there was disappointment. 'Forget about it.' As if he had – the feeling of a permanent bruise on his mouth, the remnant-taste of chlorine and wine.

Next door there was the sound of Violet slamming plates down on the table.

He could smell something plant-like on Thea's breath. 'I don't want to fight any more, Thea. About anything.'

'Nor do I.' She plucked the end of a loose thread on the arm of the chair, tugged it with detachment. 'Maybe it's a conspiracy. Like, you know, the moon landings. But on a grander scale. Maybe it's just a really involved piece of theatre.' Her smile was swiftly chased with melancholy, then despair. 'My mind doesn't know where to go. Without, you know.' Her eyes slid to her phone, which sat on the table, useless.

'I know.' He nodded at the plate. 'Do you want to try and eat?'

She sighed, an unvoiced sound of utter grace, and pushed the plate away from her by an inch with her toe. 'You have it.'

'I don't like peanut butter.'

She stared at him. 'How did I not know that about you?'

'Even the smell of it makes me want to puke.'

'God, you're so weird,' she said, and chewed on her lip again, with a smile. She picked up one cracker, looked at it seriously, and put it down again. 'I feel like I'm just waiting to die.'

'I think all we can do is live,' he said.

* * *

Luke found his little sister in the kitchen, hunched over the gardening book she'd found, deep frown-lines between her eyebrows. He realised he'd never seen her reading before.

'Hey,' he said.

She looked up with the slightest trepidation.

He was acutely aware of his height. 'I'm sorry,' he said.

'Doesn't matter.' Her eyes fell back down to her book.

He hummed a sound of discomfort. 'No. I'm... I'm really sorry I talked to you like that.'

'It's OK.' She turned a page and spoke to it. 'So did you see something out there? Or up there?'

'No.'

'But they're there.' She repeated it to herself, and he heard the innocuous rhyme, the ungraspable depths in the meaning.

'I don't know,' he said.

Violet stared at her page. 'Why aren't we dead yet? Why didn't they just do what they did in the bigger places?'

'I don't know, mate.'

'Maybe they got bored. Or ran out of stuff. "Update to Control on Operation Wipe Out Humanity",' said Violet. '"Um, we've hit a snag."'

He let out a tiny laugh through his nose, stopped himself. Knew that if he fully allowed a laugh, it would turn to uncontrollable sobbing within seconds.

He'd let her believe what she wanted to believe. At least she had something. His mind just flailed, empty, grasping at nothing, because there was nothing.

He sat down next to her. Swallowed. *One day at a time,* Connor had said. 'Where do you want me?'

'Huh?' She glanced at him, the guard let down. The dark-brown roots of her hair were showing against the dirty green.

Luke nodded down at the book. 'I'm your humble gardening servant.'

* * *

Luke taught Violet chess. Connor pulled out old books from the shelves, the classics never read by their dad and deposited here, that would never be read by him again, and tried his best to focus on more than a page at a time. Thea floated on her back in the pool, her hair in fronds, arms wide. Violet watched the sky, her camera in her lap, ready to turn it on at the slightest change.

Nothing came.

* * *

They them. Violet placed two more pieces of gravel next to each other.

Their they're there. Three ways of spelling the same sound. Not as many as words with *ough* in them, but still. She found three pieces of white gravel, clicked them together.

There, there, old people said, to make someone feel better.

She'd been lying in the grass by the pool sifting her hand through the loose pebbles of the path, listening to their *shuck*, letting them fall. Then she'd knelt up, started sorting the gravel into piles – dark grey, lighter grey, grey-brown, brickish red, white. Round or rhombus-shaped. She'd made a circle of white stones, and begun making lines coming away from it. Two pointed dark-grey stones, then one red round stone. Five light-grey stones, because there were more of them, then one white pointed stone.

The fresh stuff had run out now, apart from what was growing outside. She had spent the morning with Luke, digging rows into the hard, chalky ground. Poking seeds into it, packing soil over the top. Their diet was like an end-of-world midnight feast – chocolate, chewy bars, nuts, crisps, crackers – and the last fresh food, like tomatoes, brownish cauliflower, the hard cheeses for Luke and Thea. It had honestly been OK, eating tinned green beans and tinned carrots, even tinned artichokes, which tasted of nothing. Connor had brought back a pot with swinging handles, and Luke was able to hang it over the fire, though he didn't look that pleased about it.

They had so much food, Violet thought, stored in the garage from all of Connor's foraging trips – she preferred to think of them that way, rather than looting, which is what it was. It was kind of impolite to leave all that stuff just sitting there. They hadn't seen anyone for so long – they must have all left, because if they'd been disappeared, then surely she and her siblings would have been, too. Luke would sit there, tapping on the wood of the table the whole time Connor was gone, and would say, *Anything?* when Connor returned, later and later as he went further afield. Connor would shake his head, and Violet knew they weren't talking about supplies.

This morning, she'd dreamt of lettuces under her head instead of a pillow. Could smell them, almost minty in their greenness. Her mum used to have to make her eat salad. She'd read once about how insects were actually really nutritious, and wondered if it would be OK to break her veganism for that. Roasted grasshopper. Cricket pasta. Ladybird soup.

She felt Luke attach himself to the gardening, talking about irrigation and slow-maturing vegetables. But if there wasn't any sun or rain soon, there wasn't much point.

Another piece of grey gravel. The neon butterfly scribbled past. A white piece of gravel.

'What are you doing?' Thea said.

Connor – sitting cross-legged under one of the cypress trees, staring at his sketchbook – glanced over.

Violet looked up at her sister, who had become a shadow version of herself. She gazed back down at the gravel, and shrugged. 'Don't know. Just am.'

Art was the only useful thing, Connor thought. That's what Cage said.

* * *

Luke watched the windows, wondered if Tunde would really ever come. Thea read Violet's photography book. Violet talked to her parents and the dog, lengthy dialogues that felt as real as anything else.

Sometimes, Connor wasn't sure if the drone was still there, or if the memory of it was just lodged in one side of his head. But then it would do something new, and he'd know.

* * *

'What are you thinking about?'

Connor looked up at Thea, hovering by the door. 'Nothing. A piano piece. Kind of playing it in my head.'

A short pause, in which he imagined her thinking that he was ridiculous.

Thea sat on the chair nearest him. Her legs were now covered in long, gauged marks, like she'd been attacked by a wild beast. She curled her fingers and tapped on the side of the table. 'Dad would have got you a keyboard. If you'd asked.'

He'd never asked. He'd been so aware of her at that one concert they'd come to a year and a lifetime ago, put on by his weekend music centre. He'd marvelled at his mind, how one part could be completely focused on his fingers and right foot and the next phrase, and the other part could be somewhere else entirely.

'Wouldn't work now, anyway,' he said. 'A keyboard.'

'Play something,' she said.

He looked at her, confused.

She nodded at the table. 'Please.'

He took a breath, placed his left hand at the furthest end of the table, and began the opening of Satie's *Gnossienne No. 3*. The one he'd played at that concert.

It had an otherworldly, suspended feel, this piece. Marked *avec étonnement* – with astonishment. No shit. He played it all, more *rubato* as he tried to remember every note without the piano's rows of navigable white and black. The winding right-hand melody, the patient left-hand pedal notes and chords. The tenderness and longing that always made his ribs want to open like petals.

Thea sat perfectly still as he made tiny rhythmic patterns on the wood, his bare right foot gently padding the floor.

It had always felt better playing this piece at night. When he was at home on his own, he'd put on the lamp in the furthest corner, just enough to see by, allow the shadows to surround him.

The last recap of the melody. He heard the final left-hand chord resonate, swell in the air, fade. The flickering drone came back in. He instinctively put his hand over his ear, even though it made no difference.

'What's wrong?' she said, the words only half-articulated.

He shook his head. He felt tearful, suddenly. The drone was louder than ever.

'Does your ear hurt?'

'It's – no.' He drew his eyes up to her. 'I just keep hearing – stuff.'

'What's it like?'

It was sound and it wasn't, it had flavour and pressure. It itched. He didn't want her to think he was going crazy. He worried that he was. 'I can't describe it.'

She absent-mindedly scratched along the red marks already made on her forearm. 'It's closer, isn't it?'

'I don't know. Maybe.' *It* wasn't the right word. Or *them*. How could you articulate something unknowable? He lightly played the ghost of the melody again on the table.

She leant forward and put her hand over his, slotting her fingers in between his own. The raised bones of her knuckles, their dull gleam.

His breath winnowed to nothing. He couldn't tell if this

was just sisterly now, given what she'd said before about the kiss. Luke gave Thea and Violet hugs all the time. They'd sit couched under his arm, pack-like, on the sofa at night.

Thea turned his hand over, ran her thumb along the creases of his knuckles, around the ring on his forefinger. His mum had given it to him for his eighteenth – unblemished black titanium. *I wanted to get something with a stone, but I know my son,* she'd said, with a kiss to his forehead.

Thea was now tracing her finger around each of his, absently, as if a child drawing round his hand in pen. He listened to his heart, which seemed muffled, a sub-bass.

There was a whistle from Violet that meant tea was ready. Luke had found some new strength, begun planning their meals and how much to eat.

She removed her hand. 'I was thinking,' she said, gazing towards the window at the featureless sky.

He turned his head towards her. The long, graceful throat. The reddish skin underneath her eyes. Such stillness in her frame.

'I could read to everyone.' She looked back over with none of her old archness. Smiled.

Fourteen

Violet stood at their gate, bare feet on the edge of the tarmac. She wasn't going out, not exactly – Luke couldn't swear at her for this.

She looked one way along the road, then the other. The strange, murky heat haze and the sounds of the insects seemed to become one thing – the shimmer was the insects, and the insects were the shimmer.

Chemin de la Chèvre d'Or. Road of the golden goat. They could do with a golden goat. She would call it Ms G.O.A.T. and they could milk it, and make cheese and butter and cream. She guiltily imagined butter melting on her tongue, turning her gold. Her mum would be proud of that. Violet's great-grandparents had been farmers.

The gravel spiked into the soles of her feet. She wouldn't mind if a point or two punctured her skin, made her drip dark red onto the grey. She suddenly realised that she hadn't had the bad thoughts, since everything changed. Like the empty squares and streets they'd watched had emptied her mind, too. But in the instant she understood this, back the thoughts came. *Disgusting fucking bitch.*

She looked up at the sky, camera ready, trying to ignore them. Field reporter Violet Low.

A low rumble, over to her left. She could feel it, under her feet. The sound in her skin, travelling up her calves. She went as rigid as a guard dog and looked up at the sky. Maybe it was their time. Over and out.

But the sound grew louder, the vibrations in her soles stronger, and a vehicle appeared at the far end of the road, cresting the tiny hill and coming towards her. A truck, brownish and greenish. Military.

As it approached, she wondered if she should be hiding, but the driver would have seen her by now. She couldn't see the driver, though – the windows were silver. The main body of the truck was raised high over the massive, ridged tyres. It had a large open back end, half-full of soldiers sitting in two rows. All in camouflage gear, helmets.

Luke had come out, drawn by the sound. Connor and Thea, too. They all stood there, by the gate.

Violet tried to remember the French for *what's happening?* For *where are you going?* But she didn't really want to know any of the answers.

None of the soldiers were talking. The truck went past with a roar and one of them – a woman, a few wisps of blonde hair peeking out from her helmet – caught Violet's eye. Nodded at her, one short, sharp and definite nod.

Violet nodded back.

* * *

There were different realities, weren't there, thought Thea. The multiverse. In one universe, the Earth had just carried right on in its merrily imperfect form, and the sun stayed out and the electricity stayed on, and their dad came here and she went home and finished school and started uni and became something.

In another she had stayed at home with her mum and the dog instead, or gone with Jade and Mischa, and whatever had happened to them had happened to her.

There was another one, she supposed, in which she hadn't flirted with Philippe to mess with Connor and make herself feel better, and what Philippe had done in the kitchen hadn't happened. Another in which it still had, but when Connor came in she told him she was scared and he had hit Philippe, kicked his head in. She liked that one.

Another in which she paid attention to her sister. *You're very alike*, her mum had said, not that long ago. *More than you think. Peas in a pod.*

'You know you can tell me about stuff,' Thea said in bed, staring at the ceiling.

Violet hummed, already half-asleep. 'Mmm.'

'You can tell me anything.'

'Like what?' Her sister's voice was muffled by the pillow.

'Something happened, didn't it? Before.'

Violet was very still for a long moment, before she turned over, dragging the duvet with her. 'Kind of isn't important now.'

'It's important to me.'

So Violet told her about the caretaker and started to cry, and Thea stroked her hair as she cried, too.

'The Monday I had travelled on had been a cool temperate day, but the next day the sky was cloudless and the sun beat down.'

Thea was reading to them, her legs curled underneath her on the armchair. L. P. Hartley's *The Go-Between*, a book steeped in bucolic summer heat.

An England so far distant in time and space, and an England he'd never had a full attachment to – the fictional England of cricket and country house bullshit, usually the south, and its blithe entitlement. Perhaps it was the Irish in him as well as the Northern, or the influence of his mum's activism, or having Kaia and other non-white people around him. He'd always thought of his dad as so easily part of that world.

Violet was tucked into Luke's side, his arm around her shoulders. Connor was sitting on the floor, his back to the cool wall. All of them with one part constantly alert, prowling the walls outside, thinking where the nearest weapons were, and whether they would help.

Thea read softly, with detachment, but he knew that she'd read it better than anyone else. He kept losing focus, not listening to the individual words but to the fluidity of her voice, the faint grain of it, the light interruption of consonants.

He thought suddenly of Dave, reading to him when he was little – how he'd be listening to a child entering an enchanted world, and fall asleep midway without realising. He'd wake up to find it morning, and wonder what magic made that happen.

Thea's face, with three tea-lights around her. A moon-glow.

* * *

Violet hit a particular bulge on the wall overlooking the valley with her baseball bat, over and over, until the paint flaked, until cracks appeared, until she'd made the beginnings of a gorge. Thea arranged and rearranged the objects in the dining room, invented rituals, goddesses. Luke made lists, and added to them. Connor beat Luke at chess. Connor and Violet went out, telling Luke exactly where they'd be, taking his watch and leaving him with the clock. They brought back hot-water bottles, because they were planning ahead now, matches, lighters. Violet collected books she thought might be useful. Luke and Thea sorted the food into shelf-lives.

Connor felt the drone enter his bloodstream. Felt the world tighten.

* * *

They needed an axe. A great big, fuck-off axe. Instead, they had to use various gardening tools, a spade for leverage, and another spade for hacking at the wood. It was a serious workout.

Violet was currently on branch collection, the easier job. The weird little oak trees were best, dry and easy to reach. They made a satisfying tear and crack as they came loose. She always apologised, because it felt like pulling their arms off.

Violet had looked up French words for 'gun' in the big phrase book. The soldiers had guns strapped across their chest. Not *un revolver* or *un pistolet*. *Une mitrailleuse*, maybe, which sounded way too pretty and delicate to mean a thing that blasted people to bits. *Une arme à feu*. It would be quite cool to have an arm of fire, Violet thought, imagining it as her superhero skill. She waved her arm across the horizon, torching everything that came near them.

As she did so, she sprayed the sky, and remembered to take a photo. She'd been switching the camera on to take just one a day. Just in case.

Maybe her camera was her weapon. She fetched it from the long grass and zoomed in on a bit of sky as grey and featureless as the rest of it. *Pow*, she thought, and spread her finger and thumb in opposite directions on the screen, just to check.

Her breath hitched. She brought the camera screen right up to her face. The ripple was there. Lavender-grey, slightly shiny.

Bigger than before.

* * *

Luke couldn't sleep. If he did, it was so light that it didn't feel like sleeping at all. Every night he willed it to come, and it hid even further away. Every day felt harder, his mind more hopeless and wild, his bones juddering.

He was lying in his dad and Josie's bed. He wished they were here, either side of him. He'd asked Thea if she and Violet wanted his room, seeing as they were bunked together now. He'd spent nights listening to them talking next door, arguing and finally going quiet, and been envious.

Thea had shaken her head. *I can't go in there*, she'd said.

She was a bit better. He'd expected her to turn him down when he'd asked for her help outside, but she'd lugged the loose stones over from the dry-stone wall, and with him constructed them into an oven of sorts, gazed at it. *The Internet would tell us what to do*, she'd said. *Survivalist 101*.

He got out of bed, went to the window. You used to be able to see the tangerine flicker of the nearest town, ten kilometres away. And to the left, a glow on the horizon, a suggestion of the historic city. Now it was a flat, inky line, nothing more.

It got cold here in the winter. Properly cold. He'd only come once, was amazed by the transformation of near-tropical colours into greys and greens, the tops of the mountains on the other side of the lake shock-white. They would never get enough wood to see them through.

That taste on his tongue. Sometimes, it was almost metallic, coppery. He touched it and held it to his nose. It didn't smell of anything.

He watched the dark, flat sky. 'Fucking come on,' he whispered. 'Get it the fuck over with.' His words fogged the glass, faded again.

* * *

Thea read travelogues of Trieste and the Hebrides, more classics, some children's books of Violet's. Violet bet Connor all of her friendship bracelets that she could beat him at chess, then tied them all round his wrist. Luke kept experimenting with his wood-fired oven. Connor pulled five neighbours' recycling bins along the road to theirs to use as rain butts, in case it ever rained.

Violet continued making her gravel web, lines stemming outwards from the central circle of white, as big as a serving plate. Three round red stones, then one white diamond stone. Four pointed dark-grey stones, then one round grey-brown stone. Connor had begun to help, wordlessly passing her a handful of one colour. The lines crossed diagonally, laddered, spiked off, like someone was doodling with them.

Nothing had come for them, she thought. The web she was making was growing, and they were all still here.

* * *

Lavender and wine country. No lush acres of corn or wheat, no sheep or cows. The ground was hard, gritty, the same bone-grey as the sky. The grass fields brittle and dull. Scrubby wildflowers along the verges.

Connor listened to the fine hiss of the bike spokes in dialogue with the distant cicadas and the occasional dull goose-cry of his brakes. He listened for anything else out here.

The gnarled olive trees were planted in politely spaced rows, the leaves of the vines a perfect appley green. They would never want for olives and grapes, as long as they grew. Wild garlic, too, from the oak woods in the other direction. *For sophisticated living in the apocalypse, come to the South of France*, Violet had said.

He was learning from one of Violet's books how to identify trees, which ones might produce nuts or berries when autumn came. If autumn came, he thought, eyeing the sky again.

A little bit further each time. Luke hated him going out, but Connor knew they would always need more. He knew which houses he'd covered, the ones he avoided because they looked occupied. Though nothing looked occupied now, not exactly. When had they last seen anyone? On his first trips, he'd passed a worn-looking farmhouse and seen a kid with bright-red glasses in the window, staring out. The last time, the kid had waved, and Connor had waved back. He'd passed that house several times now and seen no one.

He turned down a single-lane road, going back over the route he'd taken from their house in his head – each turn, landmarks. Here, the ground on either side was brick red and had more plants with spikes. Gorse, rosemary.

He passed a sign for a tourist ranch, poorly designed with a photo of a solitary horse and an indecipherable drawing. You could eat horse well enough, he thought. He wondered if he'd ever eat meat again. *Someone must have chickens*, Thea had said, without commitment. *And there are fish in the lake*, Violet had said. *The eagles catch them.* But somehow, to start trying to be farmers would mean truly acknowledging that all this was here to stay. Not just temporary.

Further up, there was a gate, rusted to bronze, in the middle of a low stone wall. *Entrée interdite. Propriété privée.* Beyond it, a long white gravel track, and land that looked different to him. There were olive groves to either side, but beyond them the field looked glossy, a deep, inky green. He looked at the handwritten signs on the gate again.

213

He left his bike on the roadside, trod lightly on the grass as if someone might hear the crunch of his trainers on the gravel. Somehow, it was easier to trespass on properties that were second homes, had pools and sun umbrellas. But he just needed to know what grew there, to add to his mental map of the fig trees, the nearest grapes and olives. He wasn't convinced that Violet's carrot and cauliflower seeds were going to erupt on their lawns. No sun, for a start.

Quiet, here. A gentle, electric haze of insects, invisible amongst grass and leaves. The rasp of a single crow. There was a rectangle of pale-pink farmhouse a couple more fields away, and the darkness of a single window.

He gripped his iron bar and glanced back at his bike. Maybe this was stupid, all for the sake of a cabbage or lettuce or whatever it might be. Then he thought again of Violet, lying on her front next to her raised ridge of soil, as if daring it to grow or face her wrath. Of Luke, looking at the tins in the basement as if they were a complicated equation. Of Thea, making herself nibble peanut butter on crackers, the only thing she'd eat and only because he'd made them for her.

There was a heat emanating from the ground, if not in the air. It had presence, a near-song. A vibration that seemed to nudge at the drone in his ear, gently destabilising his body. What was that thing in acoustics – *beats*, two near-identical tones making a pulsing tremolo and another note altogether.

Here. The dark green he'd seen. The field had sprinklers strung over it, the canes aslant. He glanced one more time at the farmhouse, before bending down. Fuck it. They needed their vitamins. It was kale, maybe, the spines of the leaves luridly purple. He rubbed a leaf between finger and thumb, tore off a shred and tasted it. It was tough and bitter, but boiled it'd be fine. He felt round the base of the plant and tugged. Tugged again, to no avail. Then he stood and used his crowbar to ferret under the roots until it yielded. The row next to the kale was longer-leaved, paler. Well, he'd take one of everything and see what the chef in the family could do.

He was so focused on gently pulling at the second plant that, for a moment or two, the sound of a harsh voice didn't find its way into his consciousness. By the time he stood up, there was already a brute crack splitting the air somewhere above his head. For a moment, all thought was slammed out of him.

He ducked, dropped the plant, spun in a circle. Unable to tell where the sound had come from. He spun back the other way to see a figure, white-haired and limping heavily, approaching from the furthest end of the next field with a long rifle in his hands. He was shouting again, the words distorting on their way to Connor.

'No. I'm sorry,' he shouted back, forgetting to speak French.

The man was still advancing, still shouting unceasingly. The words hard-edged and indecipherable from here. Another shot above his head, the sound expanding.

'No, listen, I'm sorry. I was just—' Connor waved his hands before realising too late that he was holding his crowbar. He dropped it, and waved his hands again.

The third time the gun fired, it was as if the sound itself, honed to a fine point, penetrated him, blasting through skin and muscle, past bone.

The echo of it in his ears as he staggered, fell. The crow, breaking out of the tree.

Fifteen

Violet was shouting his name.

Luke had been thinking about Jamie, hating himself, thinking about Tunde. Wondering if he'd ever get to touch a man again in the ways that he loved, and pressing the heel of his hand against his cock, though there wasn't much doing.

Now, Violet was shouting his name in a way that didn't mean she needed help with the vegetable planting. He could hear Thea, too.

He got to the window, saw Connor's bike on the ground, and Connor lying beside it. Their sisters crouched over him.

'Oh, my God,' said Thea. 'Connor.'

Violet had heard the sound of the bike crashing onto the paving and come out to see what her brother had nicked today. She'd found Connor on his back, panting, his skin grey. He was topless, his T-shirt wrapped around his right forearm, soaked brown-red. Swipes of blood along one side of his chest. Her heart had dumped itself out of her.

Thea was repeating the same words, over and over.

Now Luke was here, his hands on him, swearing and saying his brother's name.

On seeing him, Connor's face stilled for a tiny moment, before he took a huge breath and began crying so forcefully that Violet almost jumped. He was saying something, but it was so lost in the fog of salt and mucus that it was hard to hear.

Luke was holding him, an arm under his neck, kissing his forehead. 'Jesus fucking Christ. What's happened to you?' he said. 'Connor. Talk to me.' There was no wound on his torso. He touched the soaked T-shirt.

Connor was crying and mumbling into Luke's shoulder, his skin looking paler by the second.

'It's happening,' said Thea, without emphasis. 'It's here.'

Violet felt a shiver prick up every single hair on her body.

'Get me a towel,' said Luke to her. 'Clean.'

As she legged it into the house, she felt Thea's words wrap around every one of her bones. *It's here.* Not *it's there.* She took the stairs two at a time and looked at the used towels in a pile in the bathroom. Dashed back down to the kitchen and found the largest hand towel, folded by her mum months ago, in the cupboard.

When she came back out, Thea was kneeling and Connor's head was on her lap. She had pulled her hoodie sleeve down and was wiping his nose and talking softly to him. Luke was beginning to carefully unwind the T-shirt from around Connor's arm.

Connor's words became recognisable. 'It went through,' he was saying, through shudders and sobs. There was a shine of sweat on his upper lip, his skin rashed with goosebumps.

Luke let either side of the T-shirt fall onto the paving below Connor's arm. His skin was a smeary mess of blood. Violet automatically glanced away, before making herself look back.

'It went right through,' Connor said, his whole body convulsing. His pupils were massive.

There was a hole the size of a chickpea halfway up his inner forearm, pulsing with blood. Luke carefully leaned over to look at the other side of Connor's arm. Violet leant over. A messier wound, jagged bits of skin. More blood.

'Connor,' said Thea. 'Did someone… shoot you?'

Connor's stomach suddenly constricted, and he made a horrible, bleak sound, before he rolled over and threw up next to Thea's knees.

Connor's mind was a flipbook of blood loss, gangrene, amputation, death. Luke's mind was suddenly, astringently clear. Violet thought, an actual bullet went through my brother's actual arm. *Mon frère a été abattu.* Thea thought, this is the other side of him. This is what he really looks like.

'He's cold,' said Thea, the back of her hand on his forehead. 'And hot.'

'We have to go to a hospital,' said Violet. She was holding Connor's other hand.

'I don't think anyone's there, mate,' said Luke.

Thea tried to imagine it, Connor's head on her lap as it was now, their car running out of petrol on an empty motorway.

Or arriving at an empty city, Connor fading with every moment. With no idea what was out there.

'But he literally got shot,' said Violet.

'We're not going out there,' said Thea. 'There are people with guns.'

A moment of silence, with everyone looking at Connor, his eyes damp, grit stuck to the side of his face. Thea brushed it away with the backs of her fingers.

'Get me that book,' Luke said. 'The big red one.'

Violet had been in charge of sourcing their growing library. The mini-Internet. Gardening, herbs, livestock, trees, DIY, crafts, first aid. All in French but the books had pictures, and they had Thea and a French phrase book.

Strange, feeling life seep out of you. Not just the blood, but energy, coherence, words, hope. The flaring feeling of being alive, because it might be gone soon. A new part of him was open to the world, in bald shock at the feeling of air. A part that was supposed to stay hidden. He would die because he felt so tired and he would leave them and they would die and Luke and Violet and Thea—

They got him inside and onto the sofa.

Connor was slick with sweat, uncontrollably shaking. Thea came down with blankets and more towels.

'OK,' said Luke. 'OK.'

In hospital shows on TV, there were drips, blood transfusions, tens of medical experts. Now, there was him and his university first-aid training, trying to remember anatomical diagrams. He'd learnt how to deal with breaks, shocks, do CPR and the recovery position, but anything severe always started with phoning the emergency services.

In Luke's head, a wound higher up or near Connor's wrist would be worse. His arm wasn't spurting with blood, the kind of spray that might mean an artery, though he was still basing this on movies and didn't know a fucking thing.

Violet came running in with three first-aid kits in her arms. She unzipped them and let everything tumble out onto the floor. 'Been stockpiling,' she said.

As Thea covered their brother in blankets and kept talking to him, Luke raised Connor's arm onto the end of the sofa behind his head, and tied a bandage as tight as he dared below his elbow, pressing down on both sides of the wound with a handful of gauze. The blood rapidly feathered along the cotton grid-lines. Violet brought a bottle of water and table salt as instructed, and Luke put a few pinches of salt into the bottle, shook it with his hand over the top. He let it run over both sides of his brother's arm. Connor arched his back, made a whimpering sound, fell back again. Luke watched the pink-white triangles of skin on the exit wound come into clearer focus as the blood diluted, before it deepened in colour again.

He gave the bottle back to Violet. 'A few more,' he said.

The pain was worsening. There was a blazing hot coal in his arm, the burn radiating outwards. A faraway sensation of pins and needles. Blank spots where he was sure he should be feeling something. The roar of blood in his head like a tide.

'What do we do now?' said Violet.

'I don't know,' said Thea, who had the first-aid book open on the sofa arm.

When Thea was eight, she'd been startled by a fox running out in front of her bike, and had fallen, slid across the gravel. Her thigh had gashed and bled and the five minutes before anyone found her had felt like hours. Since then she'd not even been able to look at her own paper cuts and hated needles. Now, she was in a different sphere – above the chaos of Connor's arm and his rattling body.

'Sorry,' Connor was saying, teeth knocking together. 'Sorry, sorry, sorry.'

'Shh.' Thea stroked his head, moved the damp curls out of his eyes, and kept turning the pages of the book. Funny, how it didn't have bullet wounds in here.

'Listen to me,' said Luke to his brother. He'd become a different person too, focused and quiet, stopping to stare into the middle distance, before instructing her and Violet to do something else. 'You're a hard Northern bastard.' He smiled at Connor. 'This is nowt.'

'Way harder than us,' said Violet.

'Exactly,' said Thea.

Connor started crying again.

'I think we need to stitch him up,' said Luke, fifteen minutes later.

222

Violet had watched her brother pack Connor's arm with gauze and padding, wrap it in bandages. But then he'd stared at the small patch of dark red growing outwards, whilst they tried to keep Connor warm and get him to drink water through a straw. His breathing was erratic, sometimes fast and shallow, sometimes with long gaps in between. Violet had sung him the guitar riffs of songs to keep him awake.

Now, Violet and Thea looked at Luke.

'There's no bullet in there,' said Luke. 'No clothing material. I think – I think that's what we're supposed to do. To stop infection.'

'Yes,' said Thea, who'd turned into some sort of weird ghost-nurse. She was looking at the book. 'If it hasn't stopped bleeding after ten minutes.'

'OK.' Luke exhaled, rubbed a palm over his mouth. 'If we have a needle.'

Violet glanced at Thea, and knew they were thinking the same thing.

'On it,' Violet said, and went up to her parents' room, opening the trunk at the end of the bed that held photo albums, spare pillowcases, and their mum's craft box. Inside was a canvas bag with a half-completed cross-stitch of an abstract painting called *Broadway Boogie-Woogie* by Piet Mondrian. *You will literally never finish it*, Violet had said once. *I might*, her mum had replied, putting out her tongue. *Just need to be in the mood.*

'Right,' said Luke.

There wasn't time to sterilise the needle. Luke had

223

poured bottled water on it and wiped it with clean tissue. He'd stared at the tangle of threads, found himself for a surreal moment trying to decide which colour would be best, and chosen blue. The threads were thin and he had absolutely no idea if this would work or if he'd be making his brother's injury – a ludicrous word for the holes in him – worse.

'Right,' he said, again. There was a rocketing sensation in his chest. His hand was shaking.

'I'll do it,' said Thea. She put out her hand, palm upwards.

Luke didn't even ask if she was sure, only felt relief. He passed her the needle and thread.

'Should we, like, make him drink something? Like whisky?' said Violet.

'I don't think so.'

Connor, his head on a cushion, made a tiny, hopeless moan. His lips were pale, tremors still passing over him. He looked spent, but there was evidently that tiniest bit of him left that couldn't take any more pain.

'I know,' Luke said to him, and knelt down, held his other hand. He wasn't going to cry now. He wasn't allowed. 'Just look at me, all right?' He forced a smile. 'Tough Northern bastard.' He put the outer side of his own hand to Connor's lips. 'Bite on me.'

Thea, who freaked out when Violet had a nosebleed and wouldn't look at any operations on TV. Thea, who shrieked when there was a dead mouse on the doorstep left by next-door's cat.

She was kneeling on the floor, pushing the needle through the edge of Connor's bigger wound, the one where the bullet had come out, and it was going through the skin and into the other side.

Violet couldn't watch and she had to watch.

Connor let out a long, raw sound, Luke's hand clenched in his mouth. His eyes shut so tightly they were just little spiderwebs.

Into the skin. Over to the other side. Connor made a smaller sound on every puncture. Again. And again. Luke was telling him about a holiday in Cumbria where they'd got lost on a mountain and the massive chocolate cake they'd had when they finally made it home.

The insane sight of Thea tying knots and snipping the thread with scissors. Connor's skin pulled together, still seeping blood. He'd gone quiet now.

Thea did the other wound, the one where the bullet had gone in. Royal blue lines in his skin. She tied the knots, put the needle carefully down on the sofa arm.

Violet did the bandages this time, pressing the thick, spongy gauze against the wounds as Luke instructed, wrapping round the stretchy fabric, sticking it down with masking tape from the garage.

She sat back on her heels and looked at Connor. His eyelids had smoothed, his head lolled to the side, Luke's hand still partly in his mouth.

'Con,' Luke said, gently. He levered out his hand and touched Connor's cheek. 'Connor.'

Violet felt everything begin to go cold and numb, as Luke

kept saying their brother's name. Like every atom in the air was turning itself off, one by one.

Luke put his thumb against the crease of Connor's other wrist, cocking his head. 'I think he's fainted. Come on, Con. Just for me.' He leant down to Connor's ear. 'Oi, our kid.'

Connor made a tiny sound, opened his eyes as if it was the hardest thing in the world. Super-slow blinks.

'You're all done,' Luke said. 'Like a total fucking badman.'

Connor shut his eyes again.

Thea stood up and slightly reeled, before walking slowly and deliberately to the kitchen and throwing up in the sink.

Sixteen

He felt barely there at all. Every inch of him faded to nothing. It took effort to open his eyes, to swallow, to turn his head. All consciousness honed down to the colossal, burning pain from his hand to his shoulder.

He would wake and find two of his siblings curled up asleep on duvets on the floor, and the other watching him. Violet, then Luke, then Thea. Cans of Coke on the table by his head. Painkillers. His right forearm had been bandaged again.

He was too tired to speak.

* * *

Connor blinked a lot in his sleep, Thea thought. She looked at the protrusion of his Adam's apple, the long line of his jaw with his head turned slightly away from her. Smooth-cheeked, unlike Luke's stubble. That accidental surliness in the lift of his upper lip. The light from the window mined copper from his curls. She was allowed to look, because she needed to check that he was still breathing.

She reached down and scratched her leg, gently. There was one single mosquito bite now, on her calf, which constantly emanated heat.

After a while, Connor shifted and with a sharp inhale was suddenly awake, eyes wide and darting.

'It's OK,' she said. 'You're home.' She heard the hollowness of the word, knowing it wasn't the one he'd prefer to be in.

She watched him try and calm himself in his contained way. She'd almost preferred him erupting into tears, needing his brother, allowing her and Violet to hold his hands. But he wasn't quite as before. She could hear his teeth, gently clattering together.

'Water?'

He took such a long time to respond that she thought he hadn't heard. He'd barely spoken since getting back. Then he nodded, and she brought over the glass and straw.

The pain cross-hatched across his face as he moved even the smallest amount, and he gave a tight, muted hum so childlike it didn't seem to come from him at all.

After he'd sipped a little, he rested his head back again, exhausted.

'Something to eat?'

He shook his head. His lips came apart, an inhalation. Silence. He was blinking up at her as if she had all the world's answers. The little boy he'd been all along, if only she'd looked.

'Please will you read to me?' he said, and his voice was small, completely unguarded.

Outside, she could hear Violet hitting the wall with her

baseball bat, the methodical dull thuds.

'Of course I will,' she said.

* * *

Luke was at home, except it wasn't anywhere he recognised – but his mum was there and Dave and a bunch of his mates, and there was a party, and he wasn't quite sure what they were celebrating, whether it was for him or someone else, but he couldn't see Connor and he needed to find him and no one was really listening, just pouring drinks and turning up the music, and he went upstairs to look for his brother and it was dark here and the bedroom was his old one, the posters of City players and club nights, and there was someone there, *here*, a presence, and—

In an instant, he'd shot awake, his gut in his throat as a shadow came through the window. There was a hand on him and he pushed off the sheet, scrambling up the bed. 'Fuck,' he mumbled.

'Hey,' said a low voice, shushing him. 'It's me. It's me. It's Tunde.' He shushed again, the sound of the sea over fine shingle.

Tunde couldn't be here because Luke was at home, or home of a sort, and—

'It's Tunde,' the figure said again, and knelt down, held up his palms. 'I come in peace.'

Luke tried to join the voice and the image into something coherent.

'I'm sorry,' Tunde said. 'I thought to come at night. Maybe better. Now I don't know.'

Yes. It was him. The gentle shape of his voice. The shaved head. Baggy vest-top.

'Fuck,' Luke said again.

Tunde put his hand on Luke's thigh on top of the duvet. 'It's OK that I come?' He spoke under his breath.

Luke nodded. He felt like he'd just sprinted sixty metres. 'Yeah. Yes.'

Tunde rose and removed his vest, a shadow-layer peeling off, and slid under the sheet next to Luke, the two of them on their backs. 'Hello,' he said, as if it was quite usual for them to meet this way. 'That hill is a bitch.' The skin of his arm was slightly cool and tacky with sweat.

'Sorry,' Luke said, trying to grasp the miracle. Tunde had said he would come, and now he was here. 'Where's your friend?'

'He went to Montpellier. Or that way. His family is there. Maybe. Bad idea, probably.'

'And Zaf? Or Gael?'

There was a pause, before Tunde blew out air, as if he'd just dragged on a joint. 'I don't know.'

The silence sat, swelled and flattened again with the infinite possibilities.

'Is anyone with you?', asked Luke.

'No. Not any more.'

'But have you seen… people?' The easier question.

'I feel like almost everyone left right away. I helped a family, but they disappeared.'

'You mean… left?'

'I don't know.' Tunde rolled onto his side and kissed Luke's

230

temple. His body smelt mossy. 'I thought to come and see if you were here.' He ran a knuckle over Luke's bicep.

Luke's mind was still flared and alert, his skin fizzing. He wanted to go and check that Connor was really next door, but he didn't want this apparition to disappear, either. 'My brother,' he said.

Tunde hummed a question.

'My brother got shot,' Luke said.

There was a long pause, and Luke wondered if Tunde knew that English word, and wished he knew the French.

'Let me see,' Tunde said.

* * *

'Where was it?'

Violet was by her brother's bed. They were still taking it in turns to be with him, so that he was never on his own. In the night, she'd heard bumping sounds and talking, and got up to find Luke and Tunde in here, Tunde strapping a wooden spoon to Connor's arm, while he looked bleary and confused.

Now, Connor looked over.

'Where it happened,' Violet said. 'Where you got shot.' *Can't have been far*, Luke had said. *I literally have no idea how the fuck he got back here.*

'Why?' Connor's voice was dry, as if he'd been stuck in a desert for days.

'So I can go and slay that motherfucker.'

It probably hurt to laugh. Connor winced as he tried. 'Don't do that,' he said.

'Why not?'

'He was just…' He swallowed, as if even that was hard. 'I'm not even sure he meant to hit me. Probably had that gun for rabbits.' His sigh was small and jaded.

Un fusil, she thought. A rifle. 'Pretty big rabbit.'

'Yeah.'

She curled her bare toes over onto the floor tiles. 'We thought it was – you know.' *They them their there.* She should tell them about the clingfilm-like ripple in the corner of every one of her photos. But if it was there, it was just there, and they wouldn't be able to do anything about it.

'I know. It wasn't.'

'You actually got shot.'

'Yeah.'

Luke had driven with Tunde to the pharmacy in the medieval village, and come back shaking his head, saying they'd gone to the next one along, too, with no luck. No luck – a nice way of saying that the windows were smashed in and everything had gone. *How much petrol do we have now?* Thea had asked. *Not much*, Luke had said.

Violet had volunteered for looting duty. Looty-duty. She knew what houses they'd covered already. Tunde had come with her, and helped her search for medication. Luke had checked with her beforehand, but even though Tunde was a man she hardly knew, she didn't feel scared. She liked him. He was calm, as if the end of the world was the kind of thing that happened here all the time. He even made jokes. She was definitely improving her French – *analgésique, éclisse*. Connor was on a double dose of *antibiotiques*, Tunde saying

232

that he didn't think they were quite the right ones, but they would hopefully still help.

'You don't have to avenge me,' Connor said to her. 'Thanks.'

'Think I could, though?'

'Definitely,' he said.

Violet knew, with a little fizz of pride in her chest, that he wasn't joking.

* * *

'Do you want to stay here?' Luke said to Tunde, that night in bed. He didn't think the others would mind – even if it did mean splitting rations, it also meant an additional pair of hands.

Tunde shook his head. 'No. My sister could come.'

'Your sister?' He hadn't mentioned one.

Tunde shrugged. 'She's in Marseilles.' A thoughtful pause. 'She *was* in Marseilles. I don't know.' He let out percussive breaths through his teeth, a staggered rhythm. 'The last thing she said is that she will come here. So I stay. I left a message on the door last night.' He breathed into the hollow of Luke's neck, his lips against skin. 'But I will go home tomorrow.'

'I wish…' said Luke, and watched the words disappear into the dark.

'What do you wish, English boy?'

He couldn't. There was no point.

'Yeah,' said Tunde. 'I wish it too.' He leant over and pressed warm lips onto Luke's, sealing up the wish forever.

Just this. Just this moment. A long, lean man against him, limbs amongst other limbs, blotting out everything else.

In the morning, Tunde wrote down everything he needed for Connor.

'And… he'll be OK?' Luke said.

Tunde shrugged. 'I don't know. We always have the things we need at nurse school.'

Somehow, it was reassuring for him not to lie.

'But—' Tunde nodded to the list he'd dictated, Luke shaking as he wrote it down. Lots of water, food with salt, food with sugar. Antibiotics. Painkillers. What to look out for in terms of infection. When he'd first seen Connor's blue stitches, he'd raised his eyebrows, before telling Thea she had done a pretty good job. She had given a half-smile, a remnant of the sort of academic pride she'd obviously had before.

'All right,' Luke said.

Tunde put his hand on Luke's arm. 'I'm sorry. But my sister.'

'I know. Of course.'

Tunde had given him the address of the apartment he'd been renting with Gael, drawn a map. Luke had already told him to come back when his sister came. Had checked with the others. Both of them could stay here.

Tunde gave a nod, his smile sanguine, and kissed him. He pulled away, and rested his nose against Luke's. 'Maybe,' he'd said about coming back, and Luke understood that the ambiguity was not a lack of commitment on his part.

The future was unknowable, that was all.

* * *

Days and days in bed. Connor did everything not to think of the pain and it was the only thing he could think of. There'd be moments, an hour or so after the strongest painkillers, when it ebbed slightly, before coming back more vehemently than ever. Sleep came in waves, his head blurred. The antibiotics made him so nauseous he could barely eat. He wanted the curtains shut all the time, found daylight intrusive.

'I don't think you'd have even liked it,' Connor said to Thea, once, from his pillow.

She looked up, folded her book over her middle finger. 'Liked what?'

'The veg. From the farm.'

She gazed at him. A gentle smile that looked so much like her mum's. 'I'd have eaten it.'

* * *

Thea looked at herself in the mirror. She'd lost weight – before, she would have been happy about it. No make-up. She looked older and younger at once. More like Violet.

She turned the tap on and ran her hand under it. The faucet spat, spat again, gushed briefly, then trickled, then stopped. She turned round and tried the bath. The same.

Quietly, she knelt down on the bathroom floor, and wept.

'We'll have to move,' Luke said. 'If – as soon as Connor is OK. Don't tell him about this.'

'Where?' said Violet. 'If we don't have water, no house will.'

'Down to the lake.'

235

'Oh, yeah.'

'No,' said Thea.

They looked at her.

'I'm not going out there.'

'There's been nothing,' said Luke. 'We've seen nothing.'

Violet took a breath, then put her thumb in her mouth and bit on it as she listened.

'We've seen Connor being shot and almost killed.'

'By a man, not – anything else.'

'So it's dangerous, no matter what.' She sat back, resolute. 'We've got water.' Big bottles of it in the garage, stacked against the wall.

'It won't last forever.'

'It might rain,' she said. They all looked out at the grey, blank sky.

Violet held her baseball bat in both hands and danced around the pool. Thea fanned her feathers underneath the shark tooth. Luke ate chewing gum to keep his mouth moist. Connor watched the candles burn, listening to the meeting of flame, wax and wick.

The drone, which had disappeared when he'd got shot, was back. As keen and bright as ever.

* * *

'I've been shit,' said Luke.

His brother was managing to sit up now, his arm splinted again. Luke had been trying to fend off his own panic for days since Tunde had left – the prospect of Connor going downhill with an infection, or any movement tearing something held only delicately together.

'What are you talking about?' Connor said. He'd only eaten half of his extra-salted bowl of soup, and Luke was polishing off the rest.

'Leaving you to go out. Like a total fucking waster.' His mum would be ashamed of him, he thought, unable to think of her in the past tense.

'I wanted to,' said Connor, as understated as ever. 'I wanted to help. I'm not very good at...' He looked out of the window.

Luke knew what he meant to say. At the emotional support, the hugging, the cheerleading, saying that everything was going to be all right. Being dad. 'It's not true,' he said. 'But anyway. I'm going to be better. Get my arse into gear. I owe you.' The water's stopped, he wanted to say. Connor, we're so fucked.

'You don't owe me anything,' Connor said. 'You're my brother.' He moved his forefinger over the raised crease of his duvet. 'How's your hand?'

Luke glanced down at it. Connor had bitten down so hard on him that he'd torn the skin. The feeling of his teeth was still there, somehow. 'I'll live.' For a moment, he didn't dare look up at him, because to do so would be to suggest that Connor still might not.

* * *

Thea read to him. She dipped into their dad's history books – the Reformation, the English Civil War, the 1970s. She read from biographies of Samuel Pepys, a naturalist, a playwright.

She wasn't always sure that Connor was listening, but he never asked her to stop, just lay gazing towards the grey light outside. 'I'm basically Radio 4,' she said, having finished a chapter of a memoir by a female novelist. Her mum always had Radio 4 on, no matter whether it was a drama or gardening or the news. He didn't look over, but he did smile.

There was weight in his body, so unlike his usual spryness. Luke was worried that he was getting worse, but somehow, Thea knew that it wasn't just the injury. Grief had finally found a way in, through the hole in him.

She read a few poems from an anthology inscribed to her gran by a headmaster in the 1950s, comforting things by John Masefield and Alfred, Lord Tennyson. She imagined herself swimming among the words, *mountain sheep* and *bells* and *larks on the wing*, a world in which things were certain and structured. The book binding was wine-red, smelt of dried herbs, and had a large worn-away patch the size of a 10p coin on the back cover. Her eyes would flicker to Connor's arm, and she'd remember with detached astonishment what she had done, the blue threads she had placed in him. She pictured the damaged skin reaching out blindly, aching to be joined again.

It wasn't like in films, Violet had realised. Rookie cops getting slammed in the shoulder by two bullets and jumping straight back up to chase the baddie. It hurt like nothing else on Earth and didn't stop hurting. Connor was the bravest person she knew and he was still in so much pain, and dead tired. He only got up to use the loo or for Luke to help him wash with bottled water in the sink. There were still bloodstains on the paving outside, and she'd tried three times to get them out of the arm of the sofa with cream cleanser. They'd burnt his T-shirt. The bruises seeped out beyond his bandages, practically black. Like ink was under the skin.

She had started doing her mum's cross-stitch. Little yellow, red, blue and grey blocks and rows, with bigger white oblongs, all made by sewing tiny overlapping crosses. It was supposed to be about New York and old jazz piano, and the yellow reminded her of taxis. Once, she brought it in when it was her turn with Connor, before remembering that he might not want to be reminded of being cross-stitched himself.

Last night, at dusk, she'd taken a photo, from the same spot she always did now. The ripple, still only ever on the screen, looked larger again, in a way that made her stomach hurt. Or was it just that she'd zoomed in more before she'd taken it? She tried to remember what those long, squashed-together shapes had looked like on TV, but couldn't picture them properly.

She wished she could somehow take the images the way William Henry Fox Talbot or Cecilia Glaisher had. With chemicals, not a machine with buttons. Or maybe they'd show up better under ultraviolet light. Nowhere to hide.

Ultra, she thought. Beyond everything.

'I'm really sorry,' said Luke. 'If I've fucked it up.'

He was unwinding the bandages again, each time terrified of what he might find under there. Yellow pus, redness, red streaks were all mentioned in the bigger first-aid book.

'Just knock me out before you amputate, all right?' said Connor. An attempt at his old gallows humour, but there was fear in his eyes.

Carefully, Luke peeled away the gauze and padding, passing it to Thea. The slight resistance of dried liquid as he pulled. He willed it not to ooze. Christ, he wished Tunde were here.

Connor rested his head back on the pillow with a sharp inhale through his teeth.

The bruises had turned from purple to a ghoulish yellow. Both wounds deeply red and angry. The skin was pale and at least partly connected.

'Does it look OK?' said Luke. 'I mean, I think it looks OK.'

'It looks disgusting,' said Violet. 'But it looks OK.'

'So they need to come out?' said Luke, mostly to himself. 'The stitches.'

Connor was staring resolutely out of the window, as if the arm had nothing to do with him.

'The book says ten to fourteen days,' said Thea.

'Let's say... yes, then?' Violet said. 'Yep. Affirmative.'

The three of them looked at one another.

'Calling Nurse Thea,' said Violet. 'Nurse Thea to Emergency Room 1.'

His thumb didn't seem to be working. He couldn't feel anything there. Couldn't bend his elbow properly. His right arm seemed to exist in a different world. 'It's totally numb,' he said to Luke.

Thea had leant over him, snipped with those tiny sewing-kit scissors. Only when she'd finished did he dare look over at the little pile of crusted blue threads, like a tiny sea anemone.

Last night, he'd woken up shouting, found Luke sitting on the bed telling him it was all right, until he crashed back into sleep.

'OK,' said Luke now, and touched his shoulder. 'That's OK. You've done enough.'

Thea watched Connor bend his little finger, then his fourth, third, second. His thumb remained stationary.

'It might just take time,' she said.

He nodded, and she realised that if she was wrong, he would never play the piano again. If there were pianos to play.

A door slamming. Cupboard. Tins set down on the table. The slightest percussive sound made Connor's breath jerk and adrenaline flood his body. Thea found him once sitting against the living-room door, shaking violently, and he'd turned away from her, wanting to curl inwards. Luke had told everyone they needed to be quieter, but Violet often forgot, and Connor would hear her shushing herself afterwards and swearing.

The drone was a comfort now. At least it was constant, didn't leap out at him.

'I made you something.'

Connor looked up.

Violet was at the door, her mouth screwed up to one side.

She came in, and he saw that she hadn't meant soup, or a drawing. She held out the contraption – the pool-net pole, sawn down to about a third of its length, with a knife strapped tightly to the top with the same masking tape they'd used for his bandages. 'I know it looks dumb,' she said. 'But it's quite light. I thought it might be easier to use with your other hand.'

He tried to imagine himself wielding it. Didn't find the thought outlandish.

'I can find something else,' said Violet. 'It's just that Luke doesn't want us going out much now.'

'It's sound,' said Connor. 'Honest.'

Violet's face lifted in an instant.

'You don't have to sleep there any more, you know,' Connor said, from his bed.

Luke looked up from the pile of duvet and blankets on the floor of his brother's room. 'I want to.' He scratched the back of his neck. 'It's as much for me as for you.' He packed his pillow's heft into the middle and put his head down.

'Should probably use your room, then,' Connor said.

A strange, dense moment, both of them doubtless considering the laughable idea of the pair of them, grown lads, sharing the double bed.

'All right,' Luke said. 'Tomorrow. Wanna blow that out?'

He listened to the short puff of air as the candle flame was extinguished. The rush of silence in with darkness. There'd been dogs barking, for a while. He hadn't noticed them for a few days.

His stomach grumbled. Before, he'd top up his blood sugar with nuts or cereal last thing at night, eat balanced meals heavy on the protein. Now he was doing his best to eat only as much as the others, and they were all on too many carbs. Still, at least his bread was tasting better. *Olives*, Violet had said tonight, looking at her slice. *Fancy.*

Luke heard Connor gently clear his throat, the way he often did before saying something of significance. 'Do you think it's gone?'

Luke stared at the ceiling, a dull bolt of dread in his chest. A desperately guilty part of him had been grateful for the distraction of these last days – timing Connor's medication, checking his temperature, working with Thea on trying to decipher the two first-aid books, thinking back over every relevant second of his studies. The only thing with Connor getting a bit better was reality coming back in.

'Your guess is as good as mine,' he said. 'Are you still hearing that sound?'

'Yeah.'

'Is it any louder? Or more… I don't know.'

Connor didn't answer right away. Luke touched his tongue to the roof of his mouth, the vegetal taste ever-present. He was getting thirstier, too, as if his body wanted to store all the water possible before it ran out.

'Yeah,' Connor said, eventually. 'It is.'

Luke lay there, listening to his brother breathe, breathing with him.

Seventeen

Violet wasn't sure if riding at night was really a good idea.
Luke had taken the lights and the reflectors off both bikes,
saying there was less chance of anyone seeing them, which
meant less chance of insane people with guns shooting them.

Luke had said he'd go out alone, and Violet had said, *No
way, José. If you get shot or whatever then I have to help you
get home.* No matter that Connor got back on his own like
some sort of superhero.

It was kind of cool, their bikes softly whizzing through
the night. Even with another starless sky, she could see the
silhouettes of the trees, and the arc of the earth. She watched
for the yellow shimmer on the horizon, though it only ever
seemed to be towards the coast, and not in this direction.

No houses had lights any more. No bulbs, obviously, but
no dull glows from candles behind the curtains either. Still,
Violet taught Luke the routine before they entered each
property – the checks, skirting the perimeter, feeling like
the soldiers from the truck, in camo with caps and massive
boots. She used hand signals like she'd seen in war films.
They did two houses, storing what they couldn't carry for

another time. The first one had a torch that you shook to power it, which was a total bonus. Look for first-aid kits, rice, matches, books for the library, juice, bottled water, sanitary towels. *God, of course*, Luke had said, when she'd mentioned them. *Sorry.*

She had got the washing-up down to a fine art – literally one wipe with the damp cloth. But clothes were harder. She'd scrubbed at the crotch of her pants with soap but needed much more water to rinse it out. The toilet needed tons – Luke said not to throw tissue down or flush *unless, you know*. But what about her period, Violet had wanted to ask, imagining the carnage. There was all the pool water, but it was going scummy now.

On the way back, Luke pointed up the hill towards the church, and she followed him, her calves working overtime. It had surprised her, that last time when they'd followed the procession – he'd gone round the back and she was certain she'd heard him crying.

But Luke got off his bike, resting it silently against a tree by the car park. 'Candles,' he said.

Before, the church had its outside lights on. Now it was one pale, horizontal rectangle adjacent to one vertical rectangle. She could hear the second hand of the big iron clock. Time, just moving on.

As they turned the corner, Violet nearly tripped up on something. Luke put out his arm, a palm against her stomach to stop her moving any further forward. He squatted down and she peered towards the gravel, trying to use her bat senses.

Luke was picking up something, replacing it, picking up something else. Eventually she crouched, too, and carefully reached out to the objects on the ground. Jars, with little tea-lights, like before. All waxless. But not just that. Her fingers inched along something cool, small. And another, and another. Stones, not the gravel from the path, in a line, with a little space in between.

'Is it, like… offerings?' she said, under her breath.

Luke's voice was quiet, but she could hear the dull, troubled tone. 'I don't know.' He remained sitting on his heels for a moment longer, before rising. 'Go wait by the bikes, all right?'

She did as she was told, not taking anything from the scattered possessions. She ran her finger along the smooth metal of her bike. Listened to her heart, *thump-thump*, and to the insect-buzz in the trees behind her. Waited for him to come back.

What was her mum doing right now, if she hadn't been disappeared? Was she in a car, driving down to them? How would she get across the Channel if nothing was working, if most people had been disappeared? Maybe she could find a fisherman and pay him to come over, but how important would money be now? China would be harder. But if her dad could, he would. He had excellent powers of persuasion. *You could persuade the fish out of the sea*, her mum had once said to him. *And these two are learning from you.* Dad had smiled. *I do my best, my darling.* Violet couldn't persuade herself now, though. She kept trying to imagine the day she looked up and one of them – or both, hand in hand, because it was a daydream after all – were coming through the gate, her mum kneeling down, sobbing, as they ran towards her. Alanna was there, too, and they'd beat up a ton of people to get down here, and everything would be OK, even if the rest of the world had turned to shit. The ripple would stop showing up on her camera.

But it wasn't going to happen. Not really. She just knew, somehow.

It was so quiet. No planes, no car engines, no sound of people on their terraces around the valley. Just the crickets and the grasshoppers, *tsk*-ing. A quiet that she could feel. Sometimes, she wondered if she could feel the ripple in the sky too, even if she wasn't looking for it. A tingling, tightening sense in her skin.

'Come on, Luke,' she said, under her breath. Her heartbeat was beginning to speed up, even though her body hadn't moved.

A shadow slipped out of the church door. She felt all the breath in her vanish.

Luke came towards her. He shook his head. 'They've all been taken already,' he said. 'The candles.'

* * *

The crop fields are becoming green and ragged. The lavender has kept its hue and is no longer in neat rows. Its sweet, smoky scent smudges the air.

In the oak forest, young truffles inflate to colossal, unnatural sizes in the soil. The juniper berries' year-long journey from green to blue-black accelerates.

In the wooded slopes nearer the gorge, a nightingale delivers its song in the bright of day.

* * *

Ravel wrote a left-handed piano concerto, Connor thought, for his friend who'd lost an arm in the First World War. He was sure there were others – Saint-Saëns, maybe.

'Sign of genius,' Violet said. She had taken her plate to the dark dining-room window, her bare feet up on the wall by the frame. 'All the best people are left-handed. I.e., me.'

There was never any question that they wouldn't eat together now. Luke, Thea and Connor were around the table, the tall candle burnt halfway. People only had so many candles, and Luke and Violet could only ride so far. Violet had found a book on making your own candles and soaps, though the experiment hadn't got any further than that. '*Flocons de cire de soja*,' she'd read, before Thea had translated. 'Where the fuck do I get soy wax flakes from?'

'Do you want me to cut that for you?' Thea said.

Connor had been staring with intensity at his fork, gripped in his left fist, as he used the edge to roughly cut a tinned peach-half. 'No,' he said, and shook his head. He looked thinner. Hollows at his cheekbones and a muddiness under his eyes. 'Thank you.'

There was a peculiar new intimacy between them, Luke thought. Perhaps that's what happened when one sewed up the other. Thea had spent hours and hours reading to him, with a dedication that seemed almost clung to. She'd not had a panic attack since Connor's injury, and seemed to scratch herself less. He'd instructed Violet not to say anything about what they'd found at the church. She'd stared at him, before shrugging.

'There's something out there,' said Violet, from the window. Her voice was so unexpressive that Luke almost missed the sense of it.

They all stilled.

'What d'you mean?' Luke said.

'There's something out there,' she said.

Connor put down his fork, looking at Luke, and at the same time, Thea's breath caught.

Not Tunde and his sister. Some-*thing*.

'Blow out the candle,' said Luke.

Violet reached down for her baseball bat.

Violet had been looking at the reflections of the little flame in the window and the shapes of her siblings. Squinting past them to the silhouetted line of the highest plants along the far wall outside. She'd imagined placing them on a metal plate, exposing them to the sun, rinsing them in pool water. Her camera battery was down to one bar now. She wouldn't be taking photos forever. And then she wouldn't know if they were there or not.

Then – a flicker of shadow, something darker against the dark. Not quite as high as the walls. Upright.

There were flashes, too, low ebbs of lemon light. She screwed up her eyes. Opened them again.

Everything in Thea grew tight in an instant. Each pore

contracting in fear. Her legs felt maddeningly itchy, crawling with heat.

Luke had gone to the edge of the window by Violet. She'd known the moment he'd seen something, too – the muscles in his shoulders stiffening under his T-shirt. Low light, there for a heartbeat, disappearing.

Thea wanted to ask what it was. What it looked like. How tall. Whether there was more than one. Couldn't speak.

'Gone round to the front,' Luke said, under his breath. He had his knife in his hand.

Connor was now holding the pool-net weapon Violet had made for him.

They moved slowly towards the hallway. Thea didn't know why they weren't going to the basement, or under the table, but she wasn't doing that alone. She stayed in the orbit of the others.

A sudden clang of something falling outside, and her heart billowed outwards. She wasn't ready to die.

'Shit shit shit,' whispered Violet.

The drone in Connor's ear seemed to intensify, hone down to its original pitch, as penetrating as a laser.

The intermittent light and movement continued around the exterior of the house, and they followed it, turning, listening, each sibling's body touching something of another. The walls of the house felt like paper, could be punched through, easily penetrated.

Connor listened to Thea's breath, its shallowness and irregular rhythm.

They followed the movement to the living room. The curtains open. They pressed themselves to the wall.

There was a shape, against the window, looking in.

A face.

For a moment, Connor thought that the old farmer had found him, wanted to finish the job. Blow holes in him.

Violet yelped.

Luke felt a clatter of sensations – utter fear, and relief that it was human, and fear again, because it *was* human.

'*Pardon*,' the man was saying, on the other side of the glass. '*Pardon.*'

After steeling himself for something unimaginable, it was utterly surreal to see an ordinary person standing there, apologising.

'Stay here,' Luke said, and went to the back door. The others followed him anyway.

The man had walked round to the back door, too, and was standing on the step. He was pointing a small, lit torch down by his feet. Hiking boots. A rucksack on his back. '*Bonjour,*' he said. '*Pardon.*' His next utterances were fluid, gently animated and unrecognisable.

'What's he saying?' said Violet.

'It's not French,' said Thea.

'*Pardon*,' the man said again, and tucked his torch under his arm, before putting his hands together in prayer for a moment.

He was in his late forties, maybe. Light-brown skin. Wearing canvas trousers with lots of pockets and a lightweight coat, the sort you got in camping shops. Taller than Violet, shorter than Connor and Thea, with greying hair. He looked quite strong, Violet thought. She watched him and Thea address each other in French, a weird dance between strangers, saying *Anglais* and *hello*, and recognised enough of his words to know that it wasn't his first language. He would say a few English words, then French, then go off on his own – maybe it was Urdu, like Violet's science partner Amil spoke. The man had seen Violet's baseball bat, Luke's knife, and Connor's weapon. He didn't seem to have one of his own.

'Um.' Thea looked at them all, and back at the man. '*Qu'est-ce-que vous voulez?*'

'*Rien,*' the man said, putting up his hands, placating. He looked at Violet's bat again, and at them all with a strange mix of fear and amiability. '*Rien, rien.*' He began talking quickly in his own language, before switching back to French.

'He says he's been travelling,' said Thea. 'I think. He hasn't seen many people on the road. *Des personnes?*' she said to him.

The man shook his head. '*Mais vous êtes ici,*' he said, looking at them one at a time, more slowly, his palms open. He said it again, stressing the *you*. He sounded almost paternally proud. He spoke again, a mix of French and his other language.

Thea asked him something else. 'I think he's saying again that he's not seen many people. But he's telling anyone he comes across what he saw.'

A pause, as they all took this in.

'What did he see?' said Luke, as if he didn't want to know.

The man was alert, fizzy with adrenaline. *Lille*, Violet heard. He gestured with his hands, their shapes an additional language. Describing people, buildings, the sky. The disappearances. As he spoke, he forked two fingers at his eyes and into the air away from them, and waved his hand in a negative.

Thea barely needed to translate, but she did anyway. 'He was working in Lille. Normal day, normal streets. Everyone, I don't know, doing their usual things. He was in his flat. Then, the sky, and people just—' She took a breath, as if to fortify herself. 'People going. Like he'd blink and more people had just disappeared. He thought he was imagining it, until the street was quiet. No—' She corrected herself. 'Silent.'

Violet's skin tingled with strange electricity. 'Why did he not... you know?'

Thea asked him.

'*Je sais pas,*' he said, quite simply. A small smile. '*Je suis pas spécial.*' He spoke again.

Thea translated. 'He walked around. The streets were almost empty. They'd all been there, and then they weren't.'

Violet remembered the shots of the city squares on that first day, and the odd person wandering around as if stoned. 'But – did he see anything?'

The man closed his eyes and breathed in, as if putting himself back there. Then he put out his tongue and lightly touched the pad of his middle finger to it, as if about to turn a page. '*Non,*' he said. '*Mais je savais.*'

'But I knew,' said Thea.

The stillness of the room.

'Knew what?' said Connor.

Thea asked him and listened, her hands in her lap. 'He just knew. Felt? Knew that there was something there. Some—' She asked him for clarification. 'Some-*one*?' He shook his head. 'Something.'

The stillness of their bodies.

'What did it feel like?' Luke asked.

The man sat for a long moment, eyes looking somewhere beyond the house, the walls, the horizon. '*Pas possible*,' he said, with a simple shrug. Smiled. '*Je trouve pas les mots.*'

'No words,' Thea said, quietly, though they'd all understood well enough.

Connor laid down his weapon.

The man's name was Ohit. He took the tinned soup and peaches offered him, saying *merci* and *thank you*, but not in a way that suggested hunger. Only gratitude.

He had been working in construction in Lille. But wanted to get home – to Dinajpur in northern Bangladesh, to his parents and grandparents, he said. He didn't seem to have a partner, or children, or at least he didn't speak of them. He had walked from Lille. Small roads, he said. He would try the ports. If not, he would carry on walking east.

Home. He spoke with such frank determination, as if it were simple to walk across continents. If he could, then their dad could. Her mum could.

Ohit asked their names. '*Vous êtes famille?*' he said.

'*Oui*,' Thea said, and felt something settle in her.

255

'*Oui*,' said Ohit, smiling. '*Je – je vois ça.*' He repeated it, put his forked fingers to his eyes again, and pointed at them all.

A fluid sound. Undulating, always moving forward, with tiny swirls of decoration. Connor thought of winds over desert mountains, of wanderers, rivers.

Ohit was singing. They hadn't asked him to. He'd just begun, after helping Luke make the fire. He'd looked at the bread oven, too, and reconstructed it for them. A song in his own language. *Bengali*, he'd said. *Chanson d'amour triste.* Sad love song.

Connor listened to the microtones in the melody, how natural and unlike his own musical language they were, the pitches he'd learnt so bordered and rigid. He wondered if that was what the sound in his body was doing, singing in microtones even finer than Ohit's – the Western scale fragmented into a million shards.

Ohit broke off. He gave a laugh heavy with melancholy, which became a sigh and a smile, before the smile faded slowly.

Luke hated that he couldn't sleep. That he'd told Violet and Thea to put a chair underneath the handle of their bedroom door. That he couldn't fully trust the man who'd refused a bed, was sleeping on the sofa downstairs, the man who was brown. He knew he would be the same with anyone at this point, but he still hated himself.

Next to him, Connor slept, a slight roughness in his breath. He saw Ohit closing his eyes earlier as he remembered the disappearances. Almost as if he'd wanted to be back there. Had wanted to be one of them.

Not possible. No words.

Violet lay in bed, thinking of the candles and stones at the church. How they hadn't seen anyone for weeks. She tried to listen inside herself, feel it. Them.

She held up her arm in the dark, Thea shifting next to her.

'Thea.'

'Mmm.'

'I think the gravel is protecting us.'

Thea gave a heavy sigh, as if trying to haul herself into consciousness. 'What?'

'The gravel. The thing I've been making. We've been making.' She knew it sounded stupid, but she kept feeling a wordless impulse, deep in her body, to add to it. She'd realised that the long stems from the central circle were like the scribbles in the air by the neon butterfly she kept seeing.

Thea gave a drained-sounding hum. 'That's just…' She scratched her thigh. 'We make up stories,' she said. 'Look for patterns. To help ourselves get through things.'

Just this little thing like the end of the world, thought Violet.

'But we're still here, even though…' Violet was going to tell her about the photos, but she didn't want to give Thea another panic attack. One day soon, she would show them the succession of images, the stretching, furrowing ripple, its increasing weight. Only when she was sure it was there.

'Even though what?'

'I just think it might be getting closer,' she said, very carefully. Best not to say *they*.

Thea scratched her thigh again. 'Yeah. Probably.' She turned over, away from her sister.

Violet held up her arm, and imagined it being rubbed out, inch by inch.

In the morning, Ohit had gone. He'd taken a few tins, two candles and a box of matches. Torn a page out of the introduction to *The Go-Between* and folded it precisely into a bird in flight, placed next to some chocolates in bright-red foil wrappers.

'I thought he might want to stay,' Violet said.

None of them said what they were thinking – that he didn't because it wasn't safe enough here.

* * *

Then, three days of rain. An onslaught. New rivulets formed. Coins and rings in the pool, the water overflowing onto the paving. A layer of water on the road. Each plant bowing under the weight. A toasted, iron-like smell.

Violet danced around the vegetable beds and her gravel sculpture, holding the ends of the baseball bat in each hand, head up and tongue out. Thea sat by the windows as they were coated with rain, her vision blurring. Luke watched the water butts fill, and put out every other receptacle he could find, his T-shirt stuck to his skin. In the garden, Connor listened to the gentle attack of rain on the pool, on the leaves, on his skull. How it harmonised with the drone.

How he could feel whatever was coming, more than ever.

Eighteen

Connor couldn't stop the nightmares. They took different forms, no longer interrupting his sleep with a great crack but seeping in slowly, a comforting premise becoming violent, and him softening into consciousness drenched in cold sweat. Luke would be next to him in the double bed, waking up to soothe his brother. *Dad*, Connor had said, once, before remembering where he was.

'My period's gone weird,' said Violet, as they put olives in jars.

'Yeah?' Thea's Pill had run out weeks ago. She'd thought about asking Luke and Violet to look for some and decided not to. Felt her body tilt and shift, wondered if she was imagining it.

'I mean, it should have come this week,' Violet said. 'I think it was this week. But it hasn't.' She glanced up. 'I haven't had sex. Obviously.'

'It'll come.'

'I don't want to have sex.'

'Not many options at the moment,' Thea said.

'No, I mean – I just don't want to,' said Violet. 'Ever. I think I'm, you know. Ace. Asexual. I mean, maybe.'

Thea poured the olive oil into the jar, and Violet screwed the lid tight.

'You be who you want to be,' Thea said. She put her hand over Violet's. 'You *are* ace. In more ways than one.' She smiled.

* * *

The sky cleared. The sun suddenly there, a miracle, an outrage, a mundanity.

Cyanotype blue, thought Violet, wondering if the vegetables might grow now. She took a photo of the sky and studied the screen, wanting something more definite to show up, like Anna Atkins's chalk-coloured algae plants. Dreading it. As she looked at the screen, it went black. The battery was dead.

Maybe it's really over, thought Luke. A god, thought Thea. An omen, thought Connor.

* * *

If Luke concentrated, it was almost as it was before. The four of them sitting on the loungers in the sun, shades on. Except there were no phones, no fresh food except for his bread, no cars. No hope.

Violet was shivering next to him, picking off a petal from her damp arm. She didn't care about the dirtiness of the cold pool, swam under the leaves and insects, emerged a swamp monster.

'You're peeling,' Thea said.

Luke looked over as Thea pulled at a papery corner of skin on Connor's shoulder.

Connor would often catch Thea's wrist as she scratched her leg, and he'd hold it firmly for longer than Luke might have. They would look at each other, an understanding passing between them, and Thea would stop scratching, at least for a while.

Luke watched now as she peeled off the shred of loose skin, rolling it into a tiny cigar-shape, letting it fall. She took up another curling end. The little well at the base of Connor's throat went taut as he swallowed, but he let her anyway.

Violet was watching, too.

Luke's mouth was dry again. The dryness had a corroding quality, almost tingling, over his inner cheeks, the back of his throat, his lips. He tried his best not to drink too much, but he had a warm carton of juice by him again. It would take away the taste, just for a moment.

Then, the sound of a car, not close. Thea stopped. They all looked up.

Violet hopped onto the wall and stayed crouched there, looking over the valley.

'Anything?' Luke called.

Violet remained a moment longer, before jumping down. 'A maroon car,' she said. 'Gone now. I thought maybe it was Tunde. You know, with his sister.'

Luke knew it wasn't. He'd got up before dawn, having been awake for hours, and using Tunde's hand-drawn map cycled to the apartment, in the nearest village on the northern side of the lake. A sodden note to his sister was pinned to the door, the green ink diluted and blotched. Signed *T x*. The door was unlocked, and Luke had gone in, sat on one of the unmade beds for a while. Telling himself Tunde had gone to find her.

Hoping he had.

*　*　*

Thea missed the parks, wet and green, and the pavements and the Greek grocery shops and the Cameroonian pancake place. The humid charge of female energy in the corridors of her school. Her friends, their fearless mix of intellect and pop culture.

Violet missed the skatepark and the freezing lido and her dad's hand, because she used to still hold his hand if no one was looking.

Connor missed his bedroom studio, all his books around him, Spike on his stomach, Kaia leaning into him, the canals, gigs under the dank railway arches.

Luke missed his mum. Her sudden, asphyxiating hugs and love of gossip. How she'd sit with an arm around him on the trams, until he was the bigger one and put his arm around her instead. How, the last time he remembered doing so, she'd rested her head on his shoulder and said, *My bloody lovely boy.*

*　*　*

Connor drew. He didn't fill his notepad with words any more, just drawings. Left-handed, with effort. Lines, connecting, crossing. To try and get closer to the sound in his head.

He wondered if the sound he could feel had always been there and he just hadn't heard it. Hadn't been listening.

There were the suggestions of melodies now, not formed into pitches, but shimmering shapes and curves. He thought of the ice-cream van coming round the corner into their cul-de-sac. Of bagpipes, played far away. A waterfall, barrelling down onto his head, with tales of higher ground. Of every tune and chord he'd ever heard, all compressed together.

He was sure that there was something at its centre, some truth ingrained deep in him. He just couldn't quite get to it.

He turned over a fresh page, drew again.

* * *

In the woods, apples swell and fall, and the trees begin to fruit a second time. Pollen dust drifts like snow. Greens become greener.

Bramble thorns, blood-red, are stretching as long as fingers into wire fences.

The dormouse nest is full of babies, tiny and brittle-boned. They open their eyes early, as one.

Ivy travels faster, into the houses of those who have left.

* * *

Time flies when you're having fun. No time like the present. What time do you call this?

They had lost track of the days. Luke had stopped marking the calendar weeks ago, and they realised that they'd missed Violet's birthday. Connor gave her the beaded wooden

263

bracelet he always wore. Luke made an upside-down cake that sagged in the middle and no one could finish, and they all ate sweets instead. Thea told stories about Violet as a toddler, and read out one of her old children's books, in animated voices. Violet thought, with guilt, that it was the best birthday she'd had in years.

* * *

Thea was slicing beetroot. There was a field towards a village to the south-west, and Luke and Violet had checked it out several times before uprooting a few at the edge. 'I hate beetroot,' Violet had said, dumping them on the kitchen table. '*Je les déteste.*'

'But you'd *better-have* them,' Thea had replied in an overtly French accent, and smiled despite herself. Even more so when Violet looked confused. 'Beetroot. *Betterave.*'

She liked how easily they stained her, the deep pink feathering along the lines of her palm underneath her thumb, a rivulet down her wrist.

'Gotcha,' said Violet, who'd been kneeling on the floor, her nose to a very long-legged spider. She stood, cupping it in her hands. 'Ugh. Tickles.'

'Just as well Dad isn't here,' said Thea, by the counter.

Violet let out a tiny laugh. 'Yeah.'

'Why?' said Luke, who was sitting on the floor against the wall, running his thumbnail along the radiator. He had a carton of juice in his hand. He seemed to need to sip something constantly, and Thea wondered if she would ever say anything about sharing it with the rest of them.

264

''Cause he's shit-scared of spiders,' said Violet, as if it were obvious, and let the spider out on the windowsill.

A small silence, in which they were all mentally correcting her. *Was* scared.

'Is that true?' said Luke.

'As true as truth,' said Violet. 'He literally shrieks and cries.' *Shrieked*, they all thought. *Cried.*

'Remember that time in the cabin in Wales?' Thea said.

Violet snorted. 'Oh, my God. Mum practically wet herself.'

Another silence, but filled with a softer colour. The colour of absence, of loss.

'I did not know that,' said Luke, and dragged his thumbnail over the metal ridges again. A tinny, cascading stutter of sounds.

'It's come back in,' said Connor, letting the spider run onto the fingers of his good hand, before wandering outside.

'As true as truth,' said Violet again, quietly, thoughtfully.

No eternal facts, no absolute truths, thought Thea. Yet she felt such love for the three of them suddenly, wholly, that she knew it was a truth. The only truth possible.

Connor came in. 'That car went past again. I think they saw me.'

They'd seen it twice now, once down in the valley, and yesterday cruising slowly up and then back past the house, all of them staying out of sight. A large maroon car, with a barely discernible engine sound.

'OK,' said Luke, rising, trying to keep his voice light. Ohit had been nice, after all. 'It doesn't matter.'

Thea put down her knife, staring out of the window. 'They've stopped.' She looked over.

Connor bit his already-bitten lip.

They watched from the living-room window as two men got out and stood at the gate, looking in. They were talking quietly to each other. Fuck, thought Violet.

The men walked through the gate, looking at her gravel-web sculpture on their way towards the house. The four of them went to the door. It was like when Ohit had come. They couldn't help being pulled towards the visitors like magnets, because they were living humans, even if they might have guns and spray them with bullets.

The pair stopped halfway up the path as Luke opened the door. Two white men, one in his late forties, with receding hair, the other taller, younger. Twenties. Maybe father and son, though they didn't much look alike.

'*Bonjour.*' The older man was wearing a black polo shirt, his head domed and with a sheen of sweat. A vein ran from the very top of his skull down to the outer edge of his eyebrow. His smile was tense.

They all replied hello. *Bonjour, ça va, où habitez-vous, quel âge avez-vous*, thought Violet, remembering her French class teacher asking every single one of them the same stupid, useless questions. Not, *Have you seen them? Are you friendly? Is it over?*

The younger man, about the same age as Tunde and his friends, caught Violet's eye. He had a shaved blond head and sharp green eyes that caught in her stomach. She flung her gaze past him.

'*Combien êtes-vous?*' the older man said.

'*Combien?*' said Thea, as if trying to bring herself out of a dream. '*Um, quatre,*' she said. '*Seulement nous.*' She waved vaguely at the four of them, and the men looked at her purple-stained palms, and stepped backwards.

The younger man quickly put his hand round to the back pocket of his jeans. A stabbing fear in Violet's gut.

'*Non, non,*' Thea said, her voice a little too panicky and high. '*Non, c'est—*' She started gabbling, pointing to the kitchen, saying the word for beetroot, *better-'ave,* and miming chopping. She wiped her hands on her shorts, leaving a dark-pink smear that didn't make it look any better.

The younger man didn't take his hand from behind his back.

Violet was aware of the unnatural pose she was standing in, legs rod-straight, one hand on her hips. Connor had his good fist tightly clenched by his thigh.

'*Anglais?*' The way the older man asked made it sound like an insult. A disappointment. Fair do's, thought Violet.

They all nodded.

The man murmured something to the younger man.

'*Oui. Pouvons-nous vous aider?*' Luke said, a little too loudly.

'*Non,*' said the older man. '*Mais nous pouvons vous aider.*'

Stay still. Wait for them to leave.

Connor watched as Thea, and Luke up to a point, talked to the two strangers. The younger man had finally slid his hand back around and put it in his front pocket. Whilst the older man talked, his voice smooth, the younger rested his eyes on each of them in turn, as if assessing them. He had a deerlike alertness that Connor recognised.

Thea seemed to be saying something about the beetroot again, with a feigned laugh. The men smiled, and the younger man looked at her legs, the briefest flicker before he scrutinised the house behind them.

The older man was gesturing back towards his car, explaining something. Pointing at the sky with a shrug. Thea looked at Luke uncertainly, and asked the man to repeat it. Connor realised, suddenly, what they were saying. To go with them.

'*Non*,' said Luke. '*Merci.*'

The older man took a breath, not responding straight away. 'You have water?' he said, in English. 'Food?'

Oh it hadn't asked for anything. The man didn't sound like he was checking that they were OK.

'We have enough,' said Luke, and Thea repeated it in French.

They all stood looking at each other.

The next moment was very fast. There was a sharp buzzing, and the younger man raised his hand. Connor flinched and went to grab his weapon, which wasn't there, and at the same time realised that the man had been swatting a wasp from his face.

'*Non, non, non,*' said the younger man to Connor, as if admonishing a child, holding his palm out. He said something else, and muttered to the older man.

'Sorry,' said Connor. His pulse was in triple time. He stepped back behind the others. He wanted to run, hide, cry. At any moment, this could change – he'd learnt about violence, how bodies could be made to open out to the world in new ways.

The older man was speaking again, low and fluid, and Luke was politely saying no.

An exasperated laugh from the younger man. '*Erreur,*' he said, shaking his head. He jabbed a finger at his own temple. '*Tous fous.*' Another mirthless laugh.

'*Non, merci,*' said Luke.

'*Ensemble.* Together,' said the younger man, before speaking too quickly to be understood, and with fury. He gestured up at the house, around the walls and at them, walking straight through one of Violet's gravel lines, the stones scattering.

'No,' said Violet, her voice tight.

'Violet,' said Luke, too late.

Violet dashed forwards and pushed the centre of the younger man's chest with both hands.

He looked incredulous at this infraction. An astringent grin, vanishing fast. He pointed a finger close to Violet's face, uttering each word with precise force. 'Do not touch me.'

'Don't fucking come near her.' Luke stepped in front of Violet, one hand behind himself to gently push her back.

The man straightened, slowly, only inches between them. They were almost the same height.

'Don't even fucking think about it.' Luke's voice was newly hard, and very calm.

The man pulled in his bottom lip with his teeth, a crude semblance of a smile. He shook his head, and lightly touched the older man's arm, before turning and walking away. '*Putains d'idiots.*' There was the black bar of a hand pistol in his rear pocket. He spat into the grass.

The older man put his chin to his chest and sighed. 'OK,' he said. '*Bonne chance.* Good luck.'

Connor listened to his pulse rattle as they watched the two men get back in the car, the older man trying to calm the younger, the younger slamming his door.

'They said it was safe,' said Thea. 'I think. That they had somewhere. To start again.'

'Did you want to go with them?' said Luke.

'Hell, no,' said Violet.

'No,' said Connor, thinking of the younger man looking at Thea's legs.

The wasp came back, investigative, persistent.

Thea waved it away. 'No,' she said.

* * *

'Yep,' said Violet. 'Higher.'

That night, Luke and Violet had gone out, taking two pairs of thick gardening gloves and wire-cutters. They returned with a roll of barbed wire from the small construction yard three kilometres away, Violet's knees scratched and bleeding. 'Fell on it,' she said, as Thea cleaned the tiny puncture points and applied plasters.

They used chairs to stand by the wall, rolling out the wire in loops, winding it around an occasional nail to stay fast. More plasters, this time for Luke's arms. Around the tall main gate, Connor had superglued a few razor blades, upended drawing pins, spare nails. Violet had made Thea one of her hybrid weapons – a small hand trowel taped to a snapped-off arm of the clothes horse. Thea had accepted it with grace, looking solemnly at it in her hands.

Luke came back out from the garage with the one bike U-lock and a tiny golden key, and slotted it around the inner rail of the gate on both sides. *Click.*

'I'm really bad with losing keys,' Violet said.

'Time to practise not losing them,' he said.

Nineteen

Cold days. Hot days. An autumn that didn't feel like autumn. Connor peeled again and Thea gently tugged away the loose skin. The paths were mostly reduced to plastic grid mats, all the gravel added to Violet's stone sculpture that snaked around the outside of the house and had begun to lodge in the wells of trees. Thea gathered the remaining ones, trod through the grass looking for strays and added them where she could, straightened others to make sure they were connected. Luke kept drinking and drinking water, his piss practically colourless, watching the road for cars, the sky for rain.

Connor looked at the grass, at the plants, at the dry-stone wall, at his siblings. Wondered if he could hear them all. Felt he could hear almost everything, including what was coming.

* * *

'What's your favourite song?' Violet asked.

Thea had stopped reading, saying she was tired. They were all sitting in the living room watching the fire, the lurid red pulsing amongst the kindling, as if there were spirits in there. Violet was obsessed with keeping it going, sitting by the hearth and adding shreds of wood if it died down too quickly, or extra scrunches of newspaper she'd brought from three houses down. She'd been secretly trying to teach herself how to start a fire from scratch – no matches, no nothing – though she hadn't managed it yet. For when they ran out. Now she was sitting on her heels, addressing the flames.

Luke blinked. 'Who're you asking?'

'Anyone,' said Violet.

He looked round at the others. Thea was stretching her neck, her chin drawing a slow circle. Connor was on watch by the window, the fingers of his good hand flexing, playing something in his head.

'Don't know,' Luke said.

'You must have one. Doesn't have to be your all-time best.'

He tried to remember the world before this one – the dreamscape of university exams, soaking tired muscles in Epsom salts, corner shops for a sneaky bit of chocolate, buses, Thursday nights out. 'Um. "Tainted Love"? Bit old-school.' It wasn't even his favourite, really. It was his mum's.

'Don't know that one,' Violet said, arms on her knees.

'Yeah, you do.'

'How does it go?'

He couldn't help smiling. 'No, you're not getting me that easy.'

'I honestly don't know it. Go on.'

Luke put his chin to his chest, saw his mates queuing in

their T-shirts so they didn't have to pay for the cloakroom, felt a remnant sparkle of cheap booze and cheap tunes and the odd pill. 'No chance,' he said.

Connor made two punchy humming sounds in the back of his throat.

Thea and Violet looked at him. Connor hadn't moved, his leg slung over the chair, eyes on the black window. They looked at Luke.

Connor made the sounds again, followed by a little low melody.

'Oh, wait,' said Violet. 'Maybe I do know it.'

'Oh, you bastard,' said Luke, at the same time.

Connor shrugged, with the faintest suggestion of a grin, still not looking over. Hummed again.

Luke sighed and started singing, and Connor added the sparest of beatboxing sounds, more back-of-his-throat bass and some cymbals in his teeth. They all did the claps, and Luke stood and did the whole song, the full works, because he couldn't help being a good sport when he was asked.

Thea wondered how often the two brothers had done this, imagined them as children, entertaining relatives at Christmas. Violet wolf-whistled and thought of prehistoric people dancing round a fire chanting, with Luke gyrating his hips with almost no self-consciousness as the modern version. Connor just marvelled at his brother, who could even now turn it on if he had to, holding his pretend microphone, pointing at the crowd.

'You next,' said Violet to Connor, when Luke sat down again. 'A cappella karaoke takes no prisoners.'

'But Connor's favourite song will be some weird operatic thing with horrible electronics that make your ears bleed,' said Thea, with an impish sidelong look at him.

Connor gave a contemplative smile, gazed into the room for a moment, and began singing a Taylor Swift song from a couple of years ago. A quiet voice, perfectly in tune.

'No. Way,' said Violet.

God bless my fucking brother, thought Luke.

They stared at him open-mouthed, before Connor lost it and they all collapsed into hysterical giggles.

* * *

'I think I want to be they them,' said Violet, in bed one night. It was cold, and she swore that the wall felt wet, was seeping dampness into the sheet. 'But I'm not sure.'

'What?' Thea sounded uncomprehending.

'They them,' said Violet, staring at the ceiling. 'You know. Like, pronouns.'

'Oh.' The word was bathed in relief. 'I thought—'

Of course. *They. Them.* The words Violet used to describe what was out there. Maybe Thea did believe it, after all. 'No. I mean me. They mean me. I mean, they them does. Or sometimes, anyway.'

A short silence, Thea's lips dryly opening and shutting. 'OK.'

'OK?'

Thea's fingers found Violet's, clasped them tight. 'Obviously.' She spoke very gently. 'You idiot.'

They lay there, legs against legs.

'What about your name?' said Thea.

'What about it?'

'Do you want to change it for real?'

Violet looked towards the grey horizontal lines of the shutters. Changing it would mean being one step further away from her parents, somehow. Her name had come from their minds, their mouths. 'Not for now,' she said. They said.

When Violet awoke in the morning, they were still holding hands.

* * *

The rain didn't come. The water level of the bins inched lower.

They hardly washed. Luke started going out two fields away, digging a hole for his shit. *The toilet field*, Violet called it. Thea refused to go beyond the walls of the house.

They told stories, of their mums, of Dad, of their friends. They made up stories. Thea did make-up on Violet, then on Luke, then on Connor. Thea beat Connor at chess. Luke timed Violet's handstands against the wall.

They used up the juice. Cranberry, mango, apple and mango, orange with bits that Violet had never liked, orange without bits in.

Luke curled his tongue in his mouth, sucked on it.

Connor kept drawing the sound in his head. He kept drawing until he found himself on the last page of his notebook, drew on the outer covers. It was sound he couldn't describe in shape and yet he had to try. He looked at his bedroom wall.

Violet watched the sky for the lavender ripple that she'd only ever seen through her camera. Sometimes, when she blinked, she thought she saw the shapes, though she couldn't be sure. Then she watched for the neon butterfly, scribbling its invisible patterns.

Thea felt the memory of the bat in her hair, and allowed it to be there.

No more cars went past.

* * *

Thorn and tendril and bud and blade. Curling, coiling. The outer perimeter of the dry-stone wall is lustrous with new flora. Insects vibrate amongst it all, shimmer with a light beyond themselves, and lift in clouds.

The griffon vulture appears again, grey head and colossal charcoal wings. Its eyrie in the cliffs is bolstering, a raucous colony.

Algae spores begin to voraciously consume roof tiles.

* * *

'Please can you make me a hot-water bottle?' said Violet, in bed, her knees tucked up to her chest.

Thea looked at her. At *them* – Violet hadn't definitely decided yet, had talked about using both, but Thea still needed to practise. 'The fire's gone down now,' she said.

Violet made a tight-lipped grumble. 'My stupid period came.'

Thea felt the pressure on her own pelvic bone, the low spread of pain along her back. 'Mine too,' she said. She'd been spotting, pointillist drops on the crotch of her pants, scrubbing at them with as little water as possible. Her mind had felt loosened, haywire – it was hard to tell what was because of her body adjusting to the lack of the Pill, and what was everything else.

It was itching there, too. Not just her scalp, her legs and arms, but her vagina. A sweat-like prickle. She didn't think she could ask Luke and Violet to find her thrush cream.

Violet curled up further, a little dormouse in the bed.

Thea wondered what it felt like, to not want to be a *she* and still to bleed. The two felt like the same thing to her.

She went downstairs and got them both painkillers. Climbed back into bed and curled around Violet's back, an arm over her waist. Their waist. Felt the mutual throb and swell. Blood, flowing into blood.

* * *

One bin of water left. Two one-litre bottles down in the basement. Luke had to stop drinking, and he couldn't. The thirst was constant.

A sudden chime on his tongue, like a bell, like a song.

He laughed.

'What?' said Thea, on the lounger next to him.

'Can you taste that?' Luke said. He touched the tip of his tongue with his finger, and eyed it.

'What?' said Thea.

Luke sat very still. There was a memory just out of reach.

'What, Luke?'

He blinked, shook his head. 'Nothing.' He breathed in, and it came to him.

Maple sap. The taste in his mouth was maple sap.

They'd gone to Canada when he and Connor were small, to stay with Dave's family – Dave's dad, large and loud, and his mum, already with the shaking hands of Parkinson's. They walked in a damp, black-green forest of trees so dense you couldn't see the sky, wrapped up in scarves and mittens, breath in candyfloss clouds. The crunch of snow underfoot. There was a demonstration of tapping a maple tree for sap – a finger-sized hole drilled into the bark, a little metal scoop plugged into it. Clear liquid dripping out into a tiny paper cup, passed around. Connor had shaken his head, but Luke had tried it. The taste of the tree shining on his tongue, cold and bitter. Then he was passed the real thing – the ice sieved off, boiled for a day on a log fire, a woody heat that made his whole body smile. His mum had squeezed his shoulders, and they'd all been standing close to keep each other warm. Family.

'I'm off for water,' Luke said.

Connor looked up. 'Taking Violet?'

'No, it's OK.'

Connor stared at his brother. 'But we always—'

'She's asleep. Don't want to bother her. I'll do a recce, and come back with her if I find much.'

'How far are you going?'

Luke looked at the map they'd drawn on the kitchen wall, the small blocks denoting buildings, some with a tick next to them. He pointed to a small row of houses a few kilometres away.

'You should take Violet,' Connor said. 'Or go at night.'

'It's fine, bro.' He leant down and kissed Connor's cheek, a startling gesture. 'Back in a sec.'

But he didn't go there. He kept riding.

He could practically see it. A golden lacquer on everything – the gentle hills, the trees, the sky. He felt like he was riding in amber liquid.

He thought of his mum, her hands on his shoulders. Proud of him for trying something new. He imagined tasting everything before him – the gentle hills, the trees, the sky.

He headed upwards. He wanted to get to the highest point.

'Where's Luke?' Violet had slept for ages. She'd lain on her arm, and it was still numb.

Her arm. Their arm. Neither felt quite right, somehow.

'Gone for water,' Connor said.

'He keeps drinking it all.' She tried to shake feeling into her arm.

'I know.'

'And then peeing it all out.'

'I know. You all right?'

Violet was still flinging her hand about, fingers loose. 'Dead arm.'

Here.

You could see for miles. The sky as big as life. Huge grey clouds spreading all the way across, touching the silvery line of mountains on the horizon.

He'd veered off, taken the brick-red track lined with gorse until he crested the hill, and had descended to a point where everything suddenly opened out. A jade-blue triangle of the lake visible, echoed by the shaded hills far beyond it. The hills looked greener, more lush.

He let his bike fall. Listened to his heart, put his fingers to his tongue.

It started raining.

Of course it did. He felt laughter rise in him, let it come in a wave. Felt tears at the far edge of it.

He lifted his head, let the rain's heavy sweetness and coldness drop on him like coins. Like sap.

And then he knew.

Thea and Connor and Violet rushed outside with all the receptacles not already waiting, listened as the spatters and clinks became resounding sounds and dampened completely.

Violet shouted her brother's name into the rain, told him he could come back now.

He suddenly knew, as if a great understanding lined his bones. They were here.

That's what they did, he imagined, after the initial work – wandered through this strange world, moving towards the lit parts of these beings, as loud as stars. Far too much for one ecosystem.

Somewhere in the crush-depth of Luke's brain, there was his mum, feeding him a spoonful of maple syrup in bed and singing him an Irish song. *Sleep, sleep, grá mo chroí.*

He felt them move up to him, tasted them as they passed straight through. His tongue swelled, his throat.

In the moment before he died, everything in him quickened to the sharp, singular pain of loving – his brother, his sisters, the world – and it was a relief to let it go.

They took him tenderly, breaking his body into webs, into atoms.

Twenty

Connor woke with the chill dawn light, and in his sleep-fog, moved his leg over towards Luke's side of the bed. Found only the cool sheet.

'Where is he?' Thea said, without emphasis.

'He'll be here soon,' said Connor.

'It's been half a day.'

'He probably decided to shelter somewhere else for the night.'

'It's not night any more,' Thea said.

'What did he bring us?' Violet said. She'd slept for ages again, woken with a headache, the heavy sense of pressure in the air. The sense of something around them. Near them.

Thea and Connor both looked up from the kitchen table with something like distaste.

'He's not come back,' said Thea.

'Yet,' said Connor.

Violet watched the second hand of the stopped clock, and a

slug draw a gluey trail from the kitchen door to the opposite wall. They'd decided to use batteries for more important things, like the FM radio, in case a miracle message came. Thea washed up everything and began cleaning the kitchen, which she had never done in her life, and then the living room, scrubbing furiously on her knees on the floor. Connor bit the nails of his good hand to the skin. Looked at the exposed pink curves of flesh.

'He'll be here,' said Connor. 'He's just got – stuck somewhere.'
  'You got shot and you still got back,' said Thea.

Auld, elder, eldest, thought Violet. Eldred. From the Proto-Indo-European root *al*.

Another night, in which none of them slept. Connor heard Thea shouting at Violet, before the door thumped and footsteps padded across the landing. For a moment, they paused outside their dad's room, where he was, before Thea's own door opened and closed.

'I'm going to go look for him,' said Violet, at the kitchen doorway.
  'You can't,' said Thea, seated at the table with Connor. 'Not on your own.'
  'Come, then.'
  Thea hesitated and looked at Connor. 'I'm not leaving Connor on his own.'
  'I'm fine,' he said. 'Let me go.'

'No,' said Thea and Violet in unison, both as bluntly.

'You can't ride,' said Violet. 'I'm going. You can't stop me.'

'Wait till it's dark, then,' said Connor, but she was already packing up her bag.

A normal day. Riding through normal air with normal birds chattering and normal insects droning. With normal lavender rows and olive trees. It was just a normal day and Luke had forgotten his phone and Violet was just going out to have a look for him, and it was just five hours earlier than it really was so nobody was up yet and that was why there weren't any cars or people. She was an early riser. An early bird. Catching the worm.

She headed to the group of houses that Connor said Luke had pointed to on the map. It was a normal day and her heart didn't need to be tolling like church bells. She was just having a look and the fact that there was a baseball bat sticking out of her bag was just because she liked baseball. The first house had big gates painted bottle green, not quite shut. She stood against the stone wall, curled her body round, peeked in. Luke always left his bike standing just inside the wall where no one could see it. Nothing there. She wanted to move on, but knew that there was a chance he'd put the bike round the back, gone inside, fallen down the stairs and broken his ankle and was lying there waiting for her to rescue him. You definitely couldn't ride back if you'd broken your ankle.

He'd broken his ankle, thought Thea. Or his leg. He'd skidded off his bike, really badly, or someone had run him down.

The men in the maroon car. Or there'd been an altercation with someone, defending their house like the farmer had been with Connor. Guns, knives, iron bars. If *they* had those things, then other people would. Or maybe it was—

The house had been empty. No sign. It had a whole cabinet of plates with photos of people's faces on them, and an electric piano, and vases of dead flowers. Violet didn't bother looking for things they needed. Luke was what they needed, nothing else. She went to the next one, and when she was halfway across the overgrown lawn saw someone in the window, freaked and felt like puking as she turned and ran, then realised it was her own reflection. Dickhead.

The last house had red-painted shutters, all open. Ivy crawling up the walls and into one window. One of the white plastic patio chairs was lying on its side.

No bike in the grounds. Violet took a deep breath, remembered not to be afraid of her own reflection, and slid the baseball bat out of her bag.

Come back, you fucking bastard, thought Connor.

The smell crawled up her nostrils immediately. It was like the watermelon that had gone off, that gross stink after it had been stabbed. Violet could practically taste it.

The kitchen had ancient wooden cabinets and the cream tiles were stained as if tea had been smeared all over them. Food everywhere. There was a jagged hissing sound in her ears. Maybe the smell was the bins – she bet there were maggots in there, and she definitely wasn't going to lift the lid to find out.

Into the living room, a mess of clothes and books and electrical leads. A framed poster of a red London telephone box, everything else in the photo black and white. There was something here. She could feel it. A pressure on her skin, like every pore was listening. But she had to keep going.

Up the stairs, which smelt damp. The smell was getting stronger, felt like it was under each fingernail, behind both ears. The smell of old meat and old vegetables and old toilets.

'Luke?' she said, too quietly to be heard.

The bathroom was carpeted, all the way up the side of the bath. One of those bum-washer things, with a rusty tap. She'd begun to sweat, the fear spreading hot into her face, her hair. The hissing in her ears was louder, like the sea.

She saved the bedroom door until last, because she knew the smell was coming from there.

Children's drawings tacked up on the mustard-coloured wall. A thin red drape pinned to either side of the window. A long lump in the bed.

Violet heard her breath come in, go out again. *'Bonjour?'* she said, the two syllables flat. Stood there, feet away, waiting for it to move. Knowing it wouldn't. There were flies, a black mass on the pillow. 'Luke?'

Two steps. She would just need to take two steps, to make sure. She wanted to throw up.

One step. Two, enough to crane over, into the fog-like smell, to see the white hair and the blue pyjamas and the gaping yellow mouth.

'We shouldn't have let her go,' said Thea.

'I tried,' said Connor.

'Not hard enough,' said Thea.

She cycled, faster than she ever had. Clean air and blue and fields and trees and she didn't care if they saw her because nothing could be worse than what she'd seen. But it hadn't been Luke.

The road ended, became a narrow, chalky path. She didn't even stop to think and took it, because no way was she going back past that house. The smell was imprinted on her bones forever. Smell with touch and taste, smell you could see, and she stopped and dry-heaved over a bush, got going again, juddering on the bumpy track. The main thing was that she was making more space between her and that room.

The lane joined a new road. She passed cypress trees, a red fire pump – but she didn't want to think about red, or mustard, or black, or white – and she was ascending a hill with dry ground and scrubby trees, and her calves and thighs were thickening, and she had to slow.

She stopped at a triangular road sign with a gracefully leaping gazelle – or deer, more likely – saying *3 km*. She would be happy to see three kilometres of leaping deer. *Oh dearie me*, as her great-gran used to say. Oh deer-ie fucking me.

'Luke,' she said, feeling broken. 'How am I supposed to know where you are?' She thought she might be able to feel it. She felt all three of them these days, always knew where everyone was and what they were doing.

She sat for a while on the roots of a tree, as twisted as one in a fairy tale, feeling the bark scrape against her skin and trying to work out where she was on the map in her head. She wasn't certain. You could just see a hint of blue that must be the river going into the *lac*. Lack lack lack. Lack of Luke. She'd have to take this road and go all the way up the other side if she was going to avoid the way she'd come. She drank half of her water, listened to it gurgle down the canyon of herself into her empty stomach. Stood. Wished she had her camera, except that she knew they were here and she didn't need a stupid ripple to tell her so.

At least she didn't have to pedal for a bit. She slid her feet outwards, felt the wheels spin faster as she began to descend the hill. The crickets or grasshoppers or cicadas were loud here, all rubbing their hands together and giving big evil laughs. Screw you, too, she thought.

The warm wind in her hair. She let out a big evil laugh, from the belly. Another, even louder. Shouted her vicious laughter over the sound of the wind, and the insects.

Then she saw it, a glint of purple amongst the trees.

'Oh, God,' said Thea.

She was sitting by the window, watching the sky ink over itself. She looked so exquisitely weary. As if crying would be too obvious.

Connor was still fighting off the possibility of one sibling being gone, let alone another. His head hurt. His arm hurt. His heart hurt.

There was the sound of a bike brake outside.

One bike, Connor thought. Not two, and felt guilty that he wanted it to be Luke.

'I couldn't bring it back.' Violet was panting, her cheeks blotched red.

'What?' said Thea. 'What do you mean? Did you find him?'

'It was too hard.'

'What was, Violet?'

Violet suddenly sat down, her knees up, and started crying, face hidden by her hair. 'The other bike,' she was saying. 'His bike.'

Later, when she'd stopped crying, she recounted how she'd found the other bike lying on the ground at a lay-by, and how his rucksack had been there too. She'd known, then, that they'd taken him. She didn't tell them about the dead person.

'You don't know that for certain,' said Connor. 'There's still a chance.'

'I do,' said Violet. 'I do fucking know.' She looked up, her cheeks gluey with tears. 'Can't you feel it? That he's gone? He's all – in the air.'

Connor tucked his chin into his chest, as if listening very carefully. 'No,' he said, but he didn't sound convinced.

'He's fucking gone. Because we're all going to be fucking gone.' *Gone, gone, gone*, she thought, feeling her mind spray, become wild.

Luke, throwing the soft football towards Connor's head in the back garden. Swapping ice creams halfway so that they could each have two flavours. Driving Connor to his first house party, and picking him up afterwards, holding his hair back while he puked into a roadside bin. Telling him he was gay with a big, half-cautious grin on his face.

'Please come back,' Connor whispered, into the dark.

Violet got into Thea's bed. Thea turned over, put an arm over her, and Violet was suddenly five, having had a nightmare about a forest of trees collapsing on her, and her mum whispering into her hair.

He could hear him. A whisper, amongst the far-spreading drone.

I'm gone, our kid.

'It's just my imagination,' he whispered. 'It's not real.'

'Thee.'

'Mmm?'

'Connor's crying.'

He was a beck, a stream, a river, a tide. It kept coming, no matter how quiet he tried to be. The door opened and he instinctively turned from them. 'Go away,' he said, through the river, the tide.

'Nope,' said Violet, who was now on the double bed beside him, just as Thea was lowering herself onto the other side. 'Hug attack, like it or lump it.'

From behind him, he felt Violet's arms about his neck, and the tears suddenly ebbed, as if by being seen they'd lost their power.

Thea's face was very close. The faint bone-gleam of her cheek. He sensed the heaviness of sleep still in her. 'I can't...' he said. 'Luke was always there.'

She put a hand on his head, stroked his hair. 'Shh,' she said. 'Go to sleep.'

Three in a bed and the little one said.

Violet lay awake, one leg hanging over the edge, wishing it was all over. Knowing she had to be the one to count the tins and watch the windows, because Connor had lost all hope and Thea didn't have the energy. *I am a badass Viking motherfucker*, she thought.

Thea lay awake, feeling the space between her and Connor like a vibration. His soft breath against her neck.

Connor lay awake, looking at the back of Thea's head. The amber threads in her hair. He imagined taking one between two fingers and slotting it into a needle, sewing together his broken, ever and forever-broken heart.

Twenty-one

He awoke on his back between his sleeping sisters. Violet had her leg triangled, a knee shoved against his thigh, a thumb in her mouth. Thea was facing him, her lips minutely open. She was still in his T-shirt, the one he'd first seen her wearing. He listened to the sandy texture of her breath, the tiny snap that began each inhale. All the world's loss in each delicate, outward sigh.

On one inhalation, she stopped, breathed in again and opened her eyes. Lay there looking at him, her breath subtler. There were brown flecks in her blue irises, he could see now, like the dead leaves on the pool. She put her hand on his cheek, so lightly it was painful, a whisper of space between her palm and his skin. Thumb resting on his cheekbone. Her forefinger on his smaller ear, running over the ridges of the tragus and antitragus. An ear that had not wanted to fully open, a closed conch. Like the rest of him.

She removed her hand, and his ear shone with the ghost of her touch. She rested her hand flat on his breastbone, as if to absorb some of the mute grief. He put his hand over the top, hooked his middle finger into her palm.

Violet, quietly awake now, knew they were touching each other, and realised that they'd wanted to for ages. Didn't care.

* * *

Ferns and mosses have begun to join the ivy in the houses around them. Wild carrot. White-flowered dittany. Orchids. Butterflies – Spanish festoons, small coppers, mallow skippers – lay their eggs on the underside of birthwort leaves.

The mould spores spread like ink blots on the walls.

* * *

There was no more gravel.

Every single stone had been taken from the path, formed multiple lines navigating around and into the house, on the ledges of the walls, into the trees. All connected to the central white circle.

Connor, Thea and Violet completed many tasks without needing to speak – chopping wood and preparing fires, tending to the vegetable beds, bringing in water from the butts, arranging the food in the basement, taking it in turns to watch by the window or sleep on their dad's bed. Luke's bed. When the other two weren't looking, they inhaled the pillows, conjured him in scent so easily it made them smile.

Violet sang all the songs she knew the words to and made up the rest. Thea read to them. Connor wrote Luke's name all over the walls of his own bedroom. The burning was always there, sometimes embers, sometimes flaring up. Sometimes he was sure that his chest would crack open, but it never did, as much as he wanted it to.

Violet shaved one side of her head using Luke's beard clippers. Grade 2. Thea gazed at her before asking her to shave one side of hers, too, and plaited the rest, the braids in lavender-rows against her skull. They gave Connor an undercut, Thea refusing to take it all off as he'd requested. Straight brown hair, dark curls and faded green all mixed together on the bathroom floor.

* * *

'We're running out of water again,' Violet said.

Thea stopped cross-stitching – she'd wanted to help finish it – and gazed out of the window. 'It's going to rain soon.'

Violet followed her gaze to the egg-blue sky, the long blast of sun. They now had to stand on a chair to scoop rainwater out. 'Thea.'

'It might,' said Thea.

Violet looked over to Connor for support. He looked tired, eyes with a chemical sheen. They didn't have to wash, but they had to drink. Wash the dishes. Flush their shit and pee. We need to move, she wanted to say. Luke had wanted them to go somewhere with water. Maybe if they had, they wouldn't have lost him.

Thea seemed to hear her. 'I'm not leaving. Nothing's ever happened to us here. Only when we've gone out.'

'Not if—'

'I'm not leaving,' Thea said, and scratched her arm.

* * *

The leverets play with their half-siblings in the meadows, tumbling in grass as tall as humans.

Under the oaks, the truffles ripen, black and lavender-veined, and heave themselves out of the soil until the forest floor is rippled and alive.

* * *

Days and days and days of hot sun. The soil desiccating. They had to tip the bins to get the last water out.

Violet woke with weak lavender light in her eyes. Long shapes.

She got up as carefully as she could and stood at the window, opened the curtain a fraction and looked out into the night. Felt the weight of them, the *them* she wanted to see so badly, so that she could know for sure. Connor's sound was hurting his head now. The heaviness sat in her chest like a boulder. They were there. They *were*.

She looked back at her sleeping brother and sister. Two long shapes in two-thirds of the bed. Not touching.

Back outside.

'I am going to kill you,' she said to them, very quietly.

She took her bat and Connor's pool-spear, stalked along the road in the dark. Felt the draw of them and a tar-black rage. It felt as if they were pulling her towards them and she didn't care.

Up on the curve of the hill, she stopped dead.

'Oh,' she said.

They were here, weren't they. They-them-their-there.

'I hate you,' she said. 'You didn't have to take him.'

She-was-and-they-were standing in the dust of the track, and they were the long lavender ripple-shapes and they were nothing at the same time and she could practically taste them surrounding her, and something made her pull back, the thought of Connor and Thea's blood running in her-their veins, the gravel coursing outwards around the house, the neon butterfly.

Violet used the spear to trace a circle in the dust around both feet. Frantically dragged lines out from it, a web of lines as far as the spear could stretch. Sensed the valley, the dip of the land and all the space above it.

She felt them see right through to her-their skeleton, salted silver and exposed. Resisted. Saw everything, and then nothing at all.

'Fuck you,' she-they said.

* * *

Thea woke to find only Connor asleep in bed beside her, his fist curled under his chin like the Rodin sculpture. *Le Penseur.* His injured arm loose in front of his chest.

She rose and looked around the house. Outside. Turned to find Connor at the back door, he understanding straight away.

She played with her shells on the windowsill, ordering them from low to high sounds. The tiny *scut-scutting* sounds of bone against terracotta. A small, framed photo of Violet in front of her. He ate olives, wondered why he couldn't taste anything. Wrote Luke's full name in black marker on his upper arm. Began to draw a 'V', and stopped himself.

'They've taken her.'

'We don't know that.'

'Just because we didn't see it doesn't mean it's not true.'

She flicked her forefinger through the candle flame. If this was real, wouldn't she feel it? She sliced her finger through, more slowly. Slower again.

Connor grasped her hand, pulled it away from the flame. Let her go.

'Tell me you're real,' she said.

'I'm right here.'

'My mum is right here,' she said. 'My dad. Our dad. Luke.' She placed her palm on her chest. 'He's right here. Don't you feel him?'

Connor nodded. 'Yeah,' he said, and there was the silver-gold of tears underneath his eyes.

She felt huge, suddenly, housing all of them. This body was only one small part of her. Her frame reached the walls. She drew in a breath. 'I thought there would be so much more.'

'More what?'

She looked at him, smiled. 'Life.' A word sheer with elegance, desolation.

His head sang.

Connor had been sitting at the window, watching. He'd given up trying to stop Thea flicking her finger through the candle flame. It gave her focus.

The music in his ears had grown louder, louder still.

It was all-consuming, split his body into vibrating cells.

The drone that was no longer a drone was birdsong and insect song and grass growing and wood stretching. It was worms pushing through soil and the rumble of life in veins and the flex of bone in wing. It was sediment binding and water travelling and the hum of something bigger than any machine. It was beyond all of that and it was light and the absence of light and it was sound and the absence of sound and it was not earth-made. It was inevitable.

'What is it?' Thea said.

They had shared a plate of crackers and tinned ham, managed almost nothing.

He shook his head with a soft, wondering grin, his eyes unfocused.

It was the same smile that Luke made the last time Thea saw him. 'Connor,' she said, and he blinked, because she hardly ever spoke his name. 'Don't.'

'Don't what?' All sound was music, all music sound.

'Don't – I don't know. Don't listen to it.'

He gave her a vague, almost admonishing look. 'I can't help it. It's right here. It's in me.'

'I know, but – just stop. Please. It's them. I know it's them. Please don't listen to it.'

Connor gazed at her, inhaled as if trying to summon courage from somewhere new. 'I think I have to go and look for Violet.'

'No. You're not going.'

'I have to go outside.'

'No.' She reached out and touched his lip and he grew still. The sounds quietened. Only his exhales, with silence in between.

Her finger was still hot from the candle. She pulled at his bottom lip with her thumb, her face very close. Her fingernail on his teeth for a moment and then moving slowly over his top lip.

He went to speak, but the click in his throat didn't become anything.

'We're all gone,' she said. 'It doesn't matter now.'

She unfolded her limbs, rose, picked up the candle. He listened to the tread of her bare feet on the stairs.

She took off her leggings, Connor's T-shirt and her bra and lay on her back on Luke's bed. Their father's bed. Their bed. Legs straight, hands on her stomach. When the door creaked, she didn't look over.

Connor stepped into the room. Stood at the side of the bed.

She breathed slowly. Pale limbs in the moon's half-light. He sat down in the narrow space between the edge of the bed and her leg. Took her hand.

She drew in a long breath and turned onto her side, still holding his hand, and he knew to follow, to twist himself and lie down beside her, a mirror-image.

There was something stale on her breath. A crust of salt in the one tiny fold of skin by her eyelid.

The two of them, the core. The outer layers peeled from them. If they died, they would die together. She couldn't imagine it any other way.

She unfolded her fingers from his and placed her hand on his ribs, feeling each one. He was terrified and yet it was exactly what would always happen in this moment. A truth. She made him come closer to her with one press on his back, so that their feet were touching. Their legs. Stomachs. Foreheads.

He touched her bottom lip, its slight tackiness. She touched his bottom lip, the serration where he'd bitten it.

Her mouth. His. Kissing, joining.

Her hand was underneath his T-shirt now, on his skin, and he began to copy her movements. Touching her side, her stomach. Outside of her thigh. He wanted to tell her that he hadn't done this before but he understood that she knew, somehow. So much of her under his skin. So much of him under hers.

His hand overtook hers, found its way downwards, felt the shine of her. Saw the shine of her eye, the moon on the edge of the pool, before her eyes closed.

There was hearing, and there was listening.

There would always be sound, as long as they were alive to listen to it. The sound of bodies. Nervous system. Blood.

He didn't know what he was doing, and yet it was easy.

Thea had a sudden memory, a bright awareness. She was very young, before Violet. Lying on the sand somewhere. Her mum's face above her, a hand letting grains softly fall on her arms, her legs. Her mum's voice, as sing-song as the sand.

'Thea?'

'Mmm.'

'Should we stop?'

~~She wanted to be in that memory forever.~~ Sand like a whisper, like a lullaby. But Connor was looking at her, those two beautiful eyebrows drawn together in the suggestion of pain, and hope.

'No,' she said. 'Don't stop.'

Her exhalations were much louder than the breaths she took in, so that he imagined her becoming smaller and smaller, disappearing to nothing, each breath taking a little more of her away. Except that she was there, on top of him, her thighs and heels and hands, and he tried very hard not to make a sound because the one he did make was a whimper.

The sound of skin moving against skin. Overlapping, as they had always done. Acoustic beats, making another note altogether.

She felt that she was all of them, somehow. Not just him, and her, but all of them.

He was too close. He made himself go still, didn't dare look at her. But she leant down to him, sliding a hand under his hip to make him move, and they headed towards the thing that everyone was looking for. The emptying of mind and body, past and present.

The silence.

* * *

A sound. At the edge of the house. In the house.

Thea listened to the dark blood of it, moving underneath the room.

Connor lay asleep at her back, one arm around her. His skin glued in places to hers, both still sticky with each other. His good ear pressed to the pillow.

Separate sounds. A scrape. Something sliding, dryly.

She should wake him.

One of her ears was against the pillow. She couldn't tell where the sound was coming from, but knew that it was moving. Getting louder.

His arm was over her. She would never move.

The sound travelled. Louder again. She rolled her head just a little to expose her other ear. A creak on the stairs. At the door of her room. At the door of Connor's room. The candle was still burning next to her head, and if she moved to blow it out, he would wake.

Connor's iron bar was behind the door. Her weapon by her clothes on the floor.

Her skin was alive and his arm was over her and he couldn't hear it and she would never move.

The door opened and the candle flame ducked, shimmied.

It stepped into the room and Thea's heart flooded. She stopped breathing.

It breathed and she listened to how the breath slowed, and how the breath was human. How it was hers. Theirs.

Their sibling stood a moment longer in the doorway, before walking over in two steps and getting into bed beside Thea, lying on her back and staring at the ceiling.

~~Behind her, Connor shifted, but didn't wake.~~

Thea moved a little closer, and put an arm over Violet's chest. Felt her sibling's heart beating, fast, less fast, slowing.

They all slept.

* * *

'I saw them,' said Violet. 'For a second. Less than a second. Except it felt like forever.'

It wasn't yet dawn. Thea was very close, her head almost on Violet's shoulder, and their words were as translucent as spiders' webs.

'What do they look like?'

Outside, there was the sound of sparrows' feet on the roof.

'*C'est pas possible,*' said Violet.

'But… how are you here?' She touched Violet's cheek. Downy skin under her fingers. 'You were gone for a day.'

'Was I?' Violet gave a thoughtful, Thea-like hum.

'What happened?'

'I don't know.' There had been thoughts, and then there had been nothing. A blankness that didn't have a name, that stretched as far as the edges of the universe.

'But you saw them.'

'Saw them. Knew them. I don't know. But they were definitely there.'

Thea took a long breath.

'We have to leave the house,' Violet said. 'We're almost

out of water. We have to go down to the *lac*. It's what Luke
wanted.'

Thea thought of the gloss of jade-blue lake, the red stone-
dust of the beaches, the limestone caves.

'Free water for life there.'

'For life?' A strange word, unknowable.

'Yeah. I'm going to keep us alive,' said Violet, moving a
shoulder so that her sister's head rose and fell.

Thea didn't move. Violet listened to the click of the back
of her tongue on her throat as she swallowed.

Behind her shoulder, Connor raised his head. He'd been
listening, numb with relief at Violet returning, and with the
fear of what she would think of them now. He met Violet's
eyes anyway, the same leaf-green as Luke's.

Violet looked at him and tried to say without speaking
that none of this was important, only that they were all
together. Violet, Thea and Connor. They and them. They
would carry whatever they could down the long, steeply
winding hill to the *lac*, find a house to settle in and learn
to fucking fish and understand the earth properly. They
would make webs around themselves everywhere they
went because though she knew it was impossible and
that Thea and Connor didn't believe it, maybe it really
had saved her and she was going to save them, no matter
what. They would remember their mums and their dad
and talk about Luke every night. He would be proud of
them, wherever he was.

It would be OK, Violet knew, somehow. They would be
OK.

Thea twisted round to Connor. A long moment, in which they gazed at each other.

Thea turned back to Violet. Nodded.

Night collects around them. Down on the wooded slopes of the lake, the nightingale begins again. A luminous feast of phrases, ringing with love.

The crickets start up their glitching, Earth-long song.

Moths rise like ash.

ACKNOWLEDGEMENTS

To Teresa Dibble and the late Rob and Matt Dibble, for introducing me to the south-east of France. To my dear, departed and irreplaceable friend Matt, for joining us on trips to the Var, jumping from great heights into the lake, coming on boat trips, playing piano while I sang jazz standards, speaking far better French than us and delighting in *tomme de savoie* cheese. You are deeply cherished and missed, Matt, now and always.

To James Roxburgh, my editor at Atlantic, for brilliant insights, patience and kindness, and incisive cuts of my more icky lines. To Joanna Lee, Rachel Wright and everyone at Atlantic.

To Jessica Woollard, my agent at David Higham Associates, for believing in me and keeping me writing against the odds.

Deep thanks to Ione and the Pauline Oliveros Trust for granting me permission to use the title of one of Pauline Oliveros's text pieces, 'We Are Together Because'. This piece, and quotes by Oliveros within the novel, are from *Deep Listening: A Composer's Sound Practice* (iUniverse, Inc., 2005). To Anna Snow, for buying me that book at a time when I needed it most.

To my mum, Sue Myers, for reading my novel, and to Sarah Dacey, for the SF knowledge and some very helpful suggestions on an earlier draft. To Laura Cole, for such kind comments and help with the French! To Matthew Ker, for some useful pointers. To Ollie Kaiper-Leach, for looking over the Mancunian.

To Dr Sandra Cass-Courtney and to Tracey Turner.

To Dave Coulson for his online videos of wildlife in his French meadowland.

To Andy Roberts, my musicianship teacher at the High Wycombe Music Centre in 1995/6, for introducing me to John Cage (I didn't understand *4'33"* at ALL at first – 'So, what?' I said, banging the table, aggravated. '*This* is music?'). To Roger Marsh, John Potter and Bill Brooks at the University of York Music Department for greatly expanding this world for me. To all my fellow students at York and colleagues over the years for keeping the experimenting going in many forms. To my own ex-students at the likes of Junior Trinity and the Sound and Music Summer School for helping me remain inspired.

To Andy, for discovering the Var with me, and being my holiday partner on our magical trips there, and for making space for me to dream and write. For always encouraging and believing in me.

To my one working ear, and my little pixie ear.